APPRENTICE QUEST

OZEL THE WIZARD 1

JIM HODGSON

For T & D and their many adventures ahead

CHAPTER 1

I t was a dark and shitty night. The rain soaked through the rider's cloak. Water was running in rivulets down his back, removing all warmth from his body. This was his fault, of course. He'd intended to leave at first light. But it had been a nice morning for waking up slowly. And then it had been a nice day for packing leisurely. Now it was a shitty night and he was suffering in the cold.

He was close. Down this lane, he thought. Or?

He cast a small spell by whispering into his cupped hand. Wisps of magic indicated that it was, indeed, this way. To anyone watching him, it would have looked like he'd been lighting a pipe.

He guided his horse down the lane and up to the house, dismounted, and looped the reins around the post. His boots clomped on the boards of the porch as he tried to kick off the mud. Then he knocked.

"Fuck off!" a voice came from inside.

"It's Wagast."

"Then fuck off twice!"

But Wagast could hear someone moving down from an

upstairs room to answer the door. It swung open to reveal a man in a sleeping shirt.

"Bartu Hamdi," Wagast said.

"Wagast," Bartu said, as though the name tasted foul.

"This was our agreed day."

Fear flashed in Bartu's eyes. He'd forgotten. Or he'd remembered and he'd hoped Wagast had forgotten. More likely the former. Bartu was an imbecile, but not malicious. Well, not overtly malicious. Well, not overtly malicious to a wizard.

"Can we not handle this in the morning?" Bartu asked.

"I'd like to be home by then."

"Right," Bartu said.

Bartu was a bully. Wagast knew that much. His bully instincts were to bluster and try to push Wagast around. But he was also just smart enough to realize that Wagast could, if he wanted to, vaporize him. Or turn his cock into a turtle's head. Bullying wouldn't be a good option. Still, the need to be a bully was churning behind Bartu's eyes like a caged fighting dog that had fire ants where its brain should be.

The house wasn't known as an orphanage. The little village wasn't anywhere near big enough to warrant anything being called that. But it was known that if one found a child—say, floating down the river in a basket of reeds—one could bring that child to Bartu's house and the infant wouldn't die. At least, not of outright neglect.

They'd be shouted at and forced to work the land, but it was better than being left to die, wasn't it? Some of them had even grown up and moved on to lead whatever lives they chose. Of course, they might have described their departure more accurately as an "escape". Life was hard, living with Bartu.

Wagast had nosed around the farm a few times using his

magical insight to make sure that Bartu wasn't doing anything untoward to the kids. He wasn't. Which was good for Bartu, otherwise Wagast might have shown him what someone with real power can do to a bully.

"I've only just gotten a new one," Bartu said. "I can't part with the ones I've trained up, of course. The new one won't be much good to me anyway, thin whelp that he—"

Wagast stepped inside, even though he hadn't been invited. He knew this would annoy Bartu. It did.

"You were saying?" Wagast prompted.

Bartu visibly decided to get this over with as quickly as possible. He turned, walked toward a door in the far wall that led to the attached barn. He returned steering a thin, blond boy by the elbow.

The boy couldn't be any more than five.

"What do they call you, boy?" Wagast said.

The boy said nothing. The fat, mean man was scary. But the tall, ageing wizard might be even scarier. He had long white hair and a beard that were stringy with rain. The brim of his pointy hat drooped.

"He don't talk much," Bartu said. "But the lord's man said some of them were calling him Ozel."

"Ozel, eh," Wagast said. "You may release him, Bartu."

Bartu let go of the boy's elbow.

Wagast climbed in Ozel's esteem for having given this command.

"I am Wagast."

"Wag ass," said Ozel.

Wagast eyed the child. He didn't look like he'd just been awakened. He was apprehensive, and seemed pretty sharp too. He would do.

"Say thank you to Mr. Hamdi, Ozel," Wagast said.

Ozel looked dubious. Wagast nodded that, yes, he should anyway.

"Thank you," Ozel said, in a small voice.

"Does he have any clothes?" Wagast asked.

"Just what you see."

The boy was wearing a pair of breeches and a shirt that were both too large, not to mention too dirty. Leather wraps on his feet might have been pieces of a worn-out saddle.

"Any physical deformities?" Wagast asked.

"None that I know of."

Technically, the boy did have a peculiar birthmark high on his back which might or might not be a physical deformity from a wizard's perspective. Bartu chose not to mention it. The boy had two arms, two legs, a mouth and an ass, same as anyone else. Why complicate things?

"I have a funny mark on my back," Ozel said.

"Oh, a birthmark, eh?"

The child nodded.

"Is that worth any extra?" Bartu asked.

Wagast blinked. "I have a birthmark on my right buttock. Is it worth anything to you?"

Bartu made a disgusted face.

Wagast flipped Bartu a coin for his trouble and for a blanket to wrap around the boy to keep the chill off. It would be a cold ride back through the rain. There wasn't an inn on the way, and they certainly weren't staying here. Within an hour Wagast wouldn't be able to resist blasting Bartu to paste, and it was unbefitting for a wizard to vaporize people, even if they were assholes.

Wagast put his hand out and the boy took it. Wagast lifted him onto the horse, then turned and went back.

Bartu was standing there in the doorway, watching, probably making sure they left.

Wagast stepped close. "Thank you for your assistance, Bartu."

Bartu gave a small incline of his head.

"The next time I come here, if I ever do, I'd prefer a more polite welcome. I have half a mind to remove the rest of the children and level this house. Then I shall ask every stick of your fences to leap from the ground. Your animals will run where they will. Are we understood?"

Bartu's eyes went wide. He nodded, as Wagast knew he would. Ultimately, he was a weak man. It was why he'd found a way to run his farm using child labor rather than by hiring farmhands. He could lord over a child in a way that no adult would allow.

"Very good," Wagast said. He gave a curt nod, then mounted the horse and rode away into the rain.

CHAPTER 2

Wagast's house needed some work. It was one of those things that turned around in the back of one's mind, and riding up to it now in the morning light he realized how much the repairs were overdue. Vines were creeping up the stonework. The shutters were cracked and weather-beaten. He'd have to hire someone to come out and replace those sooner rather than later, he thought. Perhaps he could pay that person a little extra to teach the boy some carpentry. Not a bad idea for later on.

It was close to the small town of Bilgehan, near the very northern corner of the Kingdom of Dilara. With a little over ten days' travel Wagast could be in Calan, the next biggest town, but there was rarely any need. Dilara's capital city was much farther away. In fact, it was so far away that the royalty ignored Bilgehan, which was particularly nice if one wanted to stay out of anything that might be politics or religion. In other words, the location was perfect.

To Ozel, the house looked like a palace. He'd once lived in a hut with a nice lady, Fadima, who washed clothes. She said the clothes were from a palace. Ozel had never seen a palace for himself, but to hear Fadima tell it, it was a house so big that people could run around inside it as fast as they liked and never bump into one another.

He had some fuzzy memories of being somewhere before that, but he didn't know exactly where. Fadima said she'd taken him in after finding him walking down her road. He believed her, because he remembered being on that road for a long time, and feeling hungry and scared.

The ladies from the palace came to collect the washing when it was clean and folded, and to drop off more. Ozel liked it when they came. They were nice. They hugged him and fed him bread.

But then, Fadima said the palace didn't need her to wash clothes anymore. It was all she had done for years and years, longer than Ozel had been alive. She was too old to learn how to do anything else. She was going to live with her sister in another town, and Ozel couldn't come.

But Fadima promised that she would find someplace for Ozel to live. "You are my responsibility," she said. Ozel wasn't sure what that meant, but Fadima seemed sure that she could find somewhere for him.

Ozel cried when Fadima left him with the fat, scary man who told him to shut up his blubbering. He brought Ozel some soup, which Ozel was glad to eat, but the fat man still wasn't very nice.

Wagast seemed a little nicer. Riding the horse, he actually cared that Ozel was cold. That was a step up. Now they were coming up to a building made of stone, of all things. Only bridges were made of stone.

"Is this a palace?" Ozel asked.

Wagast, despite his fatigue, laughed. The tip of his pointy hat wiggled. When he stopped chuckling he dismounted, then lifted Ozel to the ground. "I am sorry to say, young master, it is far from being a palace. I am a wizard, not a lord. But it is a house. It keeps some of the rain out, and some of the wind. Let's have a look inside, shall we?"

Ozel nodded. He wasn't used to adults asking him questions. Usually they spoke curtly, demanding something.

"What's a wassard?"

"Wizard, my boy. Wizard. A magic-user."

"What's magic?"

"An excellent question. We shall address that over the course of our lives and never come to a conclusion."

The old man walked up the path to the front door, which was set into the curving base of a tower, withdrew a key from his robes and unlocked it. Inside a round antechamber colorful lights danced across the walls. Ozel thought this might be magic, and when he followed Wagast into the house, he saw this was right. One of the windows was made of magical glass that colored the light as it shined through. There were also bits of colored crystal hanging from a piece of string, so that when a breeze blew they tinkled against a bit of metal. This made the light dance. Ozel could have watched it for hours, and it was by no means the only wonder to behold.

"Stained glass," Wagast said. "And a wind chime."

Ozel looked at him, mouth agape, then went back to staring at the lights.

"Come along," Wagast said. "There'll be plenty of time to watch stained glass later."

He led Ozel out of the entrance into a cooking area. Beyond that was a small room with stone walls. It had a wooden frame bed with proper sheets, and a bedside table with a candle. Ozel guessed this must be the wizard's private room. He was probably about to say, "This is my bedroom where I keep my grown-up person things. If I ever catch you in here, I shall thrash you within an inch of your life, you little shit."

"This will be your bed," the wizard said.

Ozel stared. He moved to touch the bed, but Wagast stopped him.

"Let's put the horse away," he said. "Then we will freshen up, have a bite to eat, and we'll both get some rest."

Ozel looked down at himself. He was at his usual level of filth, or perhaps a little cleaner than usual having been rained on for most of the night.

"For now," Wagast told him, "Your only task is to follow me."

WAGAST SHOWED Ozel how to carry buckets of water up from the creek to the house. They built a fire to heat the water, and eventually poured it into an enormous pot that Wagast called a "bathtub."

When Ozel was clean, Wagast asked him about the birthmark on his back. "It looks like someone drew a 'Q' on you."

"What's a 'Q'?" Ozel asked.

"Oh, boy," Wagast said. "We've much to learn."

CHAPTER 3

Ozel learned a lot, following Wagast around. He learned to read, to write, and even to do some simple cooking.

Beyond these, in time, he learned a lot of important things, not the least of which being that Wagast was a "wizard," not a "wissard." Wagast had to correct him quite a lot until it sank in. Ozel eventually got it, but not before he'd frustrated Wagast to the point of him saying, "You make me sound like someone who pisses too much."

Then the old wizard looked thoughtful for a moment and added, "Hmm, now that I think about it, perhaps I do. I am old, after all. In any case, however, the word is most definitely 'wizard.'"

WAGAST COULD DO AMAZING THINGS. He could make a ball of light in his hands. He knew what plants to eat and which to avoid. He knew what to do when a person fell down and scuffed the skin on their knee.

After a couple of years of living in the stone house,

Wagast decided that Ozel was big enough to start reviving the small garden. It was hard work. There were a lot of knotty old weeds to pull out. Wagast said the more food they grew, the less they'd have to buy.

Ozel was thinking about this as he was trying to turn over a big sod of earth in the garden. The clump didn't want to shift, because the roots of the weeds were holding the dirt together. Perhaps if he just got the shovel handle the right way and leaned all his weight on the end ...

The handle snapped, sending Ozel to the ground. He picked up the snapped shaft and compared the two ends. Could he wind some rope around it? No, it wouldn't work. He'd have to tell Wagast, who was most likely in his workshop on the third level of the tower. Ozel took the shovel up with him.

Wagast peered at him over a round glass ball of bubbling pink liquid. Ozel was sure he was about to be shouted at, but all the wizard said was, "I suppose we're going into town a few days early, then."

"Can't you put it back together with magic?" Ozel asked.

"No," Wagast said. "That would undermine the mystery. Imagine someone came here for some special enchantment and saw that we use magic to mend shovel handles. They'll assume our magic is coarse and common. Next thing you know we'll be living in the riverbed under a bridge, because no one considers our work valuable and won't pay a copper for it."

Ozel didn't completely understand this distinction, only that the upshot was they weren't going to mend the handle with magic. And he didn't want to live in the riverbed under the bridge.

They went into town to see if the blacksmith could

provide a new shovel handle. As it happened, he had a few on hand already.

"I'll fix yours for free, though, if you'll have a look at my youngest daughter," the blacksmith said.

"What's the trouble?" Wagast asked.

"Don't rightly know, sir. She's tired all the time. Doesn't want to move. She says her whole body is sore. The doctor's come round a few times to let her blood out, but it hasn't helped at all. We pray over her daily. Doesn't seem to help."

"I see," said Wagast. "What has she been eating?"

"Good, strong food. We've had more meat than usual these last few months. She loves a bite of steak for dinner."

"Yes. It's as I expected. You must do two things. First, stop having the doctor around to let her vital fluids leak out. That isn't doing anything more than traumatizing your poor daughter. Second, feed her fruits and vegetables."

The blacksmith looked unsure. "But she doesn't like fruit or vegetables. She only eats meat."

"If only she had someone with greater experience and greater authority to guide her in the right direction."

The blacksmith looked like he might be insulted. However, he was willing to try anything to get his daughter back on her feet.

"Tell you what, sir," Wagast said. "We'll pay you for the work on the shovel. You feed your daughter as I've instructed for two weeks. If I'm right and she recovers, send her to us with the coins."

"I don't like to wager on my daughter's health."

"Nor should you. But you're not wagering, since you can't lose. Besides, you have my word, she'll be back on her feet in no time."

The man still didn't look thrilled. He fixed the shovel

and Wagast paid for it. Then the wizard and Ozel headed back home.

A few days later, Ozel was back in the garden again when he heard someone's feet scuff on the stone path. He turned to see a girl about his own age with blonde hair and big eyes.

"Are you the wizard's sniveling wretch?" she asked.

"The what? I don't know what that is."

"Me either. It's just what my mom said you are. The bastard wizard and his sniveling wretch. Unless you're the wizard?"

"Nope. I'm just his assistant. Can I help you?"

"I'm the blacksmith's daughter, Aysu. My father sent me to bring the wizard these coins." She held out her hand and jingled the money.

"Oh!" said Ozel. "So you're not sick anymore?"

"No, I'm much better because they took out all my bad blood."

"I see," said Ozel. He'd gotten this trick from Wagast. If you ever didn't know exactly what to say, you could always say, "I see." Then he said, "Let me fetch Wagast."

Wagast came out of the house to accept the coins.

"I'm glad you're feeling better, my dear," he said.

"Yes, sir. It's because the doctor took out all my bad blood."

Wagast nodded, tossing the coins in his hand. "I see. You'd best be off before your parents miss you."

The girl smiled, which made Ozel's insides flop around in his chest like a fish being poked with a stick. She ran down the path to the road and was gone.

"Why didn't you correct her?" Ozel asked.

"Because it doesn't matter."

"But if I say something that isn't right, you correct me."

"You, my dear boy, are my apprentice. It is my job to correct you. Her parents have the right to raise her however they wish. It's not my place to correct what they've told her." He added under his breath, "Even if it is stupid and nearly killed her."

Ozel studied the wizard's face, then stared up into the treetops swaying against the blue sky.

"People believe what they want to believe," Wagast said. "It has nothing to do with the facts. It has a lot to do with their feelings. You can never change their minds about their feelings, even when they're based on something that isn't true. That's why the world needs wizards. It's our job to try to seek the truth even when we don't like it, when we find it."

"I hope I get to be a wizard," Ozel said.

"I hope you get to be a gardener. Otherwise we're both likely to starve."

CHAPTER 4

When Ozel turned ten years old, Wagast said he was old enough to begin learning to do magic. They walked across the creek to the meadow beyond. At Wagast's direction Ozel filled a grain sack with soil.

"What if I'm not magical?" Ozel asked, as he shoveled in a scoop of dirt.

"I don't understand the question."

"What if I'm bad at it?"

"You probably will be," Wagast said. "I'd expect you to lack skill on your first day. There. That's enough."

The wizard tied the top of the sack with a bit of string, then the two of them dragged it over to the base of a tree. They leaned it against the trunk.

"There we are," Wagast said. "Now tell me this, when you began as my apprentice, were you a gardener?"

"No," Ozel said. "I killed a lot of plants."

"But now you do all the garden work, and we enjoy its bounty almost every night."

"Yes."

"So you've become a gardener. Even though you were not one when you started. How did that happen?"

"You made me work in the garden every day."

"That's right. You worked every day. That is how everything good happens. You work every day. Never give up. Most people who try gardening—or wizarding, or anything else—they try it once, and then say to themselves, 'Oh, I'm not good at this' and never try it again. It's absurd. Now. Watch me."

Wagast picked up a fallen branch and broke off a single twig. He stared at the end of the stick and said quietly, "*Lux.*" The tip of the twig began to glow with a bright light.

Ozel couldn't help himself. "Wow!"

Wagast smiled, waved his hand over the stick and the light was extinguished.

"Watch again," he said. "I clear my mind. I focus my energy. I speak the word. Got it?"

"Clear mind, focus energy, speak word," Ozel repeated.

Wagast stared at the stick again, then said "*Lux*" quietly. Again the stick glowed.

Ozel gazed wide-eyed until Wagast smothered it once more. "Why don't we use that instead of candles?" he asked.

"Because it would be unseemly. Now listen. The word is 'lux.' It's Latin."

"Don't they speak Latin in church?" Ozel asked.

"They do, but don't let your mind wander." He handed the stick to Ozel. "You try."

Ozel took the stick. He glared at it and thought, "I feel silly." Then he glared harder and said, "*Lux.*"

The result was nothing like the clear white light Wagast made. The end of the stick only fizzled with a tiny orange ember. If Ozel had blinked he'd have missed it, but it was there. Definitely there.

"Good," Wagast said.

"But it didn't light up."

"That's okay, we're learning. Now I'm going to help you reach for the magic." Wagast rested a hand on Ozel's head. He spoke a number of syllables in a row which Ozel didn't catch, then removed his hand and nodded. "All right. Now try again. Remember the three steps. First you clear your mind so that you are thinking of nothing. Then you focus your energy so that the magic knows where to go. Then you say the word so the magic knows what magic you want."

Ozel nodded. He cleared his mind. This time he felt a deep well of calm come over him, like he'd just woken recharged from a deep sleep. He lifted the stick and focused his energy, and he felt the calm rise at his command. It was a terribly thrilling feeling, like a surge of power that he could either ride to the stars or fall into and be burnt to a crisp. Before either happened, though, he remembered to say, "*Lux.*"

The end of the stick glowed with a bright clear light.

Ozel shouted with surprise and delight. He waved the stick in the air and it trailed streaks of light. Ozel ran with it, twirling and swinging the light as Wagast laughed at his antics.

"All right," Wagast called, waving. "Come back."

Ozel was panting when he came back. He couldn't believe it. He had actually done magic. Real, live magic!

Wagast waved a hand and the light went out.

"Aww," Ozel said.

"Don't worry," Wagast said. "There will be thousands of those. Now watch this."

He turned to the bag of dirt leaning against the tree. He extended his hand and said something under his breath. A bolt of fire jumped from his palm and struck the sack, causing it to twitch slightly. The fire dissolved in the air and was gone, leaving a scorch mark.

"The word is 'augue.' You try."

"Why do you say it so quietly? I can't hear it."

"That's how you determine how much magic you want to use at one time. If I were to shout the word—well, I don't like to brag. Let's just say it wouldn't be a good idea."

Ozel held his hand out toward the bag. He looked to Wagast.

"Yes," Wagast said. "Go on."

Ozel cleared his mind. The calm leapt to him again and he focused his energy. "*Augue!*"

A fireball the size of a tiny bird shot out of his hand and fizzled against the bag. It might technically have left a scorch mark, but a firefly would have left a bigger one.

"Humph," Ozel said.

"Sorry?" Wagast asked.

"Wasn't very big."

Wagast gave him a sour look.

"...but I shall work on it and it will improve?"

Wagast nodded. "One more spell and your initial set will be complete. Watch closely now." Wagast held his hand out, palm up, and whispered, "*Potio sanitatem.*" A small vial of a glowing blue liquid appeared in his hands. He handed it to Ozel.

"What is this?"

"It's a healing potion. It will speed recovery from almost any ailment."

Ozel frowned. "What about that time I was sick for a week? You could have given me a potion that whole time?"

"We do not use magic frivolously."

"But I had a fever for days."

"Yes, and then what happened?"

"You said it was best that we monitor the situation. Then at the end of the week I got even worse. You made me drink that awful cough syrup and ..."

"And?" Wagast asked.

"And I was better the next day," Ozel said slowly.

"If you are going to be a wizard, you must learn never to use your magic unless you are in a situation of some consequence. If you were a swordsman, you wouldn't use your blade to stir your morning tea. If you were a singer, you wouldn't sing every conversation. It's just not done."

Ozel imagined a soldier trying to stir his tea with a sword and wanted to giggle about it. He restrained himself. "I suppose I see what you mean," he said instead. He thought so, anyway.

"You can only do so much magic in a day. Suppose you spend the afternoon using fireballs to heat your bathwater, then you're met with some emergency that evening?"

"I'd be out of luck?"

"Precisely. Now try the spell. The words are 'potio sanitatem.'"

Ozel tried again. A tiny vial of blue liquid popped into existence and dropped into his hand. It was sealed with the smallest cork he'd ever seen. He'd need a pair of tweezers to remove it.

"Excellent!" Wagast said. "When you master these three spells we shall discuss some new ones." He waved his hand over Ozel's face. Ozel felt a change, like a buzz that had been murmuring at the base of his skull was silenced. It felt a little sad to lose the power, but on the other hand, he'd done magic. Real magic!

He grinned.

He held out his hand toward the sack of dirt. He cleared his mind, focused his energy and said, "Augue!"

A spark like a firefly shot out, but nothing more.

Wagast nodded. "You must practice. Practice keeping your mind free of any thought. You can do that while you're gardening, or doing any menial task. If a thought enters your mind, you sweep it aside. Next you must learn to focus your energy. You get better at that by being confident in your actions. Some of that will come with age, but a calm mind will help as well. Come down here every day and practice these spells. Agreed?"

"Agreed," Ozel said. He knew which one he'd be spending the most time on.

"Practice them all equally. If I should walk down here and find the bag of earth burned to a crisp, but you still cannot produce a larger healing potion, I shall be very put out."

Ozel made a face.

"Yes," Wagast said. "You are not my first apprentice. And there's something else you should remember."

"What's that?"

"I was once an apprentice too."

Ozel thought about that. Something occurred to him. "Can anyone do magic?"

"Yes, if they work at it."

"But isn't it meant to be special? Something only wizards can do?"

"Not particularly, no. Some people have a natural apti-tude for it, but my opinion is that any aptitude is merely an indication that they're willing to work hard. It's the same with any other vocation. Carpenter, blacksmith, farmer."

"So why isn't everyone a wizard?"

"I think you'll answer that question for yourself over the coming years. It takes a long time and a lot of practice to become worthy of calling one's self a wizard. Serving as an apprentice helps a lot."

"I thought I was something special," Ozel said.

Wagast chuckled. "As long as you're willing to work hard, my boy, you are."

CHAPTER 5

Saban Kozen was always on the lookout for opportunities to dip a hand into the collection money for the church. As a man of the cloth he was entitled to a few coins for his daily bread, but a few more coins made their way into his pocket when he could pocket them. Those times were relatively few, but he made the most of them. He tried to recall what his father had said: pigs eat food, but we eat pigs. It didn't make a lot of sense, and perhaps Saban wasn't remembering it exactly right.

He had noticed, when he was a boy and went with his father to feed the lord's pigs, his father always kept a pocket full of feed for himself. He knew it wasn't right, and there was something about his father's demeanor that told Saban it wasn't prudent to ask about it, but he asked anyway because the question was burning him up from the inside and he was a kid. Kids, he reflected, thinking of the brats spilling cups of communion wine or shouting in the middle of a service, aren't great at impulse control.

"The way I figure it, it's a little reward for carrying the feed out here and feeding the hogs," his father had said. "I take it home, then I feed it to your mother's goat, and we all get milk and cheese as a result."

"But the goat is so skinny. She needs more food. Why don't we take a whole sack?" Saban asked.

"Shut up," his father told him.

Saban hadn't understood this at the time. Neither, perhaps, was he completely sure that he understood it fully now. But he knew one thing: if you were going to put your hand in something, gold was better than hog feed. However, you can dip your hand in every day for a lifetime, but if you steal a whole week's church collection at once you're likely to discover that your lifetime won't last long.

What he'd more recently found, though, was going to be worth a hell of a lot more than a pocketful. It was equal to a king's ransom. And he thought he knew just how to get his hands on it.

Some kid was rich. The parents had died years ago and a fortune was waiting for the child in Calan. All Saban had to do was figure out where the boy was, or get himself a child who could pass for the heir, then grab the gold for himself and dump the kid off at an orphanage a few towns over.

The birthmark thing was tricky. The scholars in Calan would be able to tell a real birthmark from a tattoo or an enchantment. But this was something that excited Saban about his plan. He'd heard someone talking about a kid with a birthmark in the shape of a Q. Who had that been? He couldn't remember for certain, but there was only one house in the area that dealt with lost kids.

He knocked on the door. There was a grumble inside, then a scraping noise. The door opened.

Bartu Hamdi looked Saban up and down. "What do you want, Father?"

"Ah," Saban said. "Brother Hamdi. A matter has come to

my attention. One which I think you'll find very interesting." Saban cast his eye about the room. Some of Bartu's little army of helper children were around. "Perhaps we could talk somewhere privately?"

"I don't have any money to give at the moment."

"No, not at the moment," Saban agreed meaningfully. That got Bartu's eyebrows up.

Bartu left his kitchen after a stern word to the kids to keep working. "You gotta be firm with them," he explained. "Otherwise as soon as you're out of the room they slack off."

"Quite," Saban said.

"Now what was it you're wanting to talk about then?"

Saban looked around. They were standing well away from the house and the road. No one could possibly be within earshot. "I believe that some years ago you had a child with a peculiar marking."

Bartu grunted. "They're all pretty peculiar, if you get right down to it. I've had some with missing limbs. That what you mean?"

"No, this child in particular would have had a birthmark on its back that resembled the letter 'Q.'"

"What's that look like?"

Saban drew one in the dirt with his staff.

"Oh," Bartu said, looking at it. "Yeah, I remember that one."

"You do? Is the child here?"

"No, I mean I remember that letter." Bartu eyed him. "Perhaps if I knew what you were driving at, Brother, my meaning would be a little clearer."

Saban looked around again.

Bartu thought, whatever this guy's sitting on must really be something. That's twice now he's looked around and we're in the middle of nowhere.

Saban decided he needed Bartu. No one would believe that he, Saban, was the kid's guardian. But he didn't have to lay out the whole plan all at once.

"It seems the deceased parents possessed a bit of wealth overseas. It's taken this long for word to reach us from the foreign bank. If you could prove guardianship of the child, well, unless the boy has come of age that money would rightfully be yours."

"How much wealth?"

"Enough to buy this farm many times over. Enough to walk away from it today and never give it another thought."

Bartu felt his legs wobble a little. Could this be real? With that kind of money he could set himself up some-where as a minor lord. He could be done with child farmhands forever. He could have staff to serve him—and abuse them with impunity. It was everything he'd ever wanted.

"Well," he said. "Why don't you just tell me how to get my hands on that money?"

"Yes, well, as I see it we need one another," Saban said. "I know how to handle the administrative tasks necessary to complete the transaction. You know where to find the child in question."

"Seems to me I could just ask around until I found someone who could tell me where to go," Bartu said.

"You might, but wouldn't your claim have more credi-bility if you had a man of the church verifying that you are, indeed, the guardian?"

Bartu considered this. Saban Kozen was smiling as though he'd won a prize. He had a point. Anyone in the land could turn up and claim to have been the child's guardian. If he had a priest with him, one who could write letters and was financially motivated to make things go smoothly, that might go a long way to making this thing actually work. Besides, he could always murder the friar once he had his money, take both shares, and disappear forever. He'd never killed anyone before. However, with that kind of coin on the line Bartu felt he could manage it.

"I see you have thought this through," Bartu said. "Very well. I shall offer you five parts in one hundred."

Kozen smiled. "I think the only equitable division is half each. This way neither of us is more motivated than the other."

It did have a certain symmetry to it, Bartu thought. And the priest had a point. If they were going to pull this caper off, they both needed to be well-motivated. And what did the agreed portion matter, if he was only going to kick the man's dead body off a cliff somewhere?

"Very well, we will split the money evenly."

Saban was well aware that Bartu had no intention of handing over half the money. He'd met devious people before. Obviously, the thick wretch was plotting murder even now. He would have to be wary. Ultimately it only affirmed his resolve. After all, what did it matter if Bartu was planning to kill him? As soon Saban got his hands on the money he'd poison this imbecile anyway.

They shook hands, each eyeing the other.

"Now what?" Bartu asked.

Saban blinked at him. "We take the child to Calan, show him to the magistrate most likely, then we collect the reward and we're on our way." They'd need to show the child to a banker, in point of fact, but Saban didn't feel the need to give every detail, especially since Bartu was already looking a little suspicious.

Bartu doubted Saban would be mounting this journey without knowing exactly where it led. The way Saban said "the magistrate most likely," sounded rehearsed to Bartu. He knew where to go, he just wasn't saying. It didn't matter anyway, though. "I don't have him."

"What?"

"The boy. I don't have him."

Saban stared. Could he get away with braining this idiot on the spot? Probably not. "Where is he?" he asked instead.

"I don't know, exactly. But I know who he's with."

"Can we get to the boy?"

Bartu shrugged. "We could probably find a way to grab him, throw him in a sack. As long as the wizard doesn't catch us."

"Wizard?"

"Yes. The boy is apprenticed to Wagast."

"Hmm," said Saban. Try to kidnap a child from a powerful wizard? He might as well knock on the door and ask to be dismembered. "I have a better idea."

CHAPTER 6

In the morning a pigeon arrived in Wagast's workshop. It cooed to make its presence known, then flew up to the cage on the roof. It must have been flying all night.

"Get that, won't you?" Wagast asked. He was moving rocks around in a wooden tray full of sand and studying their placements. Then he'd move one slightly in another direction and eyeball the new arrangement. And so on.

Ozel had his nose buried in a book. All these years and he still couldn't do any magic beyond his basic spells. Yet Wagast kept him reading, reading, reading. He snapped the book closed peevishly and stomped up the round stairs, through Wagast's bedroom, and to the floor above with the pigeons. The bird had a note tied to its leg. Ozel removed it, then took the slip of paper back down to the wizard and deposited it, still somewhat irritably, on the desk.

The wizard paid no mind to these antics. He reached an absent-minded hand out to the note, unfurled it, read the scrawl upon it.

"It's from Bugra Gurses in Calan. He says he's found— oh! He says he may have information about your parents."

"My what?" Ozel asked.

"Parents," Wagast said. "The people who engaged in a biological act that ultimately resulted in you. Says I should contact him as soon as I receive this."

"Why does Booger in Calan know who I am?"

"Bugra Gurses. 'Mr. Gurses, sir' to you. He knows, because I asked if he ever heard of anyone looking for a boy with a Q on his back to let me know. I thought you might want to know something about your history. Seemed only prudent."

Ozel thought about it. Did he want to know who his parents were? Not particularly. It seemed to him that parents were a thing that other people had. At twelve years old, so far he'd spent most of his life with Wagast learning about magic and gardening. Well, language and gardening. Wagast said he wouldn't be able to do serious magic until he became a man.

"I do wonder how I ended up on the road," Ozel said.

"Road?"

"Yes, that's where Fadima found me. Walking down the road."

"I see," said Wagast. "Well, in any case, perhaps we shall find out. Let's contact old Bugra and see what's what."

He cleared a space on his worktable by moving a number of scrolls and bottles with all colors of liquids inside. He lifted a heavy wooden disc from a lower shelf and plonked it down. The disc was shaped a bit like a chunky plate with high sides, and held green sand. Wagast let some of the grains drift between his fingers. He spoke what sounded like, "*Contactu*" followed by, "Bugra Gurses." When most of the sand had slipped through, a wispy green fire leaped upward. The remaining grains clinging to Wagast's fingers were wiped on his robe.

A face appeared in the fire. It had a pointy black beard on its chin, short hair, and wore an odd, square hat. The face looked a lot more trimmed and neat than Wagast's shaggy appearance.

"Eh?" the face said. "Oh! Wagast. You must have gotten my bird."

"Indeed I did, old boy. How are things round your way?"

"Not so bad, you know. I could use a decent apprentice. Hard to come by these days. No one wants to put in the work it takes to become a wizard."

"Too true," Wagast said, wiggling his eyebrows at Ozel. "Well, as you say, I got your bird. What's going on?"

"It seems the church has received notification that a bank somewhere overseas has a fortune waiting to be inherited by the child of some deceased clients. Apparently the boy will have an identifying birthmark in the shape of a letter 'Q.' I sent the bird straight away when I saw the notice, but I'm afraid the matter has been making the rounds here for a few days. So I thought, in view of the unfortunate delay, a bird more appropriate to gain your attention, you know."

"Well, this is disappointing," Wagast said. "I expect I'll be out of an apprentice shortly."

Bugra laughed, then he was gone.

Wagast turned to look at Ozel. "Well, there you have it."

"There I have what?"

"You must go on an adventure. Travel to Calan, find out about your parents, and possibly even inherit a fortune."

"But what about becoming a wizard?"

Wagast blinked. "I didn't think you particularly liked wizarding. You don't seem to care for reading books very much. Your gardening has certainly improved, though, I will say."

"I don't want to read books and be a gardener. I want to be a wizard. I want people to come to me with great problems that need fixing. I want to right wrongs. Help people. You know. Wizarding!"

Wagast waved a hand. "I don't know where you heard any of that. Have you seen me righting any wrongs in the years that you've been my apprentice?"

"You saved Aysu."

"Anyone would have done that."

"But anyone didn't do it. You did."

"And why did I know what to recommend for her?"

Ozel stared. He knew Wagast wanted him to say, "Because you read it in a book." He didn't want to fall for any pedagogical traps at the moment.

"Because I read it in a book," Wagast answered for him. His face was imploring. "I think you need to do this. If you still want to become a wizard when you're rich, I suppose you can, but as you can see, it's not a rich man's game." Wagast spread his hands at their surroundings.

"When I got here I was amazed that I would be allowed to sleep in a bed," Ozel said. "That feeling has never gone away. I don't want it to ever go away. Money or no money, I want to be a wizard. If I have to stay here and garden, and read books, that is what I will do."

Wagast said, "But in order to be a proper wizard you must be a man. To be a man, you must be tested and prove your worth. The journey to Calan could be just the thing. Would that I could make such a journey myself. I made a few in my younger days." Wagast looked out the window. "Sleeping under the stars. Naught but the wind in your hair and spicy sausages for dinner. Mind you, I could digest spiced meats back then. Now I'd be wrecked for the better part of a day."

"I've actually been thinking of something I could do to prove my worth," Ozel said.

"Eh?" Wagast was unwilling to leave his sausage reverie.

"I could go to Bartu Hamdi and tell him off."

Wagast looked unimpressed.

Ozel glared. "What?"

"Sounds like a shitty quest. He's only a few hours away."

"I'd be confronting an evil master who held sway over me!"

"He only held sway over you for a short time."

"But wouldn't that count as facing up to evil?"

Wagast tilted a hand side to side.

Ozel insisted, "I was terrified! I'm still terrified of him."

"True, but you also know him. I'd much prefer if you struck out into the unknown. That's a proper quest, that is. But striking out into the known?" Wagast shrugged.

"So you admit I'm old enough to choose my own quests?" Ozel said.

Wagast nodded. "And young enough to do so poorly, it seems."

Ozel kicked the leg of Wagast's desk. Several bottles made tinking sounds against one another.

Wagast made an irritated noise, but Ozel was already stomping down the stairs and through the house to his room. He threw a few things into a bag, grabbed his walking staff, and went out the front door, slamming it behind. Then he quietly came back in and went into the kitchen. Ozel put a few loaves of bread and a hunk of cheese into his bag, and stormed out again. This time he closed the door without slamming it. Once was enough, he figured.

He walked down the path toward the road, feeling that a world of possibilities was laid out before him.

"Oi!" Wagast yelled from the window. "Eat a spicy sausage if you can!"

CHAPTER 7

The road was dry and hot. When horses went past, a cloud of dust choked Ozel. He wished he was heading somewhere that was more of a footpath over rolling hills than a wide, dirty thoroughfare. But that was how quests went, didn't they? They were meant to be hard.

A cart was coming toward him. He prepared himself for yet another cloud of dust, but the dray stopped in the road.

"Whoa there," a man's voice said.

"Ozel, is that you?" a girl called.

It was Aysu and her father.

"Yes, hello," Ozel said. He waved. He was in a foul mood, but the way his lungs were slapping around inside his chest made him feel giddy for some reason. Aysu's golden hair shone in the midday sun. He hadn't seen her in a long time, but she must have been working alongside her father at the forge. She looked strong. But she was also unquestionably a young woman. Ozel knew instinctively that it was beyond rude to stare at her, but her shape demanded it.

"Where are you going?" she asked.

"I'm on a quest," he said proudly.

"Oh, aye," the blacksmith said. He smiled. "Fine thing for a boy your age, a quest. It'll put hair on your chest."

Aysu rolled her eyes at her father and jumped down from the cart. "Where's your quest taking you?"

"Did you bring any jerky beef?" the blacksmith asked. "And some coffee? Good cup of coffee will help in the morning, you know."

Ozel chose to answer Aysu. "I'm going to the home of a man who held sway over me when I was only five."

Aysu covered her mouth with her hands. "You're not going to ... kill him?"

"Well, I ..." Ozel said. He looked down at his feet. They were caked with dust the color of the road. "I mean, I'm not a madman." It sounded lame. Surely Aysu would be much more impressed if he'd been going to slay a villain, or a beast of the forest perhaps. But then again, what kind of person went around killing people?

She touched his arm. "I'm so jealous. I'd give anything to go on a quest like that."

"Ah, well," he said, feeling his cheeks getting hot. "You know how it is."

"Don't be silly, girl," the blacksmith said. "Quests are for men." He laughed at the absurdity of it. "Come along, let's be off. Good luck to you, young, er ..."

"Ozel," said Ozel.

"Yes, indeed. Good luck to you, young Ozel. Come along, Aysu."

Aysu grabbed Ozel's arm and pulled him toward the rear of the cart. There, where her dad couldn't see, she kissed him on the cheek.

"Good luck," she whispered. "I think it sounds like a fine quest."

Ozel's smile was wide. "Thanks."

She flashed him a brilliant smile, then hurried to clamber up next to her father. He gave the horse a light tap with the reins and they rattled away. Aysu gave him a final wave and another smile.

"Gosh," Ozel thought. "She's nice."

OZEL ARRIVED at the head of the path to Bartu Hamdi's house. At least, he thought it was the right place. He followed the track for half an hour, only to find the wrong house at the end of it.

He backtracked, then kept going down the road a while longer until he came to another turn-off that looked promising. Yes. This was the one.

When he got to the end, Hamdi's house wasn't there. There was only a smoking pile of ashes with a hearth and chimney standing in the middle. Fences were knocked down. The garden was torn up where someone in a hurry had wrenched vegetables from the ground. A draft horse grazed in the distance even though the fence was gone.

Ozel went closer to the wreckage. He could feel the heat radiating off it.

Something hit his backpack. He turned to see a kid with a handful of rocks. The kid threw another one and Ozel had to dodge. "Hey," he yelled. "Stop that!"

"Go away!" The kid threw another rock. This one fell well short, but bounced and glanced off Ozel's shin.

"Ouch!" said Ozel.

"Go away or one of these will hit you in the head!"

"Stop throwing rocks," Ozel shouted. "I used to live here. I'm on a quest."

The boy had his arm drawn back, ready to let loose with another stone. He lowered it. "You used to live here?"

"Yes. A man named Bartu Hamdi was my guardian. I'm on a quest to tell him off for the way he treated me."

"Oh," the kid said. He didn't seem eager to throw things anymore, but he was still clutching the rocks. "He's gone. He left us with instructions for running the place, but a couple of the older kids got into a fight and they burned the house down. Everyone has gone except me. I don't have any place to go."

"Where did Bartu go?"

"He went with a priest to Calan. Said they're going to be rich. He told the older boys he'd cut them in on some of the money, if they took care of the farm while he was gone. Then as soon as he was gone they started fighting. One of them burned the house down so the other couldn't have it."

Ozel's skin felt prickly. "Rich? How are they going to be rich?"

"Don't know. Are you going to follow them to Calan to tell him off?"

Ozel sighed. This was not at all what he'd planned. "I don't know. How long have they been gone?"

The kid shrugged. "Days. Do you have anything to eat other than radishes?"

"Possibly. Put your rocks down and we can talk about it."

CHAPTER 8

The kid's name turned out to be Alan. Ozel shared some bread and cheese with him. Even though they could have stayed near the smoldering house, they decided instead to have a campfire some distance away. Alan had been sleeping in a tarp. Now he rolled himself up in it like a tinker's little cigar. He seemed more at ease with someone else around to be in charge.

Ozel was relieved Alan was wrapped up inside the tarp because it had a limiting effect on the stench radiating from the boy.

Ozel, in his bedroll, looked up at the stars and listened to the crackling fire. He liked camping. He and Wagast went into the woods often to study herbs, collect them, and just to get out of the house.

What would a man like Bartu Hamdi do with vast wealth? Ozel didn't know—and he didn't care. As long as he never saw the man again he supposed that was enough.

"Did he ever beat you?" Alan asked.

"Bartu? A few cuffs round the head. Told me I was

worthless. Encouraged the other boys to kick me around, if they wanted to."

"Yeah," Alan said. "That was the worst part. When the other boys start in on you."

It had been over seven years, but Ozel remembered what Alan meant. It was one thing to have an oppressive master, but the way Bartu ran his farm encouraged and rewarded cruelty. The result was a culture of brutality in which no one could ever truly relax. There was always an older boy watching, waiting to slap you down for some mistake. Or a younger boy waiting to tell tales and earn you a beating.

What would a man like that do with great wealth? How many people would he oppress?

There was a snorting sound and Ozel nearly leaped out of his skin. In the darkness he saw it was only the horse. The big animal nuzzled at Ozel. He rubbed the horse's soft nose. The horse snorted again and blew snot in every direction.

Ozel cried out and wiped at his face.

Alan laughed. "He got you! He got you good!"

This wasn't what Ozel expected quests to be like.

In the morning, Ozel helped Alan onto the horse's back, holding his breath to protect himself from the boy's aroma. They set off back down the road toward Wagast's house with Ozel on foot, leading the animal.

"We shall be there this afternoon," Ozel said. "Wagast is nice. He will help find someone to care for you."

"Does he beat you if you make a mistake?" Alan asked.

"No."

"What if he already told you once and you weren't listening, and you got it wrong?"

"No, no beatings."

Alan looked amazed.

"And you'll get to sleep in a real bed," Ozel said.

"Holy shit!" Alan said. Then he looked sour. "He doesn't do anything else that's ... funny, does he?"

Ozel squinted, trying to understand. Then, seeing Alan's expression, he understood. "Oh god, no. Nothing like that."

"Why did you leave, then?"

"Because it's time for me to prove I'm a man and become a wizard, so I have to go on a quest."

"But you only came to Bartu Hamdi's house? Not even a day's ride away?"

"Bah," Ozel said. "You don't know anything about being a wizard."

"I know you ain't supposed to finish a quest in a single day."

"Shut up," Ozel said. Then, while he was trying to think of a good reason why Alan should shut up, he said, "I hear hoofbeats." He stopped so that he could listen better and the horse plodded to a halt next to him. Sure enough, down the road ahead, someone was riding hard. Ozel's insides felt like they'd drawn up into a hard, cold ball.

"We gotta get off the road," he said. He reached up to help Alan to the ground.

"What about the horse?"

"Forget about the horse. It could be Bartu coming back because he got word about his farm."

"But at least then you'd get to tell him off."

"Shut up!" Ozel hissed. They scrambled off the road to a fallen tree. The roots made a decent hiding spot. The hoof-beats were getting a lot louder now, but they kept right on going down the road.

"Is this what it's like being a wizard?" Alan asked, when they were moving again. "Hiding all the time?"

"No, of course not."

"What's it all about then?"

Ozel tried to think of an answer, but after a few moments decided to ignore the question.

It was evening when they arrived at Wagast's house.

Ozel wasn't sure how Wagast would feel about him returning with another small boy. Ozel was even a bit embarrassed about the way he'd left. At first, when he'd slammed the door behind him, he was like a triumphant breaker of rules seeking to become a man. Now, as he walked up the path, he felt a little bit like a petulant child coming back after running away.

"Well," Wagast said with a broad smile. "Whom do we have here, then?"

"This is Alan," Ozel said.

Wagast leaned forward to shake hands, then quickly pulled back. "Welcome, Alan. You'll be wanting a bath straight away, I think."

"A what, sir?" Alan asked.

"I'll bring water," Ozel said.

When Alan was bathed, they sat for dinner around the table. Even though he'd only been gone for a day, Ozel was pleased to be back with the smell of the food mingling with the herbs and magical potions.

"So, Alan," Wagast said. "How did you come to be with Mr. Hamdi?"

"My dad died," Alan said. "He got work as a soldier, went to do war and someone killed him."

"Oh, I'm sorry," Wagast said.

"He paid a nanny to watch me while he went to do war, but after he died there weren't any money. So I had to go and live at the farm and learn to work."

"Oh, my," Wagast said.

"I was going to run away from the farm, like the older kids do, when I got old enough. To be a soldier, like my dad," Alan said. "But now I want to be a wizard."

Wagast chuckled. "Do you now?"

"Yes, sir. My dad said soldiering was a nice way to make a living, but we ain't never ate a dinner like this or lived in a house with beds. Plus my dad is stone dead and here you are old as anything. Seems to me wizards have it a lot better."

Wagast said, "I agree that it is a very different life from soldiering."

"So can I?" Alan asked. "Be a wizard, I mean?"

"Perhaps," Wagast said. "The world will always need learned people. Why don't you stay for a while and make sure it suits you, before you commit to anything?"

"All right," Alan said, his mouth full of bread. "But I'm gonna be the best wizard you ever saw."

Wagast chuckled again, then said, "I think we should set about making a sleeping spot for Alan. It's quite nice by the hearth."

Alan shot a look at Ozel.

"I think I'll just roll out my bedroll by the fire," Ozel said. "I promised our new friend here he'd be able to sleep in a bed and he's quite keen to give it a shot."

Alan smiled. His eyes looked glassy.

"Oh," Wagast said, still cheerful. "Well, isn't that nice?"

WAGAST HELPED Alan settle into bed. He gave the boy an old shirt to wear. It looked like a robe on his tiny frame.

From his bedroll on the floor Ozel looked into the embers of the fire. He couldn't help feeling jealous of Alan. He remembered what it felt like to be new to this place. To know Wagast's kindness.

Wagast was still kind. More than kind. He was like a father to Ozel. Where would he be, if not for Wagast? Still with Bartu Hamdi? What would have happened when Bartu Hamdi got the news that he was suddenly sitting on a gold-mine in Ozel?

Now that son of a bitch was out to get his hands on Ozel's money. The riches meant nothing to Ozel. However, what would a man like Bartu do with that kind of fortune? Whom would he oppress?

"I want you to know," Wagast said. "That I am proud of you."

Ozel was shocked. He hadn't heard Wagast enter. The old wizard could be stealthy when he wanted to be, that was for sure. He didn't know how to respond and didn't feel that "I see" really covered it this time, so he said, "Thank you."

"I know we had a row before you left, but I'm proud of you for striking out alone. And I'm proud of you for bringing young Alan back here. Those were very wizardly things to do."

Ozel was still a little ashamed, thinking about how mad he'd been at Wagast the previous day and how he'd stormed out. But this compliment filled him with pride. Wizardly things, he thought. He knew what he had to do.

"You were right, Wagast," he said. "I must go to Calan. Stop Bartu Hamdi getting that money."

"Yes, boy!" Wagast said, shaking a balled fist. "Yes!"

"If a man like that gets his hands on great wealth ..."

"Then great suffering is sure to follow," Wagast finished.

"But he has days on me. He's sure to be on a horse. There's no way I could catch them."

Wagast looked knowingly at Ozel, the light of the embers reflecting in his eyes.

Ozel shuddered. He knew what Wagast would suggest.

He could go through the Tangul Forest. The main road skirted around the woods between them and Calan, a longer, looping route. It was much faster to go through the forest. However, there were also things in there that defied all description. Giant bears? Deadly snakes? Some people said there were dead men walking around.

He and Wagast had camped on the edges of the woods a few times and seen nothing. Wagast was of the opinion that most of the forest was quite safe. But Ozel noticed that Wagast kept a keen eye whenever they were in the area.

Still, Wagast was right. He needed a proper quest. And Bartu Hamdi was no kind of man to be trusted with great wealth.

"I suppose I could go through the Tangul Forest," Ozel said, reluctantly.

"My boy," Wagast said. "You have no idea how long I've waited to hear those words."

CHAPTER 9

I n the morning, Wagast helped Ozel pack everything he'd need for the journey, including a gift.

Wagast held out a round helmet that came to a point in the center. It had a leather pad inside and a chin strap. "I wore this on one of my first adventures when I was about your age," he said. "I've taken the liberty of placing a few enchantments on it that should help keep you safe."

Ozel tried it on, and the buckle on the side of the helmet snapped.

"Ah," Wagast said. "Yes, well, I'll give you a little money and you can stop by the blacksmith's shop on your way to the forest."

"It's very nice of you," Ozel said. "I'm proud to have it."

Alan was still in his sleeping shirt. He waved goodbye to Ozel. "I hope you kick Bartu in the nuts."

"Alan," Wagast said, in a warning tone.

"Sorry, sir." He moved closer to Ozel and whispered, "I slept in a bed!"

Ozel grinned. "Enjoy it. For every comfortable night you

have, think of me. I shall be nestled snugly between a jagged rock and a hard tree root."

"Oh," Wagast said. "The sausage—do eat some sausage, won't you? For my sake?"

Ozel nodded. He stood there staring at them. Wagast blinked, smiling. Alan was looking between Wagast and Ozel. The silence drew out.

"Right," Ozel said. "I guess I'll ..." He took a step toward the door and away from warm beds and hot meals.

Wagast nodded.

"He ain't leaving," Alan said.

"Don't be silly," Ozel said.

He pulled open the door and walked out. He went down the path. He stepped onto the road. He could still smell breakfast. He looked over his shoulder. He could still see the house between the trees and glimpse the stained glass wind chime that had so captivated him on his first day.

And then he was on his way again, alone.

WHEN HE ARRIVED at the blacksmith's shop, he found a crowd. Apparently, everyone needed the blacksmith's services that morning. He sat down to wait.

Aysu was helping her father by keeping the forge full of coal. But she had time for a smile in Ozel's direction, which made his insides do that flipping around thing they did whenever she was around.

Looking around at the tools and wares for sale, it occurred to Ozel that perhaps he should purchase a dagger? He didn't want to carry a sword. One, he didn't know how to use one. Two, he couldn't afford one, and three, it would be heavy. A dagger might be just the thing instead.

Aysu smiled as she walked over. "Broken another shovel?"

Ozel held up the helmet with its strap no longer attached.

"Ah, I can fix that. Will be faster than having papa do it. Come on."

She led him into the workshop area where her dad was pounding on a horseshoe. Ozel waved to him. The blacksmith nodded back, but warily as though he'd tolerated Ozel and his daughter having a conversation once or twice, but three times was going too far.

Aysu plucked a thin bar of steel from a bin and compared it to the broken piece on the helmet. Then using a vise she bent it into shape. A minute later the result was that the end of the bar was fashioned into a new clip just like the one that had broken.

"How did your quest go? Are you a wizard now?" she asked.

"Not exactly," Ozel said. "I was going to confront an evil man, but he was gone. Now I have to rush to Calan to stop him gaining a great fortune and using it to oppress others."

"That sounds exciting. I wish I could go on a quest." She stuck the bar into the coals and worked the bellows a few times.

Ozel puffed his chest out a bit. "Yes, well, I don't expect it'll be all fun and games ..." Ozel realized he didn't know what to expect at all. "It's just that in order to become a wizard I have to be a man. And in order to prove my worth, I have to undertake a quest."

"More fun and games than I see around here," Aysu said. She used a pair of tongs to get the clip out of the heat. "Most exciting thing that happens to me is when a hot spark goes down Papa's shirt. You've never heard such language."

"I heard that," the blacksmith called, between the ringing of his hammer on the anvil.

Aysu used big pliers to snip the clip off the end and it clonked into a bowl to cool. She worked the old broken ring off the helmet strap, then held her hand over the new one.

"Still too hot," she said. "How long will it take to reach Calan on the road?"

"Maybe twelve days," Ozel said. Then, a little quieter, "But I'm not taking the road."

Aysu looked up. Her eyes were wide, brown, gorgeous. "You're going into the forest?" Her voice was little more than a hiss.

Ozel nodded.

She was still looking into his eyes. "You must be very brave. Do you have a weapon?"

"No, I was just thinking I'd like a dagger, but I haven't the money to buy one. I have my magic, though." He'd been practicing daily for years now. He could turn anything he wanted into a light source. His fireball was dangerous enough. And he could conjure a healing vial into being which, while small, was declared by Wagast to be "better than nothing."

Aysu stood up straight. "I shall ask father if we can give you a dagger. We have a few weapons lying around. People sometimes drop them off with us, but they are so broken they don't warrant repair. Papa used to make me repair them anyway for practice."

Ozel shook his head. "No, really, that's not necessary. I have my magic. I'll be all right."

Aysu was already gone. Ozel heard her father's hammer had stopped striking the anvil.

They were out of earshot, but Ozel knew a tense discussion when he saw one. Aysu's father was shaking his head, becoming more emphatic as he spoke. Then Aysu said something by way of emphatic retort and stalked off toward the house.

With a scowl on his face, the blacksmith watched her go, then shook his head and walked over to Ozel.

"Honestly," the blacksmith said. "Women. It's as if they spend all day thinking of how to frustrate us men, eh?"

Ozel wasn't sure that he agreed. Aysu wasn't frustrating. She was interesting and nice. He was pleased to be included in "us men," though, so he just made a noncommittal noise.

The blacksmith held his hand over the clip in the bowl and grunted when he deemed it to be cool enough. With deft fingers, he worked it onto the helmet. He held it out to Ozel, who tried it on.

The blacksmith nodded. "A fine helmet, that is. Good piece of armor. I'm no wizard, but I expect old Wagast has placed a few enchantments as well, eh? Might want to work a little oil onto it, when you can. Keep the rust off."

"I will, sir. Thank you."

Ozel paid for the work, thanked the blacksmith again, and then left through the back of the blacksmith's shop towards a path that led to the Tangul Forest. He looked over his shoulder as he walked away and saw Aysu in a window, watching him go. She held her hand up. He waved back. Then she was gone.

Ahead, the outskirts of the forest spread beneath a darkening sky.

CHAPTER 10

Inside the forest, Ozel stopped well before sundown to lay out his bedroll and get a fire going. There was a clearing just off the path. Unless he was mistaken, he and Wagast had spent the night in this camping spot before. A few herbs necessary for Wagast's more complicated enchantments grew nearby.

Did he really want to start a fire? It might keep certain types of animals away, then again, it might also draw danger toward him. Murderous folk of all possible descriptions lurked in these woods, so it was said. If they were looking around for someone to kill, they could approach a fire without being seen.

He decided safety was the most important thing and laid in his bedroll at the foot of a tree. Ozel stared up at the sky through the branches, but there wasn't much to see, the stars obscured by clouds. A light rain started, which took Ozel from "slightly cool," to "shivering."

He got up, cast the light spell on a twig, then used it to find enough wood for a fire. Once it was going, he warmed himself and his bedroll. Safety might be important, he thought, but you can also safely freeze your ass off, if you're not careful.

IN THE MORNING, he felt like he'd been thrown off a cliff. He'd gotten a few hours of sleep during the night, certainly. Hadn't he? Yet he felt terrible. He rolled up his bed, packed it, and ate a bit of cheese as he walked deeper into the forest.

The sky cleared up around noon, and when Ozel found a sunny clearing he stopped to lay out his bedroll to dry. It wouldn't take long, and he'd have a better time sleeping tonight if he could get his gear dried out. He draped the blankets over a bush in some sunlight and sat down to eat something.

He heard a shout.

He couldn't make out what the person was yelling, but it sounded like someone was in trouble. Ozel stood, focused, listened intently.

There it was again. Ozel told himself that if he were in trouble in these woods, he'd want someone to come to his aid, wouldn't he? Yes, he would.

He started to move.

He caught flashes through the trees of what was happening, but it wasn't until he crept closer that he could see it properly.

In a clearing, a man was fighting a bear.

The bear was enormous. Ozel had heard stories about the big bears in the Tangul Forest, but this thing eclipsed even his worst nightmares of how big the animals could be. It lunged at the man and clamped its jaws on his leg. The man shouted with pain and surprise. He pounded his fists into the bear's face. The beast let him go, roared, then coiled itself for another attack.

If Ozel didn't do something, the bear was going to kill the man. And when that was done, the bear would come for him too, no doubt. He cleared his mind as he had practiced so many times. He focused his energy, then he shouted, "Augue!"

The biggest fireball he'd made to date left his hands and flew towards the clearing. But the man whirled to avoid another lunge from the bear, stepping directly into the path of the magic. The fireball hit him, exploded, and he was completely engulfed in flames.

The man howled and kept swiping at the bear, perhaps not yet realizing the extent to which he was on fire. His flaming arms clutched at the animal, which reared backward and decided that fighting things engulfed in flames was out of the question. It turned and ran away.

The man dropped to the ground and began rolling over and over again in the dirt, but it was no use. The flames had taken hold. He would be dead any second.

Ozel focused again and conjured a vial of healing potion. He ran into the clearing.

"Here!" he yelled. "Drink this at once. Healing potion!"

He thrust the vial at the man, who sat up and threw his charred, smoking hood back from his face. It revealed a horrific visage. His hair was all burned off, as were his lips. His eyes were still in his sockets, but they rolled around like something out of the worst dream imaginable.

Ozel screamed and backed away too fast, stumbling and falling on his ass.

"Holy fuck!" the burned man said, his words somewhat mangled by his ruined face. "You saved me."

"Drink the potion," Ozel said. He shielded his eyes with his hand so he didn't have to look. He'd be having nightmares about this for weeks, he was sure. Then, he said again, because it was the only thing his brain could think to say, "Drink the potion!"

"How did you know that setting me on fire was the only way to save my life?" The man stood and began brushing his burned clothes. "I shall need a new cloak, I think, but better a new cloak than being dismembered, eh? That bear was an asshole, and no mistake."

Ozel said, imploring, "Sir, I don't think you're aware how grave your wounds are. Your face is burned off. Please drink the potion at once. It will help you."

"Oh, my face?" the man said. "Sometimes forget how shit I look. Sorry about that. I can pull my hood up, if you like."

CHAPTER 11

Ozel couldn't think what to say, then managed, "No, please. I'm sorry. I don't mean to be rude. I'm just not used to people looking so ... injured and being calm about it."

The man put out a gloved hand. Ozel took it and the man helped him up easily. He wasn't a large fellow, but based on the way he hauled Ozel off the ground he was awfully strong.

"I am Ergam," the man said. "Ergam Sakir. You have saved my life, and for that I am eternally in your debt." He handed Ozel the vial. "A true life debt. However, I cannot accept your healing potion. Can't drink them. I'm already dead."

"Yuh," Ozel said, his power of speech not working at the moment. He stared at Ergam. He was wearing dark brown breeches, black boots, and a dark green hooded cloak. Ergam pulled the cloak to the side to examine it. There was a large hole burned into the back.

Ozel considered drinking the vial. Something had

happened to him. He'd come under an evil spell or something. That was why he was hallucinating.

"I am sorry for the shock," Ergam said. "I'm not going to eat your soul or anything. I don't know what kind of shit you've heard about the undead, but I assure you we are nice. Unless you're a fuck-off big bear trying to bite us in half, obviously."

Ozel shook his head. "No, I apologize again. I'm being rude. Sorry. I am Ozel."

Ergam put his gloved hand out again, and they shook. Ozel noticed that the other hand didn't have a glove on it. The flesh was mangled. He hoped the glove had merely fallen off in the fight and would be replaced soon.

"Do you not have a surname, Ozel?"

"Not at the moment, no. I was an orphan. I'm an apprentice wizard, so I guess my surname could be 'the Apprentice Wizard' if I were forced to have one."

"Ozel the Brave, I should think. Ozel the Savior, perhaps. All Bears Fuck Off Here Comes Ozel, eh?"

Ozel shook his head. "I meant to hit the bear with my magic, not you."

"You what?" Ergam asked.

"I sent the fireball to hit the bear. It was only by accident that you ended up on fire. I'm lucky you weren't killed." The word "killed" slipped out before he had a chance to choose something better.

"Ah," Ergam said. He seemed to search for words for a brief moment, but it was hard to tell with the hood. Then he lifted a finger and said, "Perhaps. But you could have done nothing. You could have sat down on your ass. Or run away."

Ozel inclined his head. That was true. "How are you dead and yet still walking around?"

"It's a curse. My father ran afoul of an evil wizard."

"Why are you cursed for what your father did?"

Ergam shrugged and said something in reply, but Ozel was distracted when, behind Ergam, a figure burst from the shadows of a tree, knife raised.

"Aysu, no!" Ozel yelled, but it was too late. She was already swinging at Ergam, who had no time to react.

An instant later the dagger was sticking out of Ergam's head.

Aysu stood panting, staring with wide eyes at Ergam. Then she stared at Ozel. Then again at Ergam.

Ergam asked Ozel, "Is this a friend of yours?"

"Yes," Ozel said. "This is Aysu, the blacksmith's daughter."

"Not dead," Aysu said, blinking at the dagger and Ergam's charred head. She kept looking back and forth between Ergam and Ozel.

"I assure you I am quite dead, young miss," Ergam said. He reached up and gave the handle of the dagger a tug. "Fuck me, that's really in there."

"Aysu, this is Ergam."

Ergam let go of the dagger handle and put out his gloved hand. "Charmed," he said. He smiled, but the effect was not as polite as it could have been if he'd had more face.

"What are you doing here?" Ozel asked Aysu.

"I am on a quest," Ergam and Aysu said at the same time.

"What?" They all asked each other.

"I'm the one on a quest," Ozel said, placing a hand on his chest. "To Calan, to stop Bartu Hamdi, learn about my parents, and become a proper wizard."

"I'm on that one too," Aysu said.

"I'm on a quest to find good humans," Ergam said.

"But you can't be on my quest," Ozel told Aysu. "It's mine."

Aysu's eyes became hard, her hands balling into fists.

Ergam made a coughing sound. "Ah, Master Ozel, I'd just like to point out that the young lady has shown herself perfectly willing to bury a dagger in someone's skull. Perhaps she can decide for herself what she does with her time. I'd hate to see you get your ass kicked by your own friend."

Ozel looked at the gleaming dagger still stuck in Ergam's skull. The dead man had a point.

"And don't you forget it," Aysu said. "Anyway, I'm not going back home until I prove to Father that I'm old enough to choose my own life. I'm helping on the quest to Calan, and that's that."

Her fists were still balled up. Ozel thought it might be good to change the subject. "What is the quest you're on, Ergam?"

"Ah, yes. I'm on a quest to find good humans. You see, my people's numbers are dwindling. The church's influence on magic is such that you see fewer and fewer curses."

"Surely that's a good thing," Ozel said.

"Unquestionably. But the church also regularly sends adventurers into the wood to destroy as many of us as they can. All we ask is to be left alone. Yet for some reason, they can't seem to manage it. Some among us say we should fight back. Perhaps go on a raid of our own into town."

"What town?" Aysu asked.

"The closest one ... where are you from?"

"Bilgehan."

Ergam pointed at her. "That's it."

"Then I must warn the town," Aysu said. "If I run the whole way, I might make it before sunrise."

Ergam shook his head. "That's why they've picked Bilge-han. It's too far from anywhere to call for help in time. If you go back there, you'll only be killed too when the undead hordes descend. Besides, there's a better way."

"What's that?" Ozel asked.

"Come with me to the City of the Undead. Help me complete my quest to prove to my father's advisor and the rest of our people that the living are not all bad. We can stop the attack on your town before it ever begins. In return, I will assist you on the way through the forest to Calan. I am stronger than any living man and, as you can see," he gestured to the dagger. "I can take a lot of damage."

"Does it hurt?" Aysu asked.

"Doesn't tickle."

"What do you think, Aysu?" Ozel asked.

She nodded. "Definitely looks like it hurts."

"No, I mean about Ergam's quest."

"Oh. The idea of a city of the undead is frightening, however the idea of an undead horde crushing my family is worse." She nodded. "Yes. I shall join you, Ergam."

Ergam's face rearranged horrifically.

"Is that a smile?" Aysu asked.

"I'm afraid so," Ergam said. "What about you, Master Ozel? I should say that since I am forever in your debt, I'm in a bit of a quandary. I'm not sure if my life debt to you supersedes my quest to save my people. So, I might be honor-bound to go where you go regardless of whether you agree to help me complete my quest first. But since Miss Aysu has decided to help, I think we should help her." He stood there for a second, looking off into the trees as if in thought. "I should have thought about these kinds of conundrums before I pledged a life debt."

"Especially since you're not alive," Aysu said.

Ergam made a snorting sound and his face moved around into his dreadful version of a smile again. "She's funny. You're funny, Miss Aysu. I like you."

"Yes," Ozel said. "You're quite right. Time is of the essence on my quest to Calan. But we can't allow Aysu's family to be in danger. Or yours, Ergam."

"Capital!" Ergam said. He clapped his hands together, and the tip of one of his fingers flew off.

CHAPTER 12

Ergam picked up a bow lying on the ground and slung a leather quiver over his shoulder. There was also, to Ozel's relief, a second glove. The three of them walked back to get Ozel's gear. The patch of sunlight on the bedroll had shifted, but the blankets were dry. Ozel rolled them back up and replaced them on his pack.

"So, Ergam, you were just going to walk into town and—what? Try to find someone nice?" Aysu asked.

"Yeah, I admit that it wasn't much of a plan. But if I kept my hood up, that might have helped. I thought I might try to find someone in distress, help them out, then get them to help me in return."

"That plan seems to have worked," Ozel said.

Ergam chuckled. "In a way, but backwards, right? By the way, could we get this dagger out of my head before we set off again? It won't help make the case that all the living aren't monsters if I'm wearing a dagger for a hat."

Ergam leaned forward and Aysu wrapped both hands around the dagger's handle. Even with her pulling one way and Ergam struggling in the other direction, they couldn't dislodge it. Ozel tried pulling it free as well, this time with Ergam's head braced in the crook of a tree. His hand slipped off.

Aysu produced a hammer from a loop on her belt. "I think if I give it a few taps one way, then one or two the other way, perhaps I can loosen it in the hole." The hammer had a short handle, but had a heavy head that was square at one end and a chisel point at the other.

Ergam eyed the hammer suspiciously. "That looks like it might hurt."

"I'll be gentle."

Ozel told her, "If you were gentle, the thing wouldn't be lodged so deeply in his head in the first place."

Aysu glared at him and gave the hammer a wiggle.

Ergam sighed. "It's worth a shot. Fuck it." He bent over.

Aysu gave the dagger a single tap on the side. It moved a fraction of an inch.

"All right?" Aysu said.

"Yes. Carry on," Ergam said to the ground.

Aysu tapped the dagger back the other way, then repeated the process a few more times. Eventually she was able to tug the dagger free of Ergam's rotted and charred head. She wiped the blade off on some leaves.

"Ah," Ergam said, straightening. "That's much better." He rubbed at the hole in his skull. "I think I could keep loose change in there now."

Aysu and Ozel laughed.

Aysu held out the dagger to Ozel. "I brought this for you."

"Me?"

"You said you wanted a dagger, and I wanted to join your quest. I thought it would help you decide to bring me along if I had a gift for you. It just so happened that when I found you, I saw an undead horror standing over you and I thought you were in mortal danger. So I plunged it into his head before I had a chance to give it to you properly—no offense, Ergam."

"None taken," Ergam said.

Ozel took the dagger. It was long and graceful, a thing of artistry as much as a weapon. He regarded it with awe. "Thank you, it's beautiful!"

Aysu smiled. "I made it myself. Papa helped."

"It is very sharp," Ergam said. "A formidable weapon, to be sure. Now, young master and mistress. Shall we go a-fucking-questing?"

They set off, following Ergam through the forest.

"Ergam?" Aysu said, sounding like she was treading carefully.

"Yeah?"

"Why do you swear so much? Mind you, I don't mind. My father has been known to let fly with some coarse language from time to time, especially when he accidentally hammers his own thumb."

"I guess after you die you stop caring what anyone thinks about you. As you can see, my face and body are a complete disaster. It doesn't make a lot of sense to walk around talking posh when I look like a nightmare with a day job."

"Fair enough," Aysu said.

"Besides," Ergam went on. "I was pretty foul-mouthed before I passed away."

Ozel noticed something. "How are you walking so quietly?"

"Ah," Ergam said. "I was a forest ranger when I was alive. Spent quite a lot of time not being seen or heard. I was very good at it then, and I've only gotten better at it in the intervening years."

By comparison, it sounded like Ozel and Aysu were kicking their feet through every dry bush they could find.

"I also have exceptional hearing. Might I suggest that if we should run into any danger, I will let you know when to hide?"

"Will there be a lot of danger?" Aysu asked.

"Oh my, yes," Ergam said.

"Are you any good with that bow?" Ozel asked.

"I like to think so," Ergam said. "I'll spare you a demonstration until we need a little meat for supper, eh?"

"Do you eat?" Aysu asked.

"I do not. I don't sleep either. But I do love to hunt. Precious little need for it, since my death, and I don't relish the idea of taking a life unless it is necessary. However, finding a morsel to roast over the fire for you two will be a welcome diversion. Ah, speaking of which—"

In a single fluid motion Ergam unshouldered the long stout bow and nocked an arrow, then fired towards a tree. The arrow missed.

Ozel and Aysu looked at one another, but said nothing. Ergam started walking again, also without a word, so they followed along behind.

A good many minutes later they came to another small clearing. A rabbit lay in the middle, dead as a doornail with Ergam's arrow sticking up in the air. The dead man regarded the animal with some pride. "Shot went a tick high, I think, but I got him all the same."

Ozel and Aysu stared at one another, and then Ergam.

"You should cut the arrow out, not me, I think," Ergam said. "I wouldn't want anything you're going to eat coming in contact with my deceased flesh. It probably wouldn't harm you fatally, but it could make you sick."

Ozel grabbed the arrow by the shaft close to the rabbit's body and cut it out of the meat. He handed the arrow back to Ergam.

Ozel took the opportunity to quickly skin and dress the carcass, a skill he'd learned with Wagast.

Ergam was looking up through the trees. "We should make camp."

"We have hours of light yet," Ozel said.

"True, young master. True. But I'd like to brief you on what to expect from the challenges of the forest. We are well and truly within its borders now. There might be some particulars of the environs to which you are not accustomed. Do either of you know how to cook?"

"I do," Ozel said.

"Any good with fire?"

"I've made thousands," Aysu said, before Ozel had a chance.

"Well, don't that beat all," Ergam said. "It's as if this team was meant to be questing together, no?"

CHAPTER 13

Ozel used his dagger to carve a rudimentary spit for roasting the rabbit over the flames. While he waited for Aysu's fire to die down to coals, he collected a few herbs and greens to go with the meat. The end result, once the coals were spread and the rabbit was roasted, was not bad.

"This is the best meat I have ever eaten," Aysu said, her eyes were wide, wondering.

Ozel blushed. "I could have done a lot better with a proper kitchen. Hard to control the heat properly with the spit."

Ergam said, "My experience—when I was alive, mind— was that wizards were good cooks. Gathering the components of spells and mixing things together and shit? Those are skills that lend themselves well to the culinary arts."

"My mother burns everything," Aysu said. "Sometimes it's burned on the outside and raw in the middle. I had no idea something like a rabbit could be this tender."

"Aw, come on," Ozel said. "I'm sure your mother's cooking is not that bad."

"I bet if you put my mom's cooking next to one of Ergam's feet, you'd be hard pressed to tell the difference."

They all laughed. Ozel was getting used to the peculiar noise Ergam made when he was amused.

"Don't make me take my boot off and show you how right you are," Ergam said. "You might not eat for a few days." Then he laughed again.

It was getting dark. Ozel was glad that he wouldn't have to make camp alone.

"Ergam, you mentioned some perils?" Ozel asked.

"Ah, yes." Ergam shifted slightly on the log he was using for a seat. "The fastest way to my city, Kanat, is through the swamp. We could be in Kanat this time tomorrow night, if all goes well, but if not ..."

"If not what?" Ozel asked.

"The swamp is home to a witch. Guzul the Fierce. She's a lot older these days than when she achieved the title of 'The Fierce,' but she's still no one to be trifled with. If she finds out living humans are crossing her waters, we may be challenged to pay her some form of tribute in order to pass safely."

"What are our other options?" Aysu asked.

"We could go around. It would cost us a day or two, I expect. Not nearly so much as skirting the forest entirely by using the road, but as you said, time is of the essence?"

"I need to be in Calan in eleven days at the most," Ozel said. "The sooner the better, though."

"Quite right. In that case, I think we should go through and take our chances with Guzul. She is not exactly friendly to the living, but she's not a merciless killer either. As long as we stick to the path, move quickly, and don't touch anything, we should pass easily. I've done it many times."

"You know this area much better than we do," Ozel said.

"I suppose we should listen to your counsel. What do you think, Aysu?"

"I think that I always wanted to meet a witch."

"Aren't they dangerous and unpredictable?" Ozel asked.

"No more so than a wizard," Ergam said.

"Exactly," Aysu said. "Perhaps I could become a witch someday myself? I might not mind living in a stone house like you and Wagast. Gardening and what-not."

"Sorry to say, but it's my hope that with my scouting skills we never encounter her," Ergam said. "Enjoy your dinner, and eat a big breakfast tomorrow. We may need to be moving all day, so don't count on a lunch."

"Anything we need to be worried about overnight?" Ozel asked.

Ergam shook his head. "As I've already mentioned, I don't sleep. With your permission, I'll be on watch. In fact, I'd like to have a look around the site now that it's gone full dark, if I might excuse myself?"

"You don't have to ask me," said Ozel.

Ergam nodded, then stood and with barely a noise to mark his footsteps strode out of the firelight.

"What do you think?" Ozel whispered to Aysu. "Do we trust him?"

She was gnawing at a rabbit leg bone. "I like him. He might be dead, but he seems nice. I've met living people who were a lot less fun to talk to, that's for sure."

"True," Ozel said. "But we did only just meet him."

"Did you see that arrow shot, though? If he wanted to do us harm it'd be done. And it would be justified harm, considering I stabbed him in the head and you set him on fire."

"You raise good points."

There was a rustle of leaves at the edge of the firelight.

Ozel and Aysu both whirled, but it was just Ergam dragging his feet in the forest leaves as he walked.

"I just wanted to remind you," he said. "That I have exceptionally good hearing. Even if it seems like I'm out of earshot, I might not be."

"It's okay, Ergam," said Aysu. "We trust you."

CHAPTER 14

The next morning, as they walked, the ground became soft and began to stick to their boots. The trees turned from familiar hardwoods to things with great knobby roots, which Ergam called "knees." There was a path through the soft mud, but it was crisscrossed with streams and the occasional boggy patch.

By midmorning there was deeper water on the sides of the path. Ozel thought he saw a bone-white fish under the surface, but it could have been his imagination.

"So what do you like about blacksmithing?" Ozel asked Aysu.

She looked thoughtful. "My dad says it's good work, because it takes skill and hard effort, which are two things most people don't have in them. So you're likely to always have work to do. I like it for those reasons, I guess. You have to get the metal hot, but not too hot. There are lots of tricks you can learn for making scrolls this way or twists that way. Then whatever you make stays around for a long time."

"That makes sense. Magic's not like that as much. My spells don't hang around too long."

"But if you kill a bear that is attacking your friend, then your friend stays around, right?"

Ozel coughed. "Yes, well. But if you accidentally set your friend on fire ..."

"Already forgotten," Ergam said in a sing-song voice. "No harm done."

"Do you think you'll be a blacksmith when you grow up, then?" Ozel asked.

"I haven't decided. I think I might always like to have a forge, but as for whether I run a shop like my dad's, I don't know. He says it'll be hard for a woman to be a blacksmith, but he doesn't have any sons, so ..." She shrugged.

A very large, black bird in a tree cawed reproachfully. Its dark eyes seemed to be judging the small party as it made its way through the swamp.

They didn't sit down to eat lunch, but they did stop for a few minutes so Ozel and Aysu could take their packs off and rest. The sky was filled with clouds. A mist fingered its way through the tree branches as if it were a living thing. When they walked through clouds of the fog drifting low over the path, it chilled them to the bone.

They rounded a corner. Ahead was a row of hedges that stretched across the path. On either side was murky, forbidding water. When they got closer, they could see written in pink flower blossoms on the hedgerow was, "GO AWAY."

The branches mingled and twined around one another, and the thorns looked sharp. Someone could most likely hack or shove their way through, but it would be hard work and certainly scratch your skin.

"Oh no," Ergam said. "I was afraid of this."

"What?" Aysu asked.

"Guzul the Fierce knows we're here." He gestured to the hedge. "This hedge doesn't normally grow here."

"Shame," Aysu said. "The flowers are lovely."

Ozel looked at her.

"The message isn't very nice, but the flowers themselves, I mean."

Ergam said, "I am sorry. I have passed this way dozens of times with no ill consequences. And no hedge. Certainly no flowers."

"So what do we do?" Ozel asked.

"We turn back, I should think," Ergam said. "It's the safest option. It will cost us those few days, but we might still make it to Kanat in time."

"Might?" Aysu asked.

Ergam seemed uneasy. "We'd be entering the city from a different direction. The raiding party will come *this* way. If we're even a moment late, we'll never see them or catch up."

"If we go through, will we definitely be in time?" Aysu asked.

"Probably, but we are in Guzul the Fierce's domain now and she knows we're here. Witches do love the opportunity to put people through trials."

"How can we be sure that if we turn around, we'd lose only a few days?" Ozel asked. "If she likes toying with people, couldn't she do something anyway?"

"She could, definitely. Witches are powerful."

"Then, as I see it, we might as well go forward."

Ergam admitted after a moment, "Makes sense to me. She might be more annoyed with us if we turn back. She could delay us indefinitely, have us walking in circles, anything."

"This is annoying," Aysu said.

Ozel thought a minute, then said, "I think I know what to do."

He stepped forward to the hedge. "Hello, madam," he

called, in a loud, clear voice. "My name is Ozel. I am a wizard's apprentice. With respect, I would like to speak to you, please."

There was no response. Then a bubbling sound from the far side of the hedge reached them. It grew into a frothing roar of water in the swamp. They could see the white foam through the branches. At last, a voice deep and foreboding like the shifting of the earth itself replied. The water pulsed, and the ground rumbled beneath their feet.

"Speak."

"My friends and I are sorry to cross your land without invitation, but we are in a hurry to stop an army of undead from raiding a town. If you truly do wish us to go away, we ask that you don't delay us in retracing our steps. However, if you would like us to face your trials, we are not afraid. We ask only to be treated fairly."

There was an even deeper rumbling noise, and then a twisting and popping as the branches of the hedge unwound. The flowers spelling "GO AWAY" bloomed in reverse, then shrank out of sight entirely. An archway formed in the hedge and the path again led forward through the swamp. The frothing waters to either side ceased to boil, only bubbling a little, and then were calm.

Ergam's expression was always wide-eyed, thanks to a lack of eyelids, but his jaw hung open in an unmistakable gape of awe. "I've been around a long time, but I've never seen anything like that."

"I agree," Aysu said. "Very brave. I am impressed."

"It was nothing," Ozel said. "I only offered to treat her fairly and with respect, and asked the same for us."

Ergam still gaped. "Still, I have never heard of anyone addressing a witch that way. Quite remarkable."

"Think it'll work? Will we get through the swamp in time to make it to Kanat?"

Ergam laughed. "Oh, young master, I wouldn't worry about that."

"Good," Ozel said.

"I expect we'll be killed in whatever trials lay ahead," Ergam said cheerfully. "So there's no need to worry at all."

CHAPTER 15

Aysu was the first through the hedge. Then Ozel, and last Ergam. As Ergam was coming through, the branches of the hedge closed in so quickly behind him that they snagged his cloak.

"Blast," Ergam said. "A bustle in the hedgerow." He jerked at his cloak. "Give me that, you awful shrub!" With a final tear, the cloak came free of the thorns. Ergam held it up to examine the tatters. "How do you like that, then?"

They moved along the path in the gloom. Ahead, the trees crowded in close forming an impenetrable wall on either side. The path tilted up.

The slope didn't seem like much at first, but as it gradually steepened, Aysu and Ozel found themselves panting with the effort. Ergam went up ahead and then came back down periodically to encourage them. He seemed to have no problem whatsoever with the incline.

Part of the problem was that the path was no longer soft or muddy. Hard earth was covered with very small, round rocks. Each step Ozel took, his foot slid backward a little bit. It felt like he was expending more effort every moment and making less forward progress in return. This went on for hours, until Ozel and Aysu were both soaked with sweat. Ergam shouldered their packs for them, which was a great help. The going was still rough.

Ozel was clinging to a tree and resting for a few moments when Ergam called back to him, "You're almost there, young master. The top is just ahead."

He heard Aysu begin climbing again behind him. Ozel was going to hold her up. So he put one foot in front of the other and did his best to reduce the sliding until he finally got to Ergam at the peak of the hill. There was a flat section of trail here, and the trees fell away. It offered a commanding view of the surrounding area. It was gorgeous —except for one thing.

Ahead, the trail plunged down into a valley, then up the side of an even bigger, steeper slope. Beyond that was a taller one, and so on into the distance. The tallest of the peaks was lost in misty clouds.

"We'll be lucky just to get to the top of the next one today," Ozel said. "Let alone climbing all of them in a couple of days' time."

Aysu joined them, breathing hard. She grabbed her pack off Ergam, put it on her shoulders, and nodded. "We'd best get going, if we're going up the rest of those."

And with that, she headed down the other side.

Ozel looked at Ergam, who shrugged. Ozel picked up his pack too and together they followed Aysu.

The trail only descended for a minute or two until it came to a deep ravine. The path continued ahead, but where there had once been a solid land-bridge across the ravine was now only broken up bits of rocks and dirt—with a lot of space in between. Ozel thought he should be able to jump over the gaps. But if he missed, he'd be falling for a long time and then dead for a lot longer.

Aysu kicked a stone off the edge. It clattered a few times, then fell out of sight into the abyss.

"Are we sure we want to continue?" Ergam said.

"Even if we went back, we'd never make it through that hedge," Ozel said.

"At least let me try crossing this first," said Ergam. "If I fall it'll be annoying, but I can't be any deader than I am. I've bounced down a ravine or two in my day. Nothing to it."

"If you insist," Ozel said.

Ergam readied himself, then jumped over to a section of the bridge. He made the distance easily. He made the next two in rapid succession, then turned around and leaped back towards them.

"Let me have your packs," he said. "I can do that much."

He repeated his crossing of the ravine and deposited the packs safely on the other side, then came all the way back.

"All right," he said. "Who's going first?"

CHAPTER 16

"I am," said Aysu.

"Why you?" Ozel asked.

"Because I spoke up first. And because I don't want to be standing here alone."

"I didn't think of it like that—" Ozel said.

He was cut off when Aysu took a short run-up and leaped out. She landed neatly next to Ergam.

"All right, young master," Ergam said. "Come along. We'll catch you."

Ozel eyed the distance. It couldn't be any wider than the creek back home after it hadn't rained too much. He jumped over that all the time. The fear of tumbling to his death here added a variable to the calculation that didn't have a numerical value and yet dickered mightily the outcome.

Still, he wasn't going to go back, was he? No. If he wasn't going back, and he didn't want to waste time, he might as well jump.

He backed up a step and yelled, "Here I come!" Then rushed forward. He planted his foot at the edge of the gap just as he'd planned, but the ground shifted.

Abruptly, instead of landing safely he was, at best, going to slam into the rock chest-high and then fall to his doom.

He gave an awkward yelp and flailed his arms. His impact was as expected. His knees and chest hit the rock hard as his hands groped in a futile attempt to clutch at the rim of the precipice. All the air whooshed out of his lungs and he began to fall backward.

Ergam's hand flashed out and wrapped around Ozel's arm. Aysu grabbed the other and together they hauled Ozel up until he was sitting on the ground. He gasped there, catching his breath.

"Thank you," he panted. "Thank you."

"Not at all," Ergam said. "You'd have done the same for us."

Aysu nodded and smiled. She offered Ozel a drink of water from a canteen, which he accepted.

"I suppose this means you're free of your life debt," Ozel said.

"I don't think it really counts," Ergam said. "I had Aysu's help. I shall have to serve until I have clearly saved you from certain death, I think."

When Ozel had his breath back, he stood and they went on. The next two gaps were no more than large cracks, although they had initially appeared at least as wide as the first. The three of them stepped over these to reach Aysu's and Ozel's bags.

Now the path was carved out of a sheer cliff face. On the right was a rock wall, and to their left, empty air. The view might have been stunning were it not for the mist. They walked for what felt like days. Ozel's sense of time was screwed up without being able to see the sun. He didn't know if they'd come through the hedge an hour ago or a week ago. He felt tired enough to lie down and sleep, and lagged behind the others.

There was a whooshing, crackling sound like a big bonfire. The trail wound around a rocky outcrop, then widened on the other side. Ergam and Aysu had stopped, staring into the near distance.

A section of the path was on fire, long enough that even at full tilt someone would have to run for several seconds to get through it. The flames were white hot and flickering, and looked capable of burning through a person's boots and reducing their legs to charred twigs.

Ozel took off his pack and sat down, his back against the rock wall.

"Er," Ergam said.

"Maybe if we pee on the fire we could put it out," Aysu suggested.

Ozel looked again. The flames were waist-high.

"I'm not sure there's that much pee in all the kingdoms," Ergam said.

"Blegh," Ozel said.

"I apologize for bringing up pee," Aysu said.

"Right, well, since I'm already mostly burned," Ergam said. He strode over to the flames and stuck one of his feet into the fire, then jerked it out. He examined his boot for damage. Next he bent over and put a hand into the flames, then withdrew that and looked at it.

Ergam stood up. "I think the flames are false." He strode into the fire, twirled once, and walked back out again. He wasn't burned—no more than he'd been before, anyway.

Ozel stood and put his pack back on. "All right, I'll try it." He stepped toward the flames. He could feel the heat radiating from the fire, but that might just have been part of the enchantment.

He stuck his leg in, then quickly pulled it back. There wasn't a scorch mark on his boot, neither was the foot inside burned to a nub. He could feel Aysu and Ergam watching him. He didn't want to appear a coward.

He squared his shoulders and stepped into the fire, walking through the flames as though he were strolling through a field of wheat. Behind him, Ergam and Aysu began to follow.

He was just past midway when his feet started to feel hot. He quickened his pace a little and they got even hotter. He yelped with the pain and jumped and skipped, trying to avoid touching the ground. His last few footsteps, his feet were searing with pain. He collapsed on the far side of the fire and slapped at his boots.

He heard a scream and turned to see Aysu fall headlong. She'd tripped and gone down in the fire, desperately grasping at the bare rock to pull herself forward.

Ozel cried out and lunged for her hand. Ergam had a grip on her pack as well and together they hauled her out of the fire to safety. Ozel looked her breeches over for any flames, but they were intact.

Aysu sat up. "It quit burning me as soon as I fell."

"What?" Ozel said.

"I was looking down at the fire, and then I realized you were far ahead of me, so I started running. The flames got hotter and hotter, and I stumbled, but as soon as I fell all the heat of the fire was gone."

"Perhaps it is based on speed," Ergam said. "Anyone who got here and saw the flames would surely try to run through as quickly as possible. But the faster you go, the hotter it gets. Sounds bizarre if you ask me, but that's witchcraft for you."

"Are we all right, then?" Ozel asked.

Aysu nodded. They helped each other up, and moved on.

"Good thing we had a dead man with us," Aysu said. "Or we might be dead."

"Pleased to be of service," Ergam said. He gave a grand sweep of his arm and a little bow.

CHAPTER 17

The stone path carved into the rock wall became less severe. Soon they left the craggy scenery behind as the land rose to join both sides of the path. The trees were back, and finally they came to another hedge. This one had a grand archway with double wooden doors banded with iron hinges and straps.

As they drew near, the doors opened revealing a house in a meadow with wildflowers dotting the grass and golden sunlight filtering through trees. Standing in the archway was an elderly woman in a long white dress, and wearing a white crown that looked to be made of twigs. She was smiling.

The house was a sprawling, white structure with a thatched roof and huge exposed beams. There were pea gravel paths surrounding it leading to several flower gardens. The grounds were immaculately kept, and all the plants were magnificently in bloom. Ozel guessed that a significant amount of magic was at play.

She put her arms out. "Welcome, I can't tell you how pleased I am with your performance." She hugged Ergam, apparently unconcerned that he was an undead horror. Then she embraced Aysu and Ozel in turn. Neither knew how to react, but Guzul seemed perfectly charming. She smelled like lavender.

"So, to be clear," Ergam said. "Are we done with the trials? Or is this another one?"

"I'll say you're done," said Guzul. "No one has made it through my trials in centuries. I knew when you addressed me honestly this morning you three were a different sort of group. I'm just so thrilled you're here. I feel like I might burst with pride. The last person to make it through my fire pit used a pair of wooden poles to raise himself off the ground."

"But we were in fear for our lives at several points today," Ozel said, gritting his teeth. "I asked that we be treated fairly."

"You were also aware that you were in my domain, and that I had the power to alter what you see," Guzul said. She led the three of them to a table set with four places. "That's what a witch's trials are all about. Perception."

"So we were never really in danger?" Aysu asked.

Guzul put a finger to her cheek. "Hmm, well, I wouldn't say that." She laughed. "But you made it. That's what's important, right? Come. Rest a while. Eat something."

The food did smell good. There was a roast chicken surrounded by root vegetables, some leafy greens, plus a steaming loaf of bread next to a butter dish.

"I am a lonely old woman," Guzul said. She frowned. "I don't have the power I used to have when they called me Guzul the Fierce. When I did, I could afford to place myself out in the middle of the world. People would brave my trials in order to earn powerful enchantments, or to beg me to create love potions. They were the worst, the love potion people. You can tell them until you're blue in the face that you don't do that kind of work, but they won't listen."

Ozel edged closer to the roast chicken. There was a knife on the tray next to it. He sliced off a piece of meat and popped it into his mouth. The skin was crispier, and the meat juicier, than any he'd ever tasted.

"Trials are why I became a witch," Guzul said. "I just love creating puzzles of the mind. But since my powers began to decline, my enchantments weren't as precious. People stopped braving my trials. Now the only people who set foot in my lands are already dead. No use making them face death, you know."

"This chicken is amazing," Ozel said. "How did you get it so crispy on the outside yet so tender within?"

"Oh, you know, many years of practice," Guzul said. "It's all about controlling the heat."

"Too right," Ozel agreed.

Aysu said, "Sorry, I don't mean to be rude, Madam Guzul, but is it safe to eat this food? It's not a trick, is it?"

"No, you have my word. The trials are over. They were far too short, if you ask me. I've left people out there for days. Weeks! But I understand you have bigger trials at hand. I mustn't be greedy."

Ozel had cut himself another slice of chicken. "If this roast chicken kills me, it'll be worth it anyway. It's absolutely exquisite."

"Oh, stop," Guzul said, with a coy smile. "Please, sit."

Ozel plopped into a chair and began to fill his plate. He was so hungry and the food so good that he was eating faster than he probably should.

Aysu sat too, and Ozel cut her a slice of chicken. She ate it and smiled.

"As long as you're here," Guzul said. "I'd like to offer you two enchantments. One each. I shall place one on your dagger, Ozel, and one on your hammer, Aysu. And for you, Mr. Sakir, I have a gift. But first, let's talk about my tribute."

Ozel, Aysu, and Ergam looked at one another.

"I would like the children to draw me some pictures," the witch said.

"Sorry?" Ergam said.

"Pictures. Artwork. They don't have to be good. I just don't get many children around and I always liked their drawings. Years ago mothers used to tell their children that I was their aunt or granny, when they came to ask me for potions or enchantments. The wee ones would sit and draw with bits of charcoal or what-have-you."

"We'll be happy to do some drawings for you," Aysu said.

"Thank you, dear," said Guzul. "Now, some gifts." With a flourish, she created a puff of smoke that dissolved into sparks. When the sparks and the smoke were gone, she held a perfectly white mask. She offered it to Ergam. He turned it in his hands a few times, then put the mask on, securing it with the strap around his head.

The mask blended with his remaining skin and molded itself as though made of living clay. When it was finished rearranging, Ergam had an ordinary, uninjured face. His head and neck were still badly charred and disintegrating, but from his forehead down to just below his chin he was normal again.

"What did it do?" he asked.

"Ergam!" Aysu said. "You have lips!"

"I do?" he asked, feeling his face with his fingertips. Then he smiled.

"Is that what his face looked like in life?" Ozel asked.

Guzul the Fierce nodded. "Handsome, isn't he?"

Ergam scoffed playfully at this. "It is a fine gift, madam. One that will come in handy should I ever need to pass as one of the living."

"Perhaps you should change your name to Guzul the Nice Lady," suggested Ozel.

"Oh, I don't know about that," she said. "I still have a bit of Fierce in this old body." As she said it, her eyes widened slightly.

Seeing the hardened steel in those eyes, Ozel decided he would not at all want to be on the receiving end of her Fierce-ness.

CHAPTER 18

As they were finishing dinner, Ozel asked about the distance to Kanat. Aysu was working on a drawing of a cat with a fat round belly and a circle for a head.

"Perhaps two hours," Guzul said. "You could be there tonight."

"Er, let's go in the morning, I think," Ergam said.

"Why?" Aysu asked.

Ergam shifted in his seat. He frowned. "The City of the Undead, like any city, has its issues with assho—er." He looked at Guzul the Fierce. "Bad behavior. It tends to manifest itself more in the dark hours than the daylight. It would be prudent to arrive in the daytime, that's all."

"Not to worry," Guzul said. "I'll be going with you."

"Sorry?" Ergam said.

"There is a battle coming between your kind and the church," she said. "I think the church will probably win. Forgive me for saying so, but you are a bit of a dying breed, no?" She chuckled to herself.

Ergam's face was hard to read, perhaps since it was new to his head.

"All right, that was in poor taste," Guzul admitted. "The way I see it, they're spoiling for a fight. Once the daft Cardinal and his pet king have sharpened their claws on you lot, you can bet the witches and wizards will be next. I have long hoped we might avoid conflict. After all, I am an old woman. I'd like to stay here and tend to my garden. But it does not appear that will be the way of things. I shall go with you to Kanat and speak to your father. Better to join up with you while you're still a force to be reckoned with, than to let the church squash you."

"With all due respect, madam, the City of the Undead has a formidable—"

"A formidable fighting force, yes, I agree. For now. But the church is winning the hearts of the people because it understands one very important thing about the living: They all fear death. As long as the church is comforting people's fear of death by insisting there is life afterward, it will continue to fill the coffers. How can you ever hope to win on that front? You are dead!"

"But there can be life after death," Ergam said, sweeping a hand at himself.

"True, but the reality of carrying on as an undead person juxtaposed with the Heaven the church is selling does not fare well."

"Too true," Ergam agreed.

Guzul picked up Aysu's cat drawing. Aysu had started a new picture, this one of a landscape with mountains in the background. Guzul turned the drawing around to show Ergam and Ozel. Her lip quivered. "Magnificent."

GUZUL INSISTED that they stay the night. She had rooms in her house ready to receive guests. Ozel's bed was the softest, most comfortable thing he'd ever encountered. He wondered what would have happened if this had been his first-ever bed experience. His mind might very well have shot out the top of his head.

He could hear Guzul thanking Aysu for the drawings. The old witch came to his room to say goodnight to him as well. He'd taken off his helmet and placed it near the door. She picked it up, examining it.

"Mmm," she said. "This is some quality enchantment. Is it a Wagast?"

"Yes, ma'am. He is my master."

"Is he now? Well, that explains how you've come by some of your craftiness. You mind that Wagast now, hear?"

"Yes, ma'am. I will, ma'am."

"He and I don't always agree, but he's a fine wizard. And this ..." she examined the helmet with a critical eye again. "You should be careful with this. Never let it out of your sight. I hope for your sake you never know its true value."

She placed it on the foot of the bed, and Ozel picked it up and looked at it with new eyes. He could tell from the way the light played off it that it had some sort of enchantment, but as for exactly what that was, he wasn't experienced enough to tell.

"Let me have your dagger," she said. "By morning I'll have an enchantment on it that'll show that Wagast who's boss. Mark my word on that."

Ozel handed it to her, and she turned to leave. "Sleep well, young apprentice. Tomorrow will be ... interesting."

IN THE MORNING Guzul returned Aysu's hammer and Ozel's

dagger, which both now glowed with the sheen of enchantment.

"I have placed a frost enchantment on your dagger," Guzul said, pleased with herself. "And fire upon your hammer," she said to Aysu. "You must do your best to keep those enchantments secret. They are powerful, which means they are valuable. Keep them close, only use them when necessary."

"We will, ma'am. Thank you," Aysu said.

"Thank you," Ozel echoed.

She waved this away. "Just be sure to show them to Wagast when you get back. I hope I'm there to see his face. Hah!"

Aysu and Ozel shared a look of wonder. She tucked her hammer back into the loop on her waist. Ozel slid his dagger into his belt. He'd have to get a sheath for it.

Guzul was right about the journey. It took no more than a few hours after leaving the lush green hedge surrounding her house to arrive at a foreboding black gate.

Ergam had taken his mask off so his fellow undead could recognize him more easily. "I wouldn't want them thinking I somehow fooled around and got myself alive again."

A guardhouse of stone perched over the black gate, with heavy timber walls in either direction. A guard, whose skin was in even worse shape than Ergam's, stepped forward.

"Who goes there?"

"Yogun, it's me, Ergam. I have returned from my quest to find good, living people." Ergam spread his arms to indicate his companions.

"Please state your full name and your business in Kanat," Yogun ordered.

Ergam sighed. In a loud, clear voice, he said, "I am

Ergam Sakir, son of Bilal Sakir, Prince of Kanat." In a smaller voice he said, "Which you very well know already, you dumb prick."

"Prince?" Aysu whispered to Ozel.

"Shut up," hissed Guzul.

"I am sorry, Your Highness," Yogun said. He was speaking very loudly, as if he wanted to make absolutely sure that someone out of sight could hear him. "I am under strict orders to secure this gate from any living human entry. Only the undead may pass. I will request that a messenger be sent to the palace, but until such time as that person returns I shall have to forbid—"

Guzul flicked a hand at him and his head rolled off his shoulders to bounce heavily on the ground. His body collapsed next to it.

"Oh, very nice," the head said.

"Listen to me, all within hearing," Guzul said. Her voice was terribly loud and deep. "I am Guzul the Fierce. I and my party will speak to your king today. Whether the parts of your city between here and the palace are still standing when I get there is entirely up to you."

There was some scuffling behind the gate.

"You'd better do it," Yogun's head called.

There was a clanking of chains and the gate creaked open to a cobbled street lined with houses. After the black gate, Ozel had been expecting black streets and black houses as well, but they looked just like any other city. A handful of guards stood nearby. Those who had enough facial features left to make an expression looked rather sheepish.

Guzul the Fierce led the way through into the city with her head high, as if she were the prince returning to Kanat, not Ergam.

"Sorry, Yogun," Ergam said. "I didn't know she was going to do that. But you were acting like a bit of a prick."

The guards rushed out to grab the pieces of Yogun.

"Did you see what she did to me?" his head was saying. "Flicked my head off like it was a fly on a meat pie. I was just following orders."

One of the guards told the head to shut up.

"Will he be all right?" Aysu asked Ergam.

"Yes," Ergam said. "If they sew him back together quickly enough, he should regain full function in a few days."

"So you're immortal?" Ozel asked.

"No, not hardly. When the church raids us they decimate the bodies. One wound, even a big one, can be survived given the right treatment and time, but when one is hacked to bits, well, there's not much that can be done."

"They hack you to bits? That doesn't sound very Christian."

Ergam's head snapped up as if he were listening to the wind, suddenly ignoring Ozel.

Guzul shot her hand out and caught an incoming arrow. It would have plunged into Ozel's throat. Ozel let out a small yelp. The sharp metal tip quivered in front of his neck. She handed the arrow to Ergam.

"Anyone you know?" she asked.

Ergam looked at it.

"Wow!" Ozel said, a bit late.

"I can't see enough about this arrow to damn anyone in particular," Ergam said. "It could have been bought anywhere in the market."

Guzul made a noise in the back of her throat that didn't seem to mean anything.

"This is troubling," Ergam said. "I am sorry that my city

is showing itself so poorly. All will be well when we reach the palace."

The streets of Kanat were dense. The houses were multi-storey and shouldered right up to the wall that ringed the city. Since the denizens had no need for food, there were no outlying farms or other support structures. From what Ozel could tell, the mountains formed one border. As he was looking at the misty peaks, his eye caught a face staring out of an upstairs window. Instantly, a hand snatched the curtain across.

"Ergam," Ozel said. "Do your people hate the living?"

Guzul snorted.

Ergam said, "I hesitate to use a strong word like 'hate,' but there is currently a certain leaning away from the living. We are hunted and killed by the church. It's all the contact most of my people have with those who are alive. Hence the reason for my quest. I wanted to bring some normal, living people to demonstrate to my kinsmen, particularly the advisor Aygun Incesu, that you are not all bad."

"Much good it would have done, if your kinsmen had murdered Ozel in the street," Guzul said.

Ergam raised a finger. "Let's not rush to judgment on the strength of one—"

Guzul flicked her arm out and caught another arrow. This would have struck Ozel in the chest.

"Why is it always me?" Ozel cried.

"You'd prefer I get shot?" Aysu asked.

"Perhaps relationships with the living are worse than I thought," Ergam said. "I shall speak to Father about this."

CHAPTER 19

They came to another wall with a gatehouse, but this one stood open. No one was manning the entrance. Inside, the palace was an official-looking building and did have guards outside. They held long pikes and looked ready for a fight, but they also seemed nervous, as if they'd gotten word about the witch's ability to flick heads off bodies.

A rather more regal, deceased gentleman was standing on the top step of the palace. His clothes were worked with precious metals. He motioned at the group to hurry. "Come along now. Let's not keep the king waiting."

"My father's advisor, Aygun Incesu," Ergam said under his breath. "In a forest of pricks he's blocking all the light."

They followed Aygun Incesu through an impressive archway with high ceilings and a lot of natural light from tall windows. He said, "The king will receive you in the courtyard."

A moment later they were in a long rectangular space with marble floors and two huge pools of water running the entire length. At the end was a wooden throne. A tall undead man with wispy white hair sat wearing a crown. He looked pleased.

"My son," he said. "What news from the land of the living?"

"I have completed my quest, father," Ergam said. "I am pleased to present Ozel the Apprentice Wizard, and Aysu the Apprentice Blacksmith. Guzul the Fierce you already know."

"Indeed I do. Welcome, good lady. I understand I owe you an apology for the insolence of my guards."

"Not to worry, Your Majesty," Guzul said, with a nod. "I took the liberty of correcting the behavior on the spot."

"As well you should," the king said. "Aygun, what has happened to discipline in our ranks? Do the men not know the respectful relationship we have with our neighbor?"

"It was a regrettable lapse, My King." Aygun Incesu had most of his facial features, which made him a little easier to look at than some of the other citizens of Kanat, but Ozel thought his smile was a touch too broad and his eyes too twinkly. He reminded Ozel of Bartu Hamdi in a way, but Ozel couldn't have said exactly how.

"Indeed," the king said. "To what do I owe the pleasure of a visit from Guzul the Fierce?"

"It has come to my attention that the church is spoiling for a fight. As I see it, it is only a matter of time before they march in here with a force of considerable size and raze Kanat to the ground. When that task is complete it will, sooner rather than later, set its sights on wizards and witches. I propose that the people of Kanat, with my support, march on Calan and settle accounts."

"Your Majesty," said Aygun Incesu. "We cannot simply march on Calan. Think of the collateral damage. My allegiance with the merchants of Calan would be at an end, and those men have assured me that as long as there is no aggression toward the city we will not be raided. Have they not been as good as their word?"

Guzul the Fierce walked over to Aygun Incesu and stood just a few feet from him, looking him over.

"What are you doing, madam?" he asked.

"As I please."

The king sighed. "Kanat is in a difficult position. We are lacking in trade. To our north lie the mountains. To the south and east, Calan and its outlying farms. To our west, the territory of our friend, Guzul the Fierce. We do not need food to survive, but we need resources to maintain our existence. When we settled here, in the Tangul Forest centuries ago, we had good relationships with outlying towns. Now the church demands that no merchants trade with us lest they be declared unholy." He shook his head. "I fear the day may come when we are forced to leave our city and move into even deeper forests, if they can be found."

"So you decided to raid our town for some kind of tit-for-tat?" Aysu asked. "If you had good relationships in the past, couldn't you try asking us for help first?"

"I sent my son, my dear. And he's proven that good, living people are to be found. Perhaps, with your help, we can join with the townsfolk of Bilgehan and find some means of reviving trade."

"Your Majesty, I must protest. There is no way that the living even in a small village would ever—"

Guzul stepped even closer to the advisor, looking steadily into his eyes.

"Ah," he continued. "Ever allow us, the proud city of Kanat to—"

"You have purchased magic recently," Guzul said. Her voice had taken on a sing-song quality.

Aygun Incesu took a step back. Guzul matched him.

"You have purchased magic to compel a bear," she said. "Why would you need to do that, sir? Compel a bear?"

Ozel gasped. Aysu gasped. Ergam made a surprised rasping noise.

"A bear?" Ergam said. "Why, a bear attacked me out of nowhere when I was nearing Bilgehan. Had my friends not rescued me, I would surely have been torn to shreds!"

"Your Majesty," Aygun Incesu said. "You cannot honestly believe the word of a wi—"

"Careful," Guzul the Fierce said, cutting him off. She purred the next words. "Careful, Aygun Incesu."

"Leave us, Aygun," the king said. "I would speak to these visitors in private."

"But, Your Majesty ..."

The king stood from his throne. Aygun Incesu, still trying to back away from Guzul the Fierce, got his feet tangled and nearly fell. He caught himself, bowed hastily, and quickly left the room.

"Father," Ergam said. "We mustn't let him go. If what Guzul says is right, that means—"

The king held up a hand. "It does not matter, my son. If I were willing to execute him here on the spot, perhaps. But he is backed by a sizable faction of citizens. I have kept him in my ear because I owe it to the people to hear every viewpoint."

"But he tried to kill me!" Ergam said. "My friend Ozel was nearly shot with an arrow twice on the way through the streets. We must do something or Kanat is already lost!"

The king stared at the floor, shaking his head.

"Your Majesty," Guzul said. "I recommend that you call your most trusted to you."

Ergam said, "Yes! So that they may fight at your side,

Father. Incesu will know he'll be caught and jailed for what he's done. If he has men loyal to him, he'll rally them. Maybe even try to take over the throne."

"He wouldn't dare," the king said.

"Your Majesty, I say again, call your most trusted to you," Guzul said.

"You think I need them to defend me?"

"No, I just want them set aside so that I don't accidentally murder them alongside Aygun's people."

Guzul stopped, hearing boots stomping in the gatehouse and the clanking sound of body armor.

"Too late," she said.

A dozen men ran into the courtyard, each carrying a pike as if he meant business. At their side was Aygun Incesu. The men formed up into ranks four wide and three deep, then began marching up the marble toward the throne with Aygun Incesu now at their head.

"Bilal Sakir," Incesu called. "You have led Kanat to the brink of its doom. I have tried for years to sway you toward good sense, toward just rule of your people."

Ozel stepped in front of Aysu to protect her. Aysu elbowed him aside and drew out her hammer.

The king stood and hissed, "Fuck, I wish I had my fucking sword."

The troops and Incesu advanced. "You leave me and the people of Kanat no choice."

"Don't do it," Guzul said. Then, louder, "Men of Kanat, stand down. This is not happening. If you take another step forward I will fry you like a summer sausage."

"Forward, men," Incesu cried. "Are you going to take orders from the living? I say, no!"

He kept coming and, to their credit, his little army lowered their pikes and moved with him.

Guzul raised her arms and called, "*Catena Fulgur!*"

Lightning sprang from hands, striking the two closest guards, then arcing to their brothers. The sparks jumped from guard to guard until they were all bound to one another by leaping electrical bolts that twisted and hummed. The roar was deafening.

Then the guards exploded. Ozel and Aysu put their arms over their faces to shield them from flying long-dead-corpse debris. A chunk of bone the size of a fist bounced off Ozel's helmet with a dull clang.

When Ozel opened his eyes, the courtyard was a dreadful sight. Aygun Incesu stood in the center, arms wrapped around his body, surrounded by piles of incinerated and exploded men.

"I believe that concludes this armed coup," Guzul said.

CHAPTER 20

Ergam and his father gathered near the throne to discuss their options. Guzul the Fierce suggested the king have Aygun Incesu thrown into the dungeon for the time being, which he did. The dungeon guards who came to apprehend Incesu seemed perplexed at the mess in the courtyard until they realized that the debris scattered around was the remains of their colleagues. Then they moved quickly to do as they were told.

With Incesu handled, Guzul went out onto the palace steps to see if there was anyone else in a combative mood she could explode. She returned shortly afterward looking a little disappointed.

Ozel and Aysu sat in chairs at the far edge of the courtyard.

"I don't want to be rude," Ozel said. "But I still need to get to Calan."

"I don't want to be hit with lightning and then exploded," Aysu said. "That was horrific."

"It was. But the power Guzul has! It's staggering. She

must have been studying and practicing for a thousand years to be that powerful."

Guzul came over, nodding to Ergam and his father as she passed the throne. "I believe the two of you need to make your way to Calan?"

Ozel stood. "Yes, ma'am."

Guzul said, "I think it would be best if you were out of Kanat. As long as you're by my side I can protect you, but there are certainly still some wrongheaded idiots prowling around begging for a frying. I won't be able to see all of them coming."

Ergam walked up. "I believe the savior of Kanat is right. We need to get you two out of here as quick as possible."

"But doesn't your father need you here?" Ozel asked.

"Perhaps he does," Ergam said. "But he is a wise and just man. If he has Guzul the Fierce at his side, I believe he could not possibly be better protected."

"Doesn't seem very wise or just to have planned to raid Bilgehan," Aysu grumbled.

"Kings can be very stupid people," Guzul said. "Especially if their trusted advisor is pouring poison in their ears. Metaphorically, I mean. Try not to judge King Sakir too harshly."

Ergam inclined his head at Guzul, but said nothing.

Guzul said, "I still propose Kanat should assault the church in Calan and bring those matters to an end. But we will delay any attack on Calan until we receive word that you have completed your business and left the city." She held up a round, wooden canister. "Do you know what this is?" she asked Ozel. She unscrewed the top to reveal green sand.

"Yes, ma'am," he said. "At least, I think I do. Is it a communicator? Wagast has one."

"I bet it's a lot bigger than this one though, isn't it?"

"Oh, yes," Ozel said, suspecting this was the answer the witch wanted.

"Hah!" she barked. "I knew it. I must contact him to gloat. In any case, use this to contact me when your business is concluded. Get yourself well clear of Calan, and you may return this to me at a later time." She gave it to Ozel.

"Amazing," he said.

"Indeed," Ergam said. "Right then. Let's get out of Kanat until it's settled down, eh?"

OZEL AND AYSU thanked King Sakir for welcoming them and wished him luck with his city kingdom.

"You are welcome here any time," the king said. "You have done more for the city of Kanat than you could possibly know. I hope that you will come back in less tumultuous times for another visit."

They said they would. But Ozel could tell from Aysu's face she still thought the king was a bit of an asshole.

Ergam went to his chambers in the palace and returned wearing a hooded cloak that wasn't partially burned by magic and ripped by thorns. He also brought a leather sheath he'd found, giving it to Ozel, who threaded it onto his belt. It wasn't a perfect fit for his dagger, but it would do for now. There was much less chance he'd stab himself in the leg when he sat down—always a plus. He didn't want to find out just how powerful the dagger's enchantment was by stabbing himself with it.

Ergam said goodbye to his father once more and the small party, under Guzul's watchful eye, left the palace and strode toward the far gate.

"Keep them safe, Ergam," she said. "I'll keep an eye on

your father. We'll ferret out Incesu's conspirators soon enough."

"I have every faith that you will, madam," Ergam said. Then, under his breath, "Boy, am I glad I'm not one of those unfortunate pricks. They are going to wish they never met Guzul the Fierce."

If people in upstairs windows were peeking at them before from behind their curtains, they were now doing so twice as much. Ozel got the sense that the city had been holding its breath for a long time and now was hoping it might soon be able to breathe. The faces looked—in the cases where they existed at all—hopeful.

The east gate was much more grand than the west gate where they'd entered Kanat. The guards wore blue uniforms with a raven on them. They used a big wooden crank to open the gate. Ergam thanked the guards for their service.

Before them was more forest, but this area was much less swampy than Guzul the Fierce's domain.

That night they made camp among the trees. Ergam shot them another rabbit, but Ozel was too exhausted to gather all the herbs needed for a proper feast. Still, it filled their bellies enough.

"Ergam," Aysu said. "Why do you think that man wanted to betray your father?"

"I couldn't say. He's well-respected in our city. Bit of a prick, but that doesn't seem to matter in politics." Ergam thought a moment. "Perhaps he wanted to be king himself and was willing to grab any opportunity he saw to do so. If I was dead and my father was thrown in the dungeon, it's likely he might have been crowned."

"I bet he didn't expect his little army would be exploded

like that," Ozel said. The memory of the bolts of lightning was still vivid.

"No, I expect he didn't. Scared the shit out of me and I didn't even like those guys."

"So say we all," Aysu said.

Ozel raised a rabbit leg and waved it in agreement.

Tomorrow they'd be in Calan. They'd sort out this mess with Bartu Hamdi, and then Ozel could head back to Wagast's house by way of Guzul the Fierce. He might be a full and proper wizard in three or four days' time. He'd be glad of that. Questing was exhausting. Right now, he'd give anything to go back to Wagast's house with nothing to concern him but a little weeding and some spell practice.

Those were the days.

CHAPTER 21

Ozel woke to an undead man shaking him. He tried to yell, but Ergam put a gloved hand over his mouth before he could make a sound. Next to him, Aysu was packing hurriedly. It was still night, the forest dark around them.

Ergam searched his eyes until he judged Ozel to be sufficiently awake, then removed his hand. "Patrol, from Calan. We need to move. Pack up."

Ozel extricated himself from his bedroll, rolled it up, and struggled it into his pack. Then he made sure his dagger was in its sheath on his belt. He nodded at Ergam. Aysu was ready to go. Sleepy, but alert.

Ergam pointed at his eyes, or eye sockets, then to his feet. Ozel and Aysu nodded. *Watch where I put my feet.* They followed in his footsteps out of the camp and away from the fire toward the west. Soon the ground began to tilt upward. They were walking on loose rock and sand, which was a lot like the trail to Guzul's house in that each step slid backward slightly. After a few minutes they came to a large table-like rock jutting out of the hillside. They could lie on it and be hidden from the floor of the forest below, but still keep a good watch. Ergam motioned for them to get down, then held his finger to the gaping place where his lips had once been.

They huddled together against the loose rock of the hillside. Aysu's hand snaked into Ozel's and held it. His insides, already doing gymnastics thanks to fear, redoubled their efforts.

Ergam was looking out over the forest and turning his head occasionally so that he could listen. He slithered backward and sat facing them. "I think we are safe, for now. They will certainly find our campfire within a few minutes. If they spread out and come looking for us I'll drop the closest few and we'll head north a bit more."

Ozel thought about what it must be like to be a soldier on patrol in a forest near the City of the Undead and have an arrow come out of nowhere and end your life. "I'd prefer if we just keep moving. I don't want to kill anyone we don't have to."

Ergam looked pained, as if this was only adding more work to his already hectic schedule, but he nodded. Aysu and Ozel got to their feet and continued their way along the hillside, stopping when they had good cover so that Ergam could look and listen. It was a tense hour, but after some time Ergam pointed down the hillside, and they were back in the forest again.

"I think we are well clear now," he said.

"What are Calan soldiers doing patrolling this part of the forest?" Aysu asked.

"Probably looking for a fight. Perhaps they are expecting Kanat to attack?" Ergam said.

"I think we should warn Guzul and your father," Ozel said.

Ergam appeared to think about that. "Perhaps you are right. It is peculiar that they have a force so close. Do you intend to use the device to contact Guzul?"

"I could, but I don't want her to be angry with me if I wake her. Does she sleep?"

"I don't know if witches sleep or not. Does your master Wagast sleep?"

"All the time."

"Let's wait. She said to use it for telling her we're finished in Calan. I think if Guzul the Fierce gave me a magical item like that I'd use it for what she said to use it for and nothing else." Ergam thought a minute. "Give me thirty minutes."

Ozel nodded. Ergam ran off into the night.

Fifteen minutes later an arrow ricocheted off a Kanat guardsman's helmet with a loud "Tink!" sound. He readjusted the helmet, looked at his fellow guard, and said, "What do you suppose that was?"

There was a clatter as the arrow, which had been deflected upward, landed on the stones between the two guards. The second guard looked at it.

"It's an arrow," he said.

"Well, I can see that. But who shoots an arrow at us? We don't have any flesh to pierce."

"Speak for yourself. I still have quite a bit of my left leg remaining."

"At home you do. Not here."

"All right, well, I still have it."

"Anyway, I think that's a Kanat arrow. Must be Ergam trying to tell us something."

The other guard sighed. "I guess we should be on high alert then, eh?"

"I guess."

"Right. I'll let the rest know."

THE NEXT MORNING, Ozel and Aysu ate bread and cheese at dawn while they were on the move. The road to Calan and the main gate eventually came into view with many carts heading toward the city. They blended in with the traffic. Ergam had placed his mask on his face and covered his charred head with his hood.

"I haven't entered a city since I was alive," Ergam said, so only Ozel and Aysu could hear. "It's rather exciting." His masked face smiled.

"I've never been in a city this size," Ozel said. "That I know of, anyway."

"Me either," Aysu said. "I'm excited too."

At the gate, they were asked their business. The gate guard barely cast an eye over them. Ergam said they were in town to do a bit of banking, and the guard waved them through without further delay.

"This mask is very good," Ergam said. "Perhaps I should get a wig as well? Or a wife?"

"You'll definitely be needing a wig then," Aysu said.

Down a short, cobbled street they came to a market square. Ozel suggested they look around for someone selling spicy sausages, but none of the vendors had anything like that to offer. They gave up on the sausages for the time being.

"So," Ergam said. "Let us find lodging. Once settled, we shall check in with the bank. Which bank are we going to, exactly?"

"There's more than one?" Ozel asked.

"Ah," Ergam said.

"I don't have any money," Aysu said.

"Me either," said Ozel. "How much would a room cost?"

"It has been a while, but I wouldn't be surprised if a room in Calan would be a gold piece per night."

Ozel and Aysu looked shocked.

"Right then," Ergam said. "Perhaps we have some other options?"

Ozel said, "We could go see Bugra Gurses. He is a wizard and a friend to my master Wagast. He will know where to go." A man on a cart loaded with hay was passing by and without waiting for the others to agree Ozel waved him down. "Excuse me, sir. Where can I find the wizard Bugra Gurses?"

"At the bottom of a deep hole, I hope," the man replied. He rattled away on his cart.

Ozel shrugged at Aysu and Ergam. A woman with a sack of grain over her shoulder was near. She was leading a child by the hand.

"Excuse me," Ozel said. "Do you know where I can find the wizard Bugra Gurses?"

The woman hissed at him, pulled her child close, and hurried along the street, struggling under the weight of the sack but determined to move quickly away.

"I think we should be moving along," Ergam said, looking around the square. "The living are getting restless."

Ozel looked around. Sure enough, some of the shoppers and vendors in the market were putting their heads together, looking their way. One man even pointed at them, then started walking toward the opposite end of the square where a city Watchman was peeling an apple with his belt knife.

Ergam herded Ozel and Aysu down an alley. "Let's put some distance between ourselves and this market," he said.

The alley was narrow and twisted back upon itself several times. "It has been a long time since I was in Calan, but if memory serves, we are moving southwest."

"Is that good?" Aysu asked.

"No, it's not," said a bird perched on a sign advertising prostitutes.

Ergam regarded the bird, confused.

The bird continued. "Previously, heading southwest from here would have deposited you near the Thieves Guild, which would have been a good place to ask clandestine questions about goings-on in the city. But now it would deliver you to one of the church's strongholds."

"Sorry, who are you?" Aysu asked.

"Bugra Gurses," the bird said. "Not the bird, obviously, but the wizard controlling the bird. You are Aysu, Ozel the Apprentice, and Ergam Sakir."

Aysu, Ozel, and Ergam blinked at one another.

"Follow me," said the bird. It flapped down the alleyway, swooping to avoid washing hanging from a wall, and then perched on a windowsill. It looked down the alleyway toward the trio, who were all still watching it. No one had moved. The bird held its wings away from its body as if to say, "Well? What are you waiting for?"

"It is a talking bird," Aysu said. "That seems terribly wizardly."

"Agreed," Ergam said. "Ozel? What do you reckon?"

"Better reception than we got in the market," Ozel said.

They followed the bird down the twists and turns of the alleyway. Some of the paths between dwellings and the backs of shops looked to Ozel like they were for private residences rather than communal spaces anyone could walk through. They had to flatten themselves against a wall at one point to get around a man stirring something savory in a big pot over a stove. Was this an inn's kitchen? Or had the man merely decided to cook himself a big stew in an alleyway? There was no way to know.

They emerged across a muddy street from the base of what had once been a massive black tower. The first floor of the tower survived, but above that everything had collapsed.

The bird flew to the door and landed on a metal ring.

Ozel knocked on the door.

"I already know you're here, boy," the bird said. "Go in before someone sees you here."

"Oh. Sorry," Ozel said.

He pushed the door open and entered the golden lantern light of Bugra Gurses' tower. Ergam, Aysu, and the bird followed. It was similar to Wagast's tower, in that it was a round structure with stairs leading up the wall to floors above. Except there wasn't a kitchen off to the side. Or, for that matter, a garden outside.

The bird landed on a hat rack, squawked when the door was closed, and Bugra Gurses came down the stairs. He was wearing the same square hat that he'd been wearing when Ozel saw him in Wagast's communication device.

"Welcome," he said. "Come on up to the study, won't you? You may place your bags where you like."

"Thank you, sir," Ergam said. "We appreciate your help in finding you."

"Not at all," Bugra Gurses said. "Please, you may call me Bugra. I expect you have questions. Join me in the study and I'll do what I can to help."

"But, sir," Ozel said. "Aren't we likely to be seen standing on top of the—"

Bugra Gurses chuckled. "Just come on up.".

CHAPTER 22

Ozel put his pack down and walked up the stairs. He was amazed to see that not only was the tower intact, but it was a richly appointed library with books lining the walls and several large comfortable chairs arranged to face one another.

"Remarkable," Ergam said, when he was standing in the study.

"You have no idea what it cost me to implement this illusion," Bugra said. "I bought tons and tons of stone. Almost enough to build a second tower. Had to move it in block by block, then wait for a sufficient storm. Then I had to spill the extra stone across the neighborhood without killing anyone or damaging innocent people's property all while endeavoring to cast one of the biggest illusions the lands have ever seen."

"But why would you want people to think your tower's in disrepair?" Aysu asked.

Bugra gestured at the chairs. Everyone chose one and sat. Ozel's chair was fantastically comfortable. He wondered if it had a comfort enchantment on it, or if it was simply a well-made chair.

Bugra steepled his fingers. "The church has gained great power." He said "the church" with a sneer. "They like having that power, but they do not want the extra attention. So, they must direct the attention elsewhere. At the moment, they are fomenting distrust of our extra-mortal friends to the west, and soon enough they will come after the wizards."

"Guzul the Fierce said the same thing," Ozel said.

"Hmm," Bugra said. "You saw Guzul the Fierce?"

Aysu nodded. "Oh, yes, sir. I drew her some pictures and she fed us and enchanted our weapons. She's a very nice lady."

"How did she look?" Bugra asked.

Aysu frowned. "How do you mean?"

Bugra waved. "Never mind. Hopefully I shall see her myself. It has been many long years, but I have always ..." He seemed to be reliving an old, fond memory, like a vacation he'd taken when he was young. "Admired her."

"She looks ..." Aysu began. "Well, she looks nice. Until she looks fierce. Then she's fierce."

"Mmm, yes. That's her all right. What a woman."

Ozel felt uncomfortable with the turn of conversation but didn't know how to respectfully steer it anywhere else.

"She's going to help my people in a battle against Calan," Ergam said. "We just need to sort out this financial business of Ozel's, then let my father and Guzul know we're finished. They intend to seize the city and confront the church."

"Oh, no," Bugra said. He gripped the arms of his chair. "Really? That's a terrible plan. Kanat will be destroyed utterly."

"Why do you say that?" Ergam asked.

"It's plain as day. You saw what happened when you mentioned my name in the market. The church has convinced the king and many of the citizens that it is the only organization to be trusted. They have planted the seeds of doubt about the legitimacy of wizards. Where the undead are concerned, their seeds of doubt are truly bearing fruit. And Calan is not the only city where the church holds sway. It's much, much bigger than that. Even if Kanat managed to defeat the Calanians in a great battle, which they just may do with the help of Guzul the Fierce, it would only be a matter of weeks before the king sent an even larger force. The only way forward is to negotiate with the business leaders of Calan. Hmm …" He thought a moment, staring into his fingers. "This is troubling. I shall need a word with Guzul, I think."

"In the meantime," Ozel said. "Could you help me make contact with the bank so that I may collect my inheritance? Aysu and I could return to our homes. I'm sure Ergam would like to return to his father's side for whatever is to come. But we have no rooms, and we don't know where to go."

"Yes. Inheritance," Bugra said. He was thinking. He looked out the window toward the midday sun.

"It's just that we're in a bit of a hurry," Ozel said. "You see, a man who once adopted me, if you can call it that, is on his way here. He will lie and say that he is still my guardian so that he can collect the money for himself."

"Yes, I remember the inheritance part. This man, though. He sounds like quite a scoundrel," Bugra said.

"Oh, he is," Ozel said. "He only cares about money."

"I see," Bugra said. "Then we should act without delay. I have an acquaintance who runs an inn near the banking district. I'll help secure rooms for you there while we sort out this mess with the bank. But Ergam will have to wait for you elsewhere."

"What? Why?" Ergam asked.

"I should have thought that'd be obvious," Bugra said. "The church is powerful here. They have ways of identifying undead persons. Mind you, your mask is a positively exquisite piece of magic. I assume Guzul made it? Anyway, it's good enough for any street in any city in the world. But sooner or later the church is likely to discover your true nature. They've been provided with magical items by unscrupulous wizards in distant lands. If that happened they'd—" Bugra remembered two young people were listening. "Well, it'd be nasty. I wouldn't advise you to use any magic here or the church may know."

"So how do you have a hidden tower that no one knows about?" Aysu asked. "And a talking bird?"

Bugra snapped, "I pay a lot of bribes. Do you have money for bribes? And do you know whom to pay off?" He seemed to be annoyed. "Go to the Trotting Hound Inn. Tell the innkeeper or his wife that your fine, feathered friend will clean up."

"Clean up?" Ergam asked.

"It's code," Bugra said.

"It has been a while since I walked the streets of Calan," Ergam said. "But isn't the Trotting Hound in a rough area of the city? Where the Watch usually doesn't go?"

"It's not the best. But it is the only current option. Unless you three do have coin?"

Ozel shook his head.

"Not to worry," Ergam said. "I'll escort you there. It's the least I can do."

"I think it would be best if you part ways here," Bugra said. "I'm sure you wouldn't want Ozel and Aysu to be under any undue scrutiny? The mere suspicion that they were socializing with an extra-mortal person in broad daylight in the streets of Calan would be..." he shook his head. "They could be jailed indefinitely."

Ergam wasn't convinced, but he stood and said, "Very well. If that is what we must do, then it's what we must do. Let's go."

CHAPTER 23

Ergam confirmed the directions to the inn with Bugra Gurses, then they thanked the old wizard and turned to go. Clearly, Ergam had no intention of parting ways with Ozel and Aysu at the tower.

As they walked away, Ozel turned to look at the invisible upper floors of the tower. Now that he knew it was an illusion it seemed that he could see a shimmering in the air, but that could have been his imagination.

"I didn't like—" Aysu started.

Ergam cut her off by lifting a finger and giving her a stern look. After they'd walked a bit farther, Ergam scanned the skies for any eavesdropping birds, then said in a low voice, "All right, I think we are far enough away now. For what it's worth, I am not pleased either. I don't trust that old wizard any farther than I could kick him. And I'd like to try kicking him."

"I don't like that we have to split up," Aysu said. "But I don't see how else we could complete the quest."

"Something is peculiar, that's for sure," Ergam said. "I

wish my father were here. I would like to have his advice right now."

"Perhaps you should go to him," Ozel said. "You can ask him and Guzul the Fierce what needs to be done."

"But then I wouldn't be protecting you," Ergam said. "This city can be dangerous in the best of times, and your lodging is in one of the rougher parts of town."

"You can be back in Kanat in a matter of hours though, can't you?" Ozel asked. "Especially if you don't have us slowing you down. You'll be back before we've even settled into our rooms. Besides, I have my magic, and the dagger. Aysu's got a powerful hammer. We don't drink. We'll just keep our eyes open, stay in the inn, and wait to hear from you."

"What if we use the device?" Aysu asked. "To contact Guzul the Fierce?"

"She said to use it to contact her only when we are done and out of town," Ozel said. "I don't want to use magical items to contact a witch as powerful as Guzul the Fierce unless I'm using it precisely in the way she instructed."

Aysu considered the way Guzul the Fierce had fried and exploded the soldiers in the Kanat courtyard. "That is a good point."

"I'm afraid that all of our current options are shit," Ergam said. "But it is true that I could be to Kanat and back again in a matter of hours. I am pretty fast."

"What about our original quest?" Aysu asked.

"The earliest Bartu Hamdi could be here is the day after tomorrow, I think," Ozel said. "As long as we make contact by then, we should be in good shape."

"We can do it tomorrow," Ergam said. "I'll make sure you're safe in the inn first."

"Easy enough," Ozel said.

THE TROTTING HOUND was not much to look at. It also wasn't much to smell. It was a lot to smell, actually, but none of the smells were good.

The building leaned out over the muddy track that posed for a street as if it were drunk and in danger of toppling at any moment. Inside, the public area smelled like someone had stewed a harvest's worth of cabbage, placed the cabbage on a pile of dog hair, then set the whole mess on fire.

There were a few tables where brave souls took their meals, and a bar in one corner. Stairs led up to the second floor. A big man in a leather vest without a shirt underneath came out of a back room.

"Help you," he said.

"Uh," Ozel said. "Our fine feathered friend will clean up."

The big man blinked. Ozel thought he was going to say "what?" or otherwise ask for some kind of clarification of this nonsense, but he merely sighed heavily. He plucked a key attached to a frayed bit of rope off a pegboard behind the bar, then nodded that they should follow him. The stairs groaned as he mounted them.

The room was a room in name only. There was one bed, one blanket, and no pillow. But the lack of any luxuries wasn't a major problem. Just having walls and a roof was an improvement over sleeping outside.

"Thank you, sir," Ozel said. "We appreciate the consideration."

The innkeeper looked at Ozel as though he was something thrown up on the floor, then left without a word.

Ergam tried to close the door. There was a gap at the

bottom big enough to wiggle a hand in. "This room is a joke. I'm undead and I wouldn't be caught dead in here. I didn't like it before and I like it even less having seen the proprietor and the lodgings."

"All the more reason for you to get to Kanat and back with haste," Ozel said. "We have food to eat, so we don't have to rely on the inn for that. We'll push the bed against the door. We'll be safe for a few hours. Besides, you saw the Calan soldiers outside your city. Don't your father and Guzul the Fierce need to know about them?"

"And what if Bugra Gurses is right, that the church can detect undead?" Aysu asked.

Ergam's brow furrowed, hardened, furrowed again. At last, he nodded. His eyes went to the window which was set high in the wall and looked out onto the tops of buildings. Ergam climbed out.

"What are you doing?" Ozel asked.

"Scouting," Ergam said. "Hold tight." He stepped out of sight, walking carefully along the ridge lines of the rooftops.

"Do you think they have a bard here at night?" Aysu asked.

Ozel turned to look at her.

"It's only that I've never seen a real bard before. It sounds nice. Eating dinner while someone else sings or plays the lute."

"I'm not sure I'd want to see the kind of bard you'd get at this place. Probably just drinks your drinks and farts on you."

"Yeah, fair enough."

Ergam reappeared. He had an empty wooden crate.

"What's that?" Ozel asked as Ergam climbed back.

Ergam placed the crate on the floor by the window. "It's a step stool. If you have any trouble at all, leave by the window. All right? If you head that direction," he pointed, "the wall of the city is close. There is a stairway that leads down to street level."

Ozel and Aysu nodded.

"If I'm to do this I must go now," Ergam said. "Keep your ears open and your weapons close. I shall return as quickly as possible."

"We know you will," Aysu said.

Ergam nodded, then with the agility of a cat was out the window again. A large, bony, supernaturally quick-moving, undead cat.

Aysu and Ozel shared a worried look, then both laughed quietly and nervously.

They slid the bed against the door, and unrolled their bedrolls. Ozel insisted that Aysu take the bed itself.

"No way," she said. "Then I'll be stabbed first when the killers break in."

"No, you won't," Ozel said. "They'll stab me first, because they'll be able to see me. You'll be hidden behind the door."

"Hmm," she said. She put a finger to her chin in mock consideration. "You may have a point. In that case, I shall take the bed after all."

They both lay down.

"When did you know that you wanted to be a wizard?" Aysu asked.

"It just happened gradually. At first I hated all the work I had to do. Gardening and so forth. And Wagast makes me practice my magic often. But once I started to get a little better at it I began to love it. And, I have a lot of respect for Wagast himself, so that makes me want to be a wizard too."

"Being a witch looks good as well. I meant to ask Guzul the Fierce if she thought I could be a witch, but in all the excitement I forgot."

"I'm sure you'll have a chance again soon."

"Nah, I think it was just a passing feeling. I still want to be a blacksmith, like my dad."

"How come?"

"It's just interesting work. It's like you said. It took a long time of doing work that I thought was completely useless, but then one day I realized I knew how to get the metal to do what I wanted it to do. You have to know how to ask it, and then you have to put in a lot of hard work. I like that feeling of being able to do those things."

"I envy you. Magic is like that, but you can't see the thing you're trying to control. It's always trying to slip away from you too. I'd much rather be able to look at a horseshoe or a dagger at the end of the day and say, 'I made that.'"

Aysu said, "Metal can be that way too. It can't be too hot or too cold. The only way to know how to do it is to do it a thousand times until you know what to look for."

They looked up at the dusty, wooden ceiling of their room.

"You know," Aysu said. "This has been a great quest. I'm glad I ran away. But I'd also like to go home."

Ozel could hear people downstairs. The voices sounded slurred, drunk maybe. He hoped none of them got drunk enough to come up the stairs and kick their way into the room.

"I know exactly what you mean," he said.

CHAPTER 24

Ergam was good at moving quietly, and the need for stealth at this moment was so great that he was pulling every trick he knew. Three things were working against him. One, it was still daylight. Two, he was in an urban area rather than the forest.

And three, he was tracking a powerful wizard.

When he left the Trotting Hound, he jumped from the inn rooftop across the narrow alleyway and back in the direction from which they'd come. He landed on the far rooftop so lightly that a sleeping baby in the room didn't stir. Then he leaped across the next alleyway and the next until he came to a wide street he wanted to watch.

If he went directly to Bugra Gurses' tower, he couldn't tell whether the wizard was home—short of trying to sneak in, and breaking into a wizard's private domicile was like climbing into a dragon's mouth and going at one of its teeth with a hammer. No, what he needed was to position himself on a likely thoroughfare and wait until Bugra Gurses came by—if he ever did.

Ergam couldn't actually watch the street. The wizard

very likely had some magic to protect himself from being observed, or followed. It was Ergam's understanding that sort of thing was pretty common magic. But he'd never heard of a wizard who could detect anyone *listening* for them.

So, Ergam lay on the roof with his head near the street and listened. Normally, in a town like this, he did his best to shut out his hearing because there was so much noise. Now he considered every sound. A coin jingle in a purse at the market square sounded like three coins: one large and two small. A cat was breathing in the rooms below him. Somewhere off to his left a couple was making love. Ergam couldn't say for sure, but he thought the woman sounded like she wasn't in love. Perhaps a prostitute?

Flapping wings were everywhere, all too small to be Bugra Gurses' bird. He tried to remember what the wizard's footsteps sounded like. He'd not been able to see the man's feet. From the way they'd creaked he was probably wearing leather shoes. Ergam focused on separating the sounds of the shoes and the tiny creaking of the wooden floorboards.

Yes. Yes, that was it. A horse with a noisy harness was moving beneath Ergam's hiding place and making it hard to pick out other sounds. There! No, that was a man opening a leather wallet.

Wait. No. There it was. Yes! He could hear Bugra Gurses' shoes. The wizard was in a hurry, but he didn't want to move so quickly as to be conspicuous. The dust of the road was making the creaking even louder. There was a slight difference between his right foot creak and the left foot creak. Were the shoes damaged? Perhaps the wizard had sustained some injury and walked with a slight limp.

The creaks were getting louder now, as if the wizard were directly under Ergam's hiding place. Ergam lay perfectly still, which he could do better than any living person since he didn't need to breathe.

The creaks sounded again, only occasionally. The wizard was standing, looking around.

For a long moment, Ergam feared the wizard had some unknown magic to detect someone listening for him. If he did, the fight would not be fair. Ergam would be dead after the first spell and the wizard wouldn't even be scratched.

Then the wizard started moving again. Ergam grinned. He let Bugra continue on the street as far as he dared, then got silently to his feet and began to follow, running and leaping from rooftop to rooftop. It would be dark soon. That would help.

He trailed the wizard past the market where they'd entered the alley earlier in the day. Ergam noticed that wherever Bugra Gurses went, behind his back people shared disgusted looks. Some of them made signs to ward off evil.

The guards were preparing to close the gate for the night. One of them was yelling to the remaining merchants in the market square that if any of them intended to go outside the walls they needed to get moving. In the bustle, Bugra slipped through.

Ergam climbed down a drainpipe on the back of a house into an alleyway. It required a drop to the ground, but it was nothing he couldn't handle. He made sure his hood was on properly, and then stepped into the street and headed toward the gate. His own movements made it hard to hear the wizard's boots, but as soon as he got out of the city gate that should be less of a problem in the quiet of the countryside.

Ergam walked out of the gate without being challenged. After all, the guards didn't often concern themselves with people who wanted to leave the city. He might have to get creative when it came time to get back in, especially if it were still dark. But that was an issue for later.

He was straining his ears for his quarry when he happened to overhear a conversation between the two gate guards.

"I only wish I were out there," one of them said. "Instead of chained to this bloody gate."

"Don't I know it," the other said. "They're going to go through that town like a scythe."

"If any of those demons are alive tomorrow, they'll say 'I Kanat believe how fucked we are!'"

Both the guards laughed.

Ergam's blood, if he'd had any, would have boiled. The Calan soldiers were going to attempt some kind of attack on Kanat tonight. He had to warn his father and Guzul the Fierce, and he had to do so quickly. Well, the shortest distance between two points was, as always, a straight line.

He was out of sight of the gate. Ergam turned off the road and headed into the woods. He'd lost track of Bugra Gurses, but the surprise attack by the Calan forces on his city was more important—it was what Ergam feared the wizard was up to anyway. He readied his bow and held as many arrows as he could carry in his hand, then ran into the gathering darkness.

CHAPTER 25

Bugra Gurses could tell that something was not right. He hadn't outright detected someone watching him, only a tingling sensation in the back of his neck which often meant something was afoot. Or perhaps he was just feeling guilty about the part he was about to play in the murder of two children. Desperate times, though. He didn't need an apprentice wizard sniffing around, using Bugra's name around town. Things were too delicate at the moment.

It was a pity that he could not use one of the tunnels underneath the city. He was one of the few who even knew they existed, but they had been created for the lord's use, not Bugra's. Bugra could have used the one under his tower to get to the palace in secret, then used another to move through the city toward the gate, but it was much faster to walk above ground and speed was more important than secrecy at the moment.

He reflected on how he'd gotten to this point.

Where the church saw an easy enemy in the undead of

Kanat, Bugra Gurses saw potentially valuable resources. He'd explained this in secret meetings with the merchants.

"Imagine, gentlemen, the value of workers who do not need to sleep, who do not need to eat. The undead are perfectly suited to back-breaking work that would kill a human. They walk through fire without pause. They could be submerged indefinitely in a faulty well. The bad vapors in mines that kill workers would be nothing more to the undead than a bad smell." He didn't actually know for sure whether all of that was true. It didn't matter, the merchants were interested.

"But we can't be seen publicly to have dealings with Kanat," one of the merchants said.

"Exactly," Bugra agreed. "That is where I can be of service. The church wishes to destroy the undead. I say we instead gain their trust. Put them to work."

They'd taken some convincing from there. Eventually they'd come around to the plan. Now it was about to all be wrecked by two children who had somehow waltzed into Kanat with Guzul the Fierce and knocked everything into a cocked hat. He could still sort it out, though. He'd have the kids taken care of, then he'd have a word with Aygun Incesu and all would be well.

Bugra paused outside the gate, next to a large tree, and cast an illusion to hide himself. No sooner was the spell complete than he saw what he'd expected. A very thin figure leaving the gate and then searching around.

So, Ergam Sakir had a method of following a wizard's movements that could defeat Bugra's precautions. That was interesting. He remained motionless as the undead man walked almost directly toward him. Then Ergam stopped, looked around, and cocked his head as if he were listening.

Bugra could see two guards at the city gate were speaking. Then they laughed heartily.

When they did, Ergam Sakir grunted in frustration, then removed his bow from his back and began running toward Kanat.

When he was gone, Bugra let the illusion spell drop. Was it possible that Ergam Sakir's hearing was good enough to have overheard the guards all those many yards away? If so, could he track someone through a city, based on the sound of their movements alone? It seemed far-fetched to Bugra, but a lot of things that were previously far-fetched were coming to the fore. He'd have given anything to know for certain what the men at the gate had been joking about, but if it alarmed Ergam then he could guess. The Calan soldiers laughing probably spelled bad news for the citizens of Kanat. Something must be happening tonight.

Bugra needed to hurry.

BARTU HAMDI and Saban Kozen were both ready for the journey to be over. Neither enjoyed their colleague's company one iota and was secretly glad that the other would soon be of no consequence.

It was unfortunate that they hadn't made it to Calan today. Bartu was certainly keen for a bed rather than another night on the road. It was not to be. He laid wood for a fire, got it started, then relaxed on his bedroll.

Saban Kozen returned from the woods. "Well, it is our last night. I look forward to some proper cooking."

"Indeed," said Bartu. "When I have received my money, I believe I shall hire a cook."

"Oh, yes. A good choice."

"Maybe a lady cook."

Kozen frowned. "Why would it matter if the cook is female?"

Bartu gave him a look to communicate the depth of his stupidity.

Kozen shook his head. "It seems to me, friend, that if you intend some romantic entanglement, you can hire professionals for that purpose. It doesn't make sense to pre-occupy the cook with such matters. Better to have a cook who can focus on meal preparation."

Bartu had not considered this, and he didn't intend to discuss it further. Among the many irritating things about his partnership and travelling with the priest, high on the list was the man's tendency to talk at length about literally anything.

Kozen lifted a finger. "Remember, you will be wealthy. You might secure a lordship somewhere. If that happens, you'll have families far and wide offering their daughters to you."

That part sounded good. Some of Bartu's irritation with Kozen lessened.

Bartu stared up at the night sky. At least it wasn't raining. Kozen began to snore lightly, then more loudly. Bartu lay awake for hours, fantasizing about being a lord. He didn't care what Kozen said. He would employ women all over his house. And they would call him "Lord." Lord Hamdi. That sounded good.

Bartu woke with a start when someone cleared their throat. There was another noise nearby and his guts twisted with fear. It could be one of the undead raiders, come to claim their heads as they slept.

A man in fancy dress, wearing a square hat on his head, stepped into the firelight. "Gentlemen, pardon me for a moment." He stopped short when his eyes fell on Saban Kozen. "Saban Kozen? Is that you?"

"Bugra Gurses," Kozen said, wiping at his eyes. He didn't seem pleased. "It is me, indeed. Why have you woken us? What brings you to our fire?"

Bugra ignored this question. "And I believe you are a Mr. Hamdi?"

"So I am. Bartu Hamdi." Bartu's voice sounded thick and sluggish.

"A pleasure. Well, gentlemen, I believe I have some information for you. Ozel the Apprentice has arrived in Calan ahead of you."

"What?" Bartu demanded, springing into full awareness. "How did he manage that?"

Bugra shrugged ignorance, which was a lie. "It's not important. What's important is that he will certainly lay claim to the money you are going to collect, if he is not stopped."

"How do you know he's in Calan?" Kozen asked warily.

"He is an apprentice of my friend, Wagast. He came to me for help when he arrived in Calan. I have provided rooms for young Ozel and his companion, the girl, but I cannot guarantee they will stay there forever. Sooner or later they will venture out and make contact with the bank."

Bartu put his boots on and got to his feet. He paced back and forth. What could they do about this?

"Blast," said Kozen, sitting up. "We are too late."

"Well now," Bugra Gurses said. "That may not exactly be the case. If you were to leave at this very moment you could be at the city gate when it opens in the morning. Then, once in the city, you might be able to find a way to deal with the kid."

"A way?" Kozen asked. "What way?"

Gurses shrugged. "I don't mean to tell you gentlemen your business. You'll figure something out."

Kozen's face was aghast. "Are you suggesting that we ..." He paused, mouth open. "Harm the children?"

Bartu's mind had been wandering the same direction. Would he be willing to resort to violence against children in order to get his hands on the gold? Surely not. Well, not murder anyway. But if he could grab the kids, maybe tie them up, that might work. They didn't need to die. They just needed to be out of the way for a few days while he transacted any business required and then disappeared.

"Don't be grotesque," Gurses said. "I am suggesting that you have a problem and that you should deal with it as quickly as possible."

"Oh, no," Kozen said. "Don't try to walk backward, Gurses. We all know a wizard is very nearly as bad as the undead when it comes to underhanded dealings. Don't listen to this man, Hamdi. He is nothing if not evil. We should go to town with haste, but I will not be party to touching a single hair on a child's head."

Gurses sighed. "You were happy to be party to stealing a child's inheritance, though, am I correct?"

Kozen scoffed and made some other disagreeable noises as he began to pack his things. He didn't outright deny that he'd been intending to profit mightily.

"What about you, Hamdi? Will you see reason?"

Bartu thought about it again. Could he find a way to delay a young girl, and a boy not yet old enough to grow a beard? He thought he probably could, yes. If he failed, he'd lose the time he'd spent in this pursuit. If he succeeded, he'd gain the world. He nodded.

"Excellent," Gurses said. He pointed a finger at Kozen and barked the word, "*fulgur!*" A crackling bolt of lightning shot out of the wizard's hand and caught the priest square in the chest, blowing a fist-sized hole through him. Kozen staggered, his face wide-eyed, then stumbled again, and finally fell flat on his back, dead.

Gurses grunted with satisfaction. "I've had about enough of the church," he said. He turned to Bartu. "Oh, don't look at me like that. You were planning to dispense with him and take his share anyway, were you not?"

"How do you know that?"

"It's just how partnerships tend to go." He pointed his hand again and muttered, "*augur*." A fireball leapt to the dead man and set his clothes on fire. "I think you should start heading toward Calan, Bartu Hamdi. You have business there."

Bartu gathered his few things as quickly as he could. At least the moon was out, providing some light. He wouldn't be likely to lose his way on the road. He started walking, doing everything he could not to look at the burning corpse.

"Oh, Hamdi?" Gurses said.

Bartu Hamdi looked over his shoulder.

"Wait, I have some instructions for you."

CHAPTER 26

Ergam considered his options as he used what he could hear to form a picture in his mind of the locations of the Calan soldiers in the forest ahead. He needed to get through quickly. The easiest way to do that would be to send a few arrows through the middle of the camp. The men were expecting to begin a fight sometime this evening, not be attacked themselves. Surprise was with Ergam. If he felled a few soldiers quietly, it could clear an easy path through their midst.

Ozel had asked him not to kill any soldiers unnecessarily, and Ergam was inclined to honor that request if it was possible. He could put an arrow through a few soldiers' feet on the west side of the camp and use their howls to draw attention away from his position. But no. It would be too unpredictable. At least some of them had to die.

He listened carefully, then fired three shots into the air in rapid succession. He listened again and fired two more, then a final shot, and he began running.

As he broke from the tree line he saw three men at a campfire. Two were having a meal and one was tending to the flames. One of the men eating was facing Ergam's direction. His eyes got wide and he was about to raise the alarm when the first of Ergam's arrows plunged into his body. The other two men sprouted arrows as well and fell to the ground. The one nearest the fire fell into it.

Ahead, two soldiers sharing a smoke fell dead in opposite directions. Ergam bounded over their bodies. When he reached the front line, a soldier was slumped over a cart.

A few moments later, Ergam reached the east gate of Kanat and identified himself to the guard by yelling, "Oi! Gulden! Fuck yourself!" Gulden was indeed on duty and recognized the call. The gate was opened and he was let through.

At the palace, Ergam warned his father of the force gathering in the forest. Guzul the Fierce listened as well.

"I see," Bilal said. "We will reinforce the wall at once." He motioned to an aide, then gave orders. "Everyone capable of wielding a sword must get to arms. We expect an attack from the east, but we must not let our guard slip in any direction."

The aide nodded and disappeared to convey the king's wishes.

Guzul the Fierce was tapping her chin with a finger. "You say Bugra seemed irritated, eh?"

"Yes, ma'am."

"Something underhanded is going on here, and I mean to find out what it is. But first, we need to get you back to Calan to protect those children. Gurses will have something nasty planned."

"You don't think a wizard like Gurses would do something to—" Ergam began. He stopped when he saw Guzul's face.

"You must go," she said. "How did you get through the Calan camp?"

"I shot everyone I thought I might encounter."

Guzul's eyebrows went up. Ergam's father grunted.

"That likely won't work a second time," Guzul said. "I shall help. Let's go."

Ergam followed Guzul back to the east gate. When the gate was open, she reached her hands out to him and said "*invisibilia.*" A wave of freezing cold hit him and he looked down to make sure he hadn't been turned into a frozen statue. He had a terrible sense of vertigo as he looked straight down to the ground. He had no body!

"Hurry," Guzul said. "Before the magic wears off. You can be quiet, can't you?"

Ergam nodded, then said, "Yes, ma'am," when he realized she probably couldn't see him nod.

He set off east again. After moving through the forest for a few minutes he began to hear the telltale clank of armor and weapons. The Calan soldiers were coming. From the sound of it, they were walking closely together. If they were shoulder to shoulder when he reached them, it would be hard to slip through even given that he was invisible. Ergam nocked and loosed a few arrows off to his right, and heard a distant yelp and a cry of pain. There were shouts to reinforce that area of the line.

He ran east, hoping that when he finally saw the soldiers there would be enough chaos that he could leap between them and be on his way. He dodged to avoid a man in the front line, then had to turn sideways to scoot between the next man and a tree. No sooner had he navigated through this problem when there was a squad bearing down on him, talking excitedly about the upcoming battle. He dove under a cart, then scrambled out the rear when it began to move. There were a few more dodges and moves, and eventually he was once again on the east side of the Calan line and headed back to the city. He needed to hurry. It was nearly daylight.

GUZUL THE FIERCE and King Bilal eyed Aygun Incesu in his cell as the dungeon master left them alone. The dungeon master had protested that it was never safe to leave a king and a traitor in a room together. He caught a stare from Guzul the Fierce which, while not technically magical, had a nearly magical effect on the dungeon master. He nodded, then mumbled something about special circumstances and made to leave.

"Well?" Guzul the Fierce asked Incesu.

"Well what?"

"We want to know about the depths of your treason," Bilal said. "I cannot believe that behind my back you would do such things."

"Time is of the essence, Your Majesty," Guzul said.

The king glared at her, then nodded.

Aygun Incesu waited.

Guzul raised a hand. "I wonder how long you could live as just a head and neck?"

"All right," Aygun Incesu said. "I have seen what you can do. My King, I regret what happened. I was looking for alternative ways to come to an agreement with Calan. I thought there must be some mutually beneficial arrangement. That's when I met the wizard Bugra Gurses. He has connections to the merchants of Calan who are very interested in employing some of our people. We could have been a thriving town again."

The king nodded. "And what sorts of roles would we be given, working for the merchants, do you suppose?"

"Well, Your Majesty, I'm sure there are many ..."

"Many deep holes they could put us down," the king finished. "Do you not think those relationships have been attempted? Why do you think Kanat is where it is, far from Dilara? Do you not know that the undead are slaves in Dilara? Can you imagine what kind of existence that is?"

Aygun looked aghast.

"Well," the king said. "You may yet find out."

A FEW MINUTES later inside the east gate of Kanat, Guzul said, "I will go talk to them. Open the gate, please."

The guards looked to King Bilal for his orders. The king nodded vigorously. "Do as Guzul the Fierce commands. Her will is as good as mine."

They opened the gate. Guzul stepped out, and the king ordered the gate closed and barred once more.

"Your Majesty," one of the guards said. "I have no undue love for the living. But I don't feel good about letting one elderly, living woman face a small army of trained Calan soldiers."

"These are no ordinary circumstances. And Guzul the Fierce is no ordinary woman."

CHAPTER 27

I t had been a long day for Lieutenant Alper Usta. He had been assigned to Calan because his parents were connected, and because he needed to have some military service on his record before he returned to the court at Dilara. Calan seemed like the perfect opportunity to drill the men a bit, perhaps handle some drunken idiots in a small tavern or two, but nothing more.

It was just his luck that as soon as he'd arrived, the leadership of the city decided to demolish, at the behest of the church, a city of undead. It seemed peculiar to Usta to destroy the undead. They were a resource for labor that men weren't willing to do, as far as he knew. He supposed that out here in the far reaches of the kingdom the people did more farming than anything. Perhaps the undead couldn't be used for that, because they frightened the livestock too badly.

Whatever the reason, he and his command were poised to lay siege to Kanat, the City of the Undead.

"No, sir," Sergeant Alabora said. "With respect, sir, it cannot be a siege. The undead do not eat. They do not need fresh water. They do not even need sleep. We cannot wait them out." Alabora was quite a bit older and more experienced. Too old, probably, to be doing this anymore, but it was a backwater posting after all. His advice and rapport with the men were invaluable.

"Then what do you suggest?"

"Their fortifications aren't high. We must breach the gate by any means necessary, and fight house to house until the city is empty."

"Sounds messy."

"Oh," Alabora chuckled. "It will be."

Usta sighed. "Very well then, Sergeant. Carry on."

Alabora nodded, saluted, whirled to ready the men. Usta followed, hands behind his back, head high. He would relish the opportunity to send word home about his first victory. Not much of a fight against a tiny city of the undead, but a victory all the same.

Two men were digging graves next to a pile of bodies.

"What's this?" Usta asked.

The two men snapped to attention and saluted. "They're graves, sir."

Usta fixed him with a calm gaze, as his father had done to him when he was a boy.

The soldier continued. "For the five men who died in camp overnight. Arrows to the back, sir."

"Arrows to the back?" Usta repeated.

"Yes, sir. Very irregular, sir. Patrols have been searching the last few hours but haven't found anything."

"Carry on then," Usta said. He hurried to catch up with Alabora. "Sergeant, what's this about five dead men in camp?"

Alabora frowned. "Nothing to trouble yourself with, sir. Most likely a farmer shooting at us from a tree-top.

Happens from time to time, local boys get a bit uppity, you know."

"But five men are dead. Shouldn't I be notified?"

"Oh, absolutely, sir. It's just that with the impending assault, I'd have thought your attentions would be on the many more deaths we're sure to see today, sir." The subtext was pretty clear. Alabora was trying nicely to say, "Going by the letter of the law I should certainly have let you know. But what with this being your first actual battle and all, and you still having your mother's milk around the corners of your mouth, I thought I'd just handle this little tidbit and let you get on with playing officer."

Usta frowned. Alabora had a point hidden between the lines he was saying, which Usta found irritating. He knew this was how it would be with the older enlisted men. His father had warned him.

"It bothers me deeply when men under my command are hurt or killed, Alabora," Usta said.

Alabora nodded. His face softened a bit. "Right you are, sir. I should have let you know more swiftly."

Usta nodded. He rejoiced quietly, but didn't let it show. He could tell from Alabora's reaction that he'd scored a small point or two with the old battle axe.

"Thank you, Alabora."

An hour later, the men were in their positions. The excitement in the air charged Usta, making him want to tap his feet. However the men would look to him for calm and strength, so he did his best to show it.

Alabora lumbered up and down the line, shoving soldiers into position, checking their weapons and armor. Then he joined Usta and nodded. "The men are ready, sir. It's time."

Usta was peering ahead.

"What's that?" Usta said. There was what looked like a figure in a white dress with long white hair and a white crown of some kind. "Is that an old woman?"

Guzul came closer, walking as though she owned the forest.

Usta stepped forward, elbowing his way past Alabora to get a better look. This mad old lady was lucky she wouldn't be still standing in the way when they charged. The infantrymen were little more mindful than animals. They'd run right over an old lady without even noticing the blood on the forest floor.

He looked again. Sure enough, it was definitely an old lady. He waited patiently until she marched to within ten yards of where Usta was standing and stopped.

"Madam," Usta began. "Can we help you?"

"Yes," the old woman said. "You can fuck off back to Calan before every one of you lies dead where you stand."

Alabora was leaning forward from his position in front of the enlisted men. "Lieutenant," he hissed. "Lieutenant."

"What is it, Sergeant?"

Alabora was sweating heavily. His old age and general fatness did not lend themselves to pressure situations. "That is Guzul the Fierce. She is a powerful witch, sir."

"Oh yes?" Usta said. Then, to the old woman, "Madam, my sergeant informs me that you are known as Guzul the Fierce. Is that so?"

"Indeed it is."

"I am Lieutenant Alper Usta. I would very much like to introduce myself properly to you, it's just that you are standing in the way of a military operation. Would you please follow me this way so that we can talk out of harm's way?"

"No," Guzul said. "There will not be a military operation

today. You and your men have two choices. You can turn around and go home—or wherever you like, for that matter —or I shall begin hurting you."

Usta frowned and looked taken aback.

"Quite a lot, in fact," the witch added.

Usta didn't understand. "Madam, I assure you, there—"

Alabora was pawing at his uniform. "Sir. Please, sir. That is Guzul the Fierce. If she says she will hurt us and our men, she means it. If we stand against her, we will be lucky to crawl home to Calan." Usta saw true terror in Alabora's eyes. The man wasn't joking around.

"Listen to your man, boy," the witch said.

"Madam," Usta called in a loud, clear voice.

Alabora put his face into a gauntleted hand.

Usta stood as tall as he could. "I represent the city of Calan and the Kingdom of Dilara." He drew his sword. "I am under orders to take the city of Kanat. I must follow my orders or I disgrace the men who follow me. I am going to approach you now and ask you, respectfully, to stand aside."

He took a step forward, and his uniform fell off.

He looked down to see that he was not only completely naked, but he had an iron-like erection that would have been suitable for driving roofing tacks. He screamed and threw his sword down, then used both hands to cover himself. The blade of his sword had been replaced with a wooden phallus, but he didn't notice it. He tried to stand proudly while hiding his erection from the men and the old woman. It wasn't easy or comfortable. He didn't know what to do next.

"Now," Guzul the Fierce said. "The rest of you listen to me. I have spared this boy's life and embarrassed him instead of killing him, because he showed courage, honor, and respect on your behalf. I could just as easily have removed his skin from his body as his clothes. Unless you want to die, *today,* you should go back to your camp."

Usta picked up the ruins of his uniform breeches and tied them around his waist. They still stuck out in the front, but at least he was covered. Then he picked up his sword, saw what had happened to it, and threw it back down in disgust.

He stood tall, turned to face his men. They looked worried.

"We have met a more powerful force," Usta announced. "Stand down."

There were so many sighs of relief it sounded like a storm rattling through the treetops.

"Alabora," said Usta.

"Yes, sir."

"Find me some pants, please."

"Right away, sir."

"Lieutenant Usta."

Usta turned again. The witch was approaching. "Yes, ma'am."

"You did well here today. A much worse lieutenant would have ordered his men to attack me rather than fighting himself."

Usta wasn't quite sure how to react. "Thank you, ma'am."

"You're lucky I'm not a few centuries younger or I'd teach you a few more things as well," she said. She pinched Usta on his bare bottom as she passed.

Usta yelped, then tried to cover it with a cough. Hopefully no one had seen it.

CHAPTER 28

Ozel had not slept well, neither had Aysu. They were both glad the sky was getting lighter. They packed up their things and shouldered their packs.

"We must sort this out today," Aysu said.

Ozel nodded. "So that we don't have to come back here tonight."

The drunks downstairs had not, thankfully, come upstairs and kicked their way into the room, but they had made a lot of noise late into the night. Ozel had considered going out to ask the innkeeper if he could tell the patrons to keep the racket down, but Aysu gave him such a look that he abandoned the idea. They'd talked about wizarding and blacksmithing to pass the time, which was nice. If only the exchange of life histories had not taken place over an undercurrent of nervousness and fright, it would have been highly enjoyable.

When they were packed, they dragged the bed frame out of the way and opened the door. They tiptoed down the stairs in hopes of avoiding any confrontation with the owner. He didn't seem a particularly nice man. Aysu poked her head into the public room, made a shushing sound at Ozel, then motioned for him to follow.

The innkeeper was asleep against the far wall. At some point in the night he had thrown up on himself.

Ozel shook his head in disbelief. Aysu made her way toward the door. When she pushed it open, light streamed in and the innkeeper stirred.

"Ay," he said, his speech thick and slurred. "No one's paid me. You gotta pay!"

"Run!" Ozel said. Aysu darted out the door and Ozel was hot on her heels. She went up the street and he followed, legs pumping. When they'd climbed to the top of the hill Ozel turned to look back toward the inn. No one was following them.

He ran a few more steps and then they slowed, panting. They smiled at one another. Aysu jumped on him and hugged him.

"Oh," he said. Then he laughed.

She released him, smiling, then continued walking. "Today will be easier."

"Why's that, do you think?"

"Because up until now people haven't wanted to help us. Today they will. Bankers will be lovely. No one hates banks, do they?"

Ozel didn't know, but he hoped not.

BEHIND THEM, Bartu Hamdi stepped out of a doorway. He couldn't believe how close he had come to having those two little shits run right into him. He knew the city a little bit, but not well enough to walk directly to the Trotting Hound. He'd had to find his way, which meant he'd missed his chance to bribe the innkeeper to keep the kids under wraps for a few days. Now he'd have to improvise.

Did he really want to get mixed up in this mess? His gut said no, wanting no part of this nonsense, whatever it was. He wanted to be as far as possible from wizards of any kind, let alone those willing to strike a man stone dead on the side of the road and then set his body ablaze. If that Gurses fellow would blast a priest like that, there was no telling what he'd do to Hamdi, if he had a mind to.

Bartu stood in the street, watching Ozel and Aysu in the distance walk away. What would it look like to try to handle them right now, anyway? He'd have to run up, grab the two brats, and then shove them down an alleyway. Then what? He might be able to hold one of them down, but two? What if one of them had a knife or something? Too many questions.

When faced with too many questions, what do you do? Forget most of them.

He turned on his heel and headed toward the bank. With luck, he could be out of town before the wizard ever realized he'd disappeared, and Bartu Hamdi would be rich that night.

He stepped into the marble building and was met by a pinched-face man in colorful clothes. The doorman looked Bartu Hamdi up and down disapprovingly. Hamdi realized he was wearing the garb of a farmer, covered in dust from days on the road.

"Good morning," the doorman said.

"Good morning. I am Bartu Hamdi. I run a farm near Bilgehan where I receive orphaned children. I understand one of my charges has an inheritance. I have come to claim it."

The banker looked Bartu up and down again. He

seemed to expect this to communicate something—perhaps that Bartu should leave. Was Bartu Hamdi supposed to abandon a veritable fortune here, at this bank, merely because the man out front looked him up and down a few times? Surely not.

"I see," the doorman said.

Bartu Hamdi squinted at him. The banker wasn't going anywhere or doing anything. "What happens now?"

"Ah!" the doorman said. "Yes. I'll just see if someone is available to speak with you." He disappeared down a hallway. Bartu could see him knock on a door, stick his head in, then remove it. He walked farther down to the end of the hallway and repeated the process there. Then he came back to the entranceway, wringing his hands. "Yes. I tried Mr. Debakey, but he's indisposed at the moment. See Mr. Barnard. Room twelve." He swept his hand at the hallway as if he were drawing aside an invisible drape.

"Thank you," Bartu said, loading the words with vinegar.

At the end of the hall, the doorway to room twelve stood open. There were some letters on the door as well, though Bartu couldn't read them. He'd learned basic numbers when negotiating prices for livestock and other farm goods. Perhaps over the coming months he'd learn to read as well, since he was going to be a nobleman with time on his hands.

Barnard was an older gentleman with white hair except for a bald spot on top. The hair merged with a beard that grew on his jaw and connected with a thick white mustache. He stood to welcome Bartu.

"Welcome, sir, welcome," he said. He also looked Bartu up and down. "Toran Barnard." He stuck his hand out.

Bartu shook it. "Bartu Hamdi. I apologize for the state of my clothes. I have been travelling."

"Not at all, not at all. The wife and I like to get over to Dilara now and again, and the dust in the carriages can be positively maddening, eh?"

Bartu chuckled and didn't admit that he'd been on foot.

Barnard sat, indicated a chair for Bartu, who took it.

Barnard smoothed his mustache. "Yes. So. I understand you are the man Saban Kozen spoke of?"

Bartu's guts went ice cold. He had a memory of the last time he'd seen Saban Kozen, only a few hours ago. It seemed like a thousand years. "Yes, well, he let me know about the situation. When I heard, I left my farm at Bilgehan and came straight to Calan."

"I see. Yes. As well you might. And the boy in question. He was one of your charges?"

"Indeed he was."

"And I take it the boy is, er, no longer among the living?"

Bartu had been working on this part of the plan. "He is alive. Very much so. But he has been struck infirm these recent months. I believe with some extra money for treatment he could see improvement, however."

"Oh, yes? Oh, I see." Barnard pushed a few scrolls around on his desk, opened one, grunted, closed it. Then he opened another. "Hmm, I see. Well, that does complicate matters."

"It does?"

"Yes. You see, if he were dead, I'd have just issued the coin to his next of kin, which in this case would be you. You would have been walking out of here with a chest of gold. You are a good man to be honest about this." Barnard smiled. "Many people in your position might not have been."

Bartu could feel his teeth grinding together. He wanted to rip the wooden armrests of his chair from their sockets and beat himself senseless with them. "Yes, well, it's entirely possible that he's died while I've been away, you know. He was so *very* infirm."

Barnard eyed him. "Hmm. Yes. Go on."

Bartu blinked. Go on?

"I don't mean to bore you with the trivialities of banking, Mr. Hamdi. Nothing of the sort. But you see, the state of the law is currently in a great amount of flux."

"Flux?"

"Change. Quite a lot of change. The church holds great sway with his lordship these days, which means that any large transactions we undertake must also include a hefty tax which goes directly into the church's coffers."

"We all pay taxes," Bartu said.

"True. Quite true. In fact, taxes are a necessary evil to keep the lord's coffers full of enough gold to pay the City Watch, keep the roads passable, gates functional, that sort of thing. But an additional tribute to the church on top of the lord's tax, well, that seems arbitrarily burdensome to ... some people."

Bartu felt sweaty and uncertain. He could smell his own body, like an animal's, and he was just as out of place in this office as would a plow mule have been.

Barnard's bushy white eyebrows went up. "Now, me, I've never been a religious man. I'm like you. I work hard, I do my bit. Keep my head down, right? No need to be wondering what makes a cloud. All I need to know is whether it's going to rain."

Bartu nodded. This sounded like something he might be able to understand. Rain was important.

"What these taxes mean to hardworking people like us, is, that in the case where a guardian such as yourself is recognized as being the guardian of a child, like your, ah ..."

"Ozel," Bartu said. He was a little surprised he'd been able to remember the boy's name.

"Ozel. Exactly. The guardian of a child like your Ozel would have access to the coin on an ongoing basis. However, every time there is a transaction ..." Barnard paused, eyeing Bartu. He seemed to decide this bit needed spelling out. "As you know, a transaction is when you take money out of the bank. Anyway, any time that happens, the church will get to dip its hand into the money and take some of it away. On the other hand, if the boy were deceased, I could send you out the door with the balance of the account this afternoon. So ... you were telling me about the boy's condition a moment ago. Exactly *how* would you say he's doing?"

"Oh, he's dead. Dead as anything. All bloated and green on one side and smelling pretty bad, most likely. Completely dead."

"Ah! My condolences. So sorry to hear that very detailed diagnosis. Well, as I say, that being the case, I think we can expedite matters. We should have the coin ready for you in three or four days."

"Three or four days?" Bartu's skin felt worse than sweaty. Clammy and cold in some places, and hot and prickly in others.

"Yes. Well, we don't keep the money here, you know. We'd have no end of trouble with bandits and brigands trying to break into the place. We'll have to gather it."

"But you said I could be walking out today."

"Well, that would normally be a possibility, of course, but we didn't have any warning of your arrival. Mind you, if you were willing to pay a rush fee we might be able to accommodate."

"How much?"

"One hundred gold pieces is standard."

Bartu closed his eyes. He forced them open again. His farm back in Bilgehan was only worth maybe one hundred and fifty gold pieces and he'd worked all his life on it. Now this Barnard wanted a hundred gold pieces to speed up a little? Bartu couldn't help but make some small choking sounds as he tried to gather his thoughts. "How much is there in total?"

"Oh, let me see," Barnard said. He looked at some papers on his desk. "Ah, here we are. It looks like 4,378 gold pieces altogether."

Bartu Hamdi laughed out loud.

Barnard smiled too. "Yes, it's quite a sum, isn't it? Now, of course, you know, we can only fit around one thousand gold pieces in a chest, so that'll be four large chests that are very heavy. Two strong men should be able to manage each one. You have a few men in your employ, I assume?"

"Er, no."

"Ah. Well, we'd be glad to provide a few of Calan's finest. You'll want them on the road anyway. Won't do you much good to have the gold, if you're robbed as soon as you leave the city gate."

"Robbed? But the roads in this area are safe. Why, I've been back and forth to Calan a dozen times with no trouble of any kind."

"Oh, yes. I'd expect that to be the case. But the trouble with great wealth is that it makes its own dark magic, you know. A man who would see you walk down the road will offer nothing but a nod in your direction when you're alone, yet he will be mightily tempted to get up to some mischief if you're in a cart with four large chests."

Bartu was being fleeced. He knew it. But he had no leverage and anyway, some of what Barnard was saying was true. Bartu could get up and walk out the door and live the rest of his life the way he'd lived it up until now, or he could play along and walk out of here with a completely new life. That said, his ego wouldn't let him just sit there and take it. He suspected that if he didn't spring for the protection Barnard was offering, Barnard would tip off a couple of brigands and his throat would be slit by morning. Better to just get fleeced.

"Mr. Barnard, I am a simple man. I will ask simply. What will it cost to get me and my gold safely to Dilara?"

"Well, you'll need five strong men, the chests, daily wages for them for the journey ..." he scratched on a paper with a quill. "Let's call it two hundred."

"So one hundred for the rush fee and two hundred to get safely to Dilara?"

"That should do it, yes."

"Can you give me, say, twenty gold pieces now? I would like to have a bath, buy some clothes, then perhaps do a bit of whoring."

"We might be able to manage it by the end of the day," Barnard said.

Bartu sighed. "What if I were to accidentally drop one of the gold pieces here in your room? Say, on your desk?"

Barnard smiled a very big smile. "I believe you're getting the hang of banking, Mr. Hamdi."

CHAPTER 29

Bugra Gurses arrived at the east gate of Kanat long before dawn. He hadn't intended for this plan to include murder, but time was getting short, Bugra was getting testier by the minute, and he certainly didn't need any low-level priest like Saban Kozen getting in the way. Still, if Bugra could just speak to Aygun Incesu and get his help in finding a way to delay Guzul the Fierce, the deal with the merchants could go through as planned.

The guards at the gate stopped him. "Ho there, who goes?"

"Bugra Gurses, friend to Aygun Incesu and the crown. Admit me at once, please."

There was some talking that Bugra couldn't hear. Any sound other than the gate opening wasn't a welcome one.

"What is going on?" Bugra demanded.

"A moment, please, sir. We are dealing with a security matter and will be with you shortly. Your presence is important to us and we thank you for your patience."

What could they be doing? Were they merely incompetent when it came to opening the gate? It was possible that this gate didn't get enough use to be in good repair. But there were other concerns. What if Incesu had decided to do something rash? Was he on the throne? Was he dead? Thrown in the dungeon?

Any of that could be the case. One thing he knew for sure was that Guzul the Fierce was in play somehow. If she had gotten face to face with Aygun Incesu, she'd have sniffed him out as a rotten sneak in under a second.

Bugra couldn't help himself. "Shit," he hissed.

Obviously, Aygun Incesu hadn't made any bold moves. Or, if he had, it had blown up in his face. He was probably rotting in the dungeon at this very moment. These guards had certainly sent word that Bugra was at the gate. Next they'd send Guzul the Fierce out and then he'd ... what? Duel with Guzul the Fierce?

That wasn't what he wanted. If he imagined a perfect future for himself, it was ruling with an iron fist over all the kingdoms and having Guzul at his side. Perhaps she'd be wearing something low-cut. Yes. But no, he didn't want to fight her. There was a decent chance that she'd split him open like a dropped eggplant if it ever came to a fair magical fight. The thought of her dominating him made Bugra tingle a little.

He'd wasted his time coming out here, but it couldn't have been helped. He'd had no way of knowing that Incesu was compromised. He had to rush back to Calan. If he could speak to the merchants, perhaps he could get them to put pressure on the lord. If not, well, perhaps he could get an audience with the lord himself.

He turned and headed back toward Calan. He had added a touch of enchanted haste to his feet before so he could cover ground more easily, but the spell was wearing off. After a few minutes he was slowing down. It ended up being a blessing though, because he found himself just east of Kanat. He could see a line of soldiers through the trees. This must be the Calan force about to attack Kanat.

But—wait ...

What was this? Was that Guzul the Fierce talking to the men? Who else would be out here in that shining white gown? It had to be her.

Bugra slowed to a stop and made himself fade into the darkness. He couldn't hear what was going on, but thought he got the gist with the body language and gestures.

The leader of the troops wanted Guzul to get out of the way so he could attack. Now he was moving toward Guzul. Bad move, kid. They don't call her Guzul the Fierce because she steps aside. Bugra held his breath for the impending explosion.

Rather than splatter his brains all over the forest, she merely made his clothes fall off. She must be going soft in her advanced years. Her hair looked a little bit grayer than the last time he'd seen it. Time. It comes for us all, he thought.

Now the soldiers were moving backwards, breaking rank. They weren't going to attack Kanat. This was good news. This was very good news. Bugra made a mental note to thank Guzul the next time he saw her. He didn't know what reasons she had for protecting Kanat, but he was glad of the small break of good luck. Now to get himself back to Calan to broker some deals before the soldiers got it in their heads to try something again.

He cast haste on his feet once more, laying it on thick this time. He would have to be careful not to run into a tree. At this speed he was likely to be badly injured.

At last, he was back on the road and nearing Calan. The sun was up, its golden light shining on the open city gate.

Perhaps it was a dawn of some changing luck for Bugra Gurses as well.

THE CITY WAS BEGINNING to wake up as Bugra stalked the streets. He decided to try Odabasi at home, before going to the office of the merchant association Odabasi led. He didn't know whether the man liked to get to work early or later, and the home was closer to the west gate. The man at the door wasn't forthcoming with information, but everything suggested that Odabasi wasn't home. He wouldn't say for certain whether his master would be at work.

"Where else could he be?" Bugra demanded.

"Indeed, sir," the doorman said.

Bugra whirled with a grunt of irritation and stalked away. Odabasi would be at his office, certainly.

As it happened, Bugra ran into Odabasi, literally bumping into him as he was stalking down the street.

"Ah, Odabasi. I am looking for you."

Odabasi looked over first one shoulder then the other. "Not here. I can't be seen with you, remember?"

"I remember, but circumstances have changed. We need to speak at once."

Odabasi frowned. "Alleyway, behind my office. Fifteen minutes."

Bugra nodded and turned at the next intersection. He wasted the time by taking a long route to Odabasi's office.

Bugra was pacing in the alleyway when Odabasi opened the door, looked both ways, and then motioned Bugra inside.

They were in a small kitchen which looked like it did double duty as a storage room. Chairs were stacked up in two rows.

"Well," Odabasi said. "What is it?"

"I've just come from Kanat. Calan planned to attack tonight. They would doubtless have razed the city completely."

"Oh? Interesting. That would have been unfortunate."

"Yes, to say the least."

Odabasi looked around. "Was there anything else you wanted?"

Bugra stared. "Well, we got lucky this time. Guzul the Fierce quelled the Calan soldiers somehow and there wasn't an attack. I suspect my man in Kanat is no longer in a position to negotiate. We'll have to act fast, if we're to preserve Kanat for our purposes."

Odabasi was shaking his head. "This is becoming more trouble than it's worth. The other merchants and I like the sound of undead labor, and those programs have been shown to work to great effect in Dilara, but Calan is a very different kettle of fish. Perhaps it's time to cut losses."

"No, it is *not* time to cut losses, Odabasi. It's very easy for you to say this is becoming more trouble than it's worth. You're not the laughing-stock of the city. Women don't draw their children close when you walk by. This is my ticket back to the status that is rightfully mine."

"I very much hope that it works out for you, Bugra Gurses. But I believe I have done everything I can to help."

"You selfish idiot," Bugra spat. "Don't you know they'll come for you next? When the undead are gone and the wizards are all persecuted, they will come for the merchants."

"I believe honest businessmen are very different from the undead and wizards, sir."

Bugra was losing control of this situation. He could sense it, making him feel very small. Was he even standing up straight? The weight of the conversation seemed to be making him stoop over, shoulders bowed. Worse, this self-assured prick was going to abandon him in his time of need.

"All I want is for you to put a little pressure on the lord, get him to hold off on destroying Kanat until I can come up with a new strategy."

"I can't do that. Even if I could, I wouldn't. Look around you, Gurses. The city is not controlled by the lord in anything but name. He will not go against the church, and neither will I. I'm sorry that you have gotten yourself into an unfortunate place, but that is not my fault. Now, I must ask you to please leave."

Bugra felt himself so full of fire that it threatened to burst out of his eye sockets. He let his hand fly and it slapped Odabasi hard across the face. The fat merchant stumbled backward, hand to his cheek. Bugra hadn't meant to slap the man, but now that he had, the feeling was good. He wondered how many years it had been since someone stood up to wealthy Odabasi.

"Very well, then. If you will not help me, if you and your ilk are determined that Bugra Gurses is a monster, then I will show you what manner of monster I can be."

"Well, I—" Odabasi sputtered. "I'm sure there's some arrangement that can be made?"

Bugra sent the stacked chairs flying through the air to hit Odabasi. He was knocked backward again and cried out in pain.

"We already had an arrangement," Bugra growled. He liked the way his voice sounded. Angry, sure of himself. Vengeful. He was standing up straight now, certainly, looming over a terrified Odabasi. "But yes, now we have a *new* arrangement."

The fireball struck Odabasi and the broken chairs. Both

burst into flame. As Bugra was walking away he could still hear the man's screeching as he burned.

Shouts came from behind him. People were discovering the fire and the source of the screams. They might even get Odabasi extinguished before he died. It didn't matter. Bugra Gurses wasn't bound by the law of this place anymore. He wasn't bound by the church. He was bound only by the limits of his power to wield magic, and those were all theoretical. Anything was possible.

On the way to the palace Bugra considered his options. Should he give the lord the chance to comply with his wishes? He might as well, but just the one. He decided that, going forward, he would give people a choice to not be killed. Sure, Bugra was angry and he intended to take that anger out on the people who had maligned him these long years. Namely, the city of Calan, its lord, and its church for a start. He wouldn't murder people for the sport of it. No, he was merely demonstrating his dissatisfaction with the way he'd been treated. It was a needed readjustment. Not a purge.

When he arrived at the palace, two sentries crossed their pikes at the guard house. He'd expected this.

"Halt!" the men shouted together.

"Bugra Gurses would speak with your master," said Bugra.

"We have not been informed of any visitors."

Bugra blasted a hole in the guard's chest and the man clanked to the ground stone dead.

"Bugra Gurses would speak with your master," he said again.

The surviving sentry hastily moved his pike to the side

to let Bugra pass.

A handful of guards came running out to investigate. Lightning bolts streaked out of the clear blue sky as Bugra decapitated the four of them with a blade of energy. He decided on the spot not to do that again unless absolutely necessary. It made a terrible mess.

The more Bugra thought about it though, what was he doing here? Was he going to ask the lord's permission to go on a killing spree? Bugra Gurses needed no one's permission. He was here to inform the lord that Calan was his city now. And if that were the case ...

He turned and went back out the gate. From here he could see his tower—or he would have been able to without the illusion masking it. He raised his hands, shouted a few words, and the destroyed structure was replaced with its true form. He admired it a moment, then realized he was standing in a pool of blood. Irritated and preoccupied with stepping out of the gore, Bugra didn't hear two men approaching.

"What devilry is this?" a voice asked.

Bugra Gurses turned to see Lord Tebrik and Bishop Erkan.

"It is a readjustment, Erkan," Gurses said. "I have let you turn this perfectly acceptable backwater into a simpering chamber pot. I have abided your false piety and the resulting disrespect in the street because I knew I would certainly outlive you and everyone else in this town. Now I am sick of it and I've taken control of Calan."

"Do you see, My Lord?" Erkan said. "This is why we must put a stop to this filth they call magic. Look at these good men, cut down with but a word, I expect? They'd have had the courage to face you with a blade, Bugra Gurses, had you the stomach for it."

"Does the bear wait for the rabbit to grow bigger claws, Bishop Erkan?" Bugra asked. He decided to try something. He'd always wondered how a transformation spell would work on a human.

"Wh—what?" Erkan said. The bishop cried out as his face began to elongate. The noise of bones creaking and stretching was like the sound of a great tree falling over and over again. The twisted form that used to be Calan's head holy man fell to the ground and writhed, screaming. Then his skin sprouted hair as he shrank. His ears elongated and his teeth pushed themselves forward.

Ah, thought Bugra. That's why no one performs this magic on humans. It's horrifying torture beyond imagining. He smiled.

A white rabbit lay gasping for breath among the fine clothes once worn by Bishop Erkan.

"Now, Lord Tebrik," Bugra said, walking toward the nobleman. "I believe you should call the city populace to your palace. You and I will address them. You will let them know that I am now in charge of their fate. If they want to live, they will bend to my will. For if they do not ..." Bugra brought his boot heel down on the head of the rabbit. Its skull made a crunching noise as it collapsed.

The terrified look on Tebrik's face was so utterly perfect. If Bugra could have bottled the experience of seeing the lord's face like that and drunk it every night before bed, he might die a happy man.

"Very well," said Tebrik. "I will call them. Just, please. Stop killing people."

"Perhaps I will. Perhaps I won't. The way I see it, the city has a lot of derision to make up for. And I will have my satisfaction."

CHAPTER 30

One of the problems with looking for a bank in a city like Calan was that many of the buildings didn't have any signage. Presumably, most people who did business here already knew which buildings were what. Ozel and Aysu didn't. Another problem was that no one seemed terribly interested in talking to them.

"I'm starting to think someone might have cast an invisibility spell on us," Ozel said, after trying to get the attention of a man in nice clothes and asking directions to the banking district. The man waved him away, annoyed.

"I think it's the way we look," Aysu said, pointing to herself, dirty from sleeping out of doors. She could be right. After all, they were asking well-dressed people about the banks—which made sense to Ozel.

"We'll just have to keep trying. Sooner or later we will meet someone who is nice."

Ozel decided to try getting a little more aggressive. He stepped into the path of the next merchant who came along. "Excuse me, sir, but I'm looking for the banks in—"

The merchant shoved Ozel aside. As Ozel stepped backward, his boot caught on a cobble and he tumbled into a wooden table piled high with cloth. The table slid, then tipped over. A man came out of his shop, saw the mess and Ozel struggling to his feet. He sighed heavily and began picking up his cloth. Ozel tried to help.

"I'm so sorry, sir," Ozel said. "I didn't mean to knock the table over."

"It's all right, boy. All right. The table has folding legs so it can be brought inside at night. It is easy to knock it over. I'll handle it."

"At least let us help pick the cloth up," Aysu said.

"No, no, it's all right. I know how they go back on the table. I need to bring them inside anyway." He picked up a bolt of material and scrubbed at it, but the dust refused to brush away.

"Let me pay for that," Ozel said.

"We don't have any money," Aysu whispered at him.

"True. But my master, Wagast, could help."

The man turned to look at Ozel. "Your master is Wagast the wizard?" A smile crept across his face.

"Yes?"

The man laughed. "Well, in that case, I shall accept your offer of help and repayment. I can't wait to see old Wagast's face when he learns he's in my debt." He had a wise, wrinkled face and gray hair. His beard was short and his body under the robes was wiry. He seemed a little bit like a friendly old squirrel.

"You know him?" Aysu asked.

"Of course," the man said, standing straight. "I've been making robes for Wagast for years. He helped me when I had a coughing ailment that nearly killed me. Mended my brother's broken leg too. That's how I met Wagast over near

Bilgehan." He smiled again with the memory. "How's he doing? Is he still gardening?"

"He is, but—"

"No, wait, let me guess. If you're the apprentice, you do most of the gardening, eh?" The man's eyes twinkled.

Ozel smiled. "I do indeed."

The man laughed. "I bet you do, son. I bet you do. I believe I have seen that helmet before as well. I'm Arier Enver." He stuck his hand out first to Ozel, then Aysu, who introduced themselves. "Pleased to meet you both. Now, help me get this cloth inside, won't you?"

They helped Arier take his cloth bolts inside the shop. He showed them how to stack them, and then how to fold the legs on the tables.

"Perhaps I shouldn't have put my cloth out this morning since I have to close up for a meeting, but I figure you never know when a buyer might come looking."

"Mr. Enver, sir," Aysu said. "We are looking for a bank. Can you help us?"

"Please, call me Arier. Which bank?"

"We're not sure. We got word that I inherited some money from family. That's all we know."

"Hmm. The only office I know that might handle something like that is old Barnard's bank. He has some dealings with Dilara and places even farther away. Do you know the street off the small market, near where the old stable burned down?"

Ozel and Aysu looked at one another.

"No, I guess you wouldn't, would you. Right. You'll just have to come with me and I'll show you. I have a quick meeting with some members of the merchant council and then I can show you the way. How's that?"

"Very good, sir, thank you. We appreciate it."

Arier shooed them out the door and into the street. He turned a slate in a wooden holder around so that it read "closed." And wrote "after noon" on it with chalk.

"I'm sorry I can't take you straight away, but I agreed to serve on this blasted council. Bunch of old fools saying nothing over and over again, if you ask me. But I agreed, and if I don't go they'll be snide about it. I've gotten word there's an emergency meeting. We'll stop by, I'll shake a few hands, then we'll be off to the bank and back here before the afternoon shoppers are in the street, eh?" He walked as he talked. Ozel and Aysu followed.

"Thank you again for your help, sir," Aysu said. "We've not had much luck asking for directions until now."

"No, I expect not. Forgive me for saying so, but you two look like street urchins."

"Given that we don't have any money or lodging here, I guess we are," Ozel said.

Arier was a fast walker. His robe looked like a sail on a ship as he marched along into a light breeze. He took them down a side alley, then another. When they made the next turn, the street was full of people. The smell of burning and damp ashes was in the air.

"What's this?" Arier asked.

The first floor of one of the buildings was pouring smoke. Arier went to a well-dressed man. "Ho there, Ilhan. What's going on?"

The man turned to Arier. His face was grave. "It's Odabasi. He's dead. They found him in the back kitchen of his office, burned alive. It was only the quick thinking of the neighbors and their buckets that saved this whole block from burning down."

"What? Odabasi? How did this happen?"

Ilhan lowered his voice. "I don't know. But some of the

neighbors are saying there's no way Odabasi could have started this fire. And his body was under a stack of chairs, like someone set a fire on top of him. Some of them are saying it was magic."

"Magic? But who would do that?"

Ilhan stared at him as if to say, "you know very well who."

Arier laughed uncomfortably. "Oh, come now. I don't think even that old fool would be so bold."

Ilhan's eyebrows went up. He clearly thought that old fool *would* be so bold.

"What's going on?" Ozel asked.

Ilhan glanced at Ozel and Aysu, then stalked away without another word.

"This is troubling," Arier said. "I don't like to say such things aloud on the street, or with children present for that matter, but given that you're Wagast's apprentice you might as well know." He looked around warily. "Ilhan thinks this was done by a wizard."

"Bugra Gurses?" Aysu asked.

Arier's eyes widened and he gestured at her. "Not here. The meeting will be cancelled. Let's get you to the bank and on your way back to Bilgehan. Come on." He began walking quickly in the direction they'd come.

"Why would Bugra Gurses want to kill that man?" Ozel asked, catching up.

"I don't know that he did—or if he did, why he would. What I do know is that I don't want to be involved. I told the other merchants it was foolish to get into a relationship with Gurses. Not because he's a wizard, mind, just because he's a man under pressure."

"You mean like how he hides his tower?" Aysu asked.

"Hides his tower?"

"Yes. It's not really destroyed. He just makes it look that way so people won't think he's a powerful wizard."

Arier shook his head. "That's exactly the kind of behavior I mean. From what I hear, the wizard Gurses used to be influential in Calan politics. But when the church began to rise in power he just withdrew. Perhaps he thought it was just a passing phase and he could wait it out. I don't know."

"Is that why people don't like to talk about him?" Ozel asked.

"Lord Tebrik is religious and prefers to deal with religious people. If you want to make money in Lord Tebrik's Calan, you are religious whether you want to be or not. One cannot easily be religious and simultaneously respectful toward wizards."

"Why not?" Ozel asked.

"The church would never allow it."

CHAPTER 31

Arier led them down several more turns until they arrived, at last, at a building with a little more carved stone and decoration than others. Arier pushed through the door, and they were met inside by a well-dressed man with a face whose features appeared to be trying to get as close to one another as possible.

"Ah, Mr. Enver. To what do we owe the pleasure?" The last word came out a little uncertain as the man's eyes flitted over Ozel and Aysu.

"Is Barnard in? I'd like a quick word."

"He is, Mr. Enver. Go right ahead."

Arier nodded and strode down the hallway. Ozel and Aysu followed. Under his breath, but loud enough so Ozel and Aysu could hear, Arier said, "I do a bit of business here, so they're civil to my face. They still charge me for every transaction though."

At the end of the hall, he tapped on the door. "Barnard, you in there? Arier Enver."

There was the scraping sound of a chair. "Yes, please do come in, Arier. Welcome, welcome."

The office was small, but there was room for all three of them if they stood.

"Mr. Barnard, I'd like you to meet Aysu, an apprentice blacksmith from Bilgehan," Arier said.

"Oh, very nice. A pleasure, young lady. A fine trade. You come see me when you need some financial assistance in a few years, eh?" He chuckled.

"And this is Ozel, apprentice wizard."

Mr. Barnard did not stick his hand out. "Did you say ... Ozel?"

"Yes," Arier said.

"From Bilgehan?"

"Yes."

Mr. Barnard looked like he'd just realized he'd eaten week-old fish. "I don't suppose you were once, ah, in the charge of a man named," he shuffled some papers on his desk, "Bartu Hamdi?"

OZEL SAT in Mr. Barnard's office. He still couldn't believe it. Apparently, just a few hours previous, Bartu Hamdi had walked into the office, told Barnard that Ozel was dead, and then left with a fortune in gold coins after arranging a small group of strong-armed men to protect him.

Barnard looked concerned and sorrowful, especially having seen Ozel's peculiar Q birthmark, but it didn't stop Ozel wanting to yell at the banker. He did his best to stay calm.

"As I say," Barnard said. "I believe this can all be sorted out before close of business today."

"Well, we wouldn't want you to miss any other appointments," Aysu said coldly.

This comment appeared to strike Barnard like a fist to

the gut. At least he had the good grace to know sarcasm when it was directed at his incompetence. "Yes, ma'am, you're absolutely right. You shall have my full attention until it is resolved."

The pinched-face doorman wedged himself into the room and handed a slip of paper to Barnard, then was gone again. Barnard read it. His face brightened. "Here we are. It is as I'd hoped. Mr. Hamdi mentioned he'd like to stay in town tonight because he ..." Barnard coughed. "Well, he just wanted to stay in an inn before getting back on the road, I think. We should be able to get our hands on the money tomorrow with the help of the City Watch. I will send notice to them right away."

"So what do we do?" Ozel asked.

"For the moment there isn't much else to do, I'm afraid. Legally the money is Mr. Hamdi's for the course of the evening until the Watch can get to him in the morning. The inn will have a note of his spending, for which we will reimburse up to half of the amount."

Arier cleared his throat.

Barnard started again, "Ah, as I was saying, reimburse the *full* amount of the losses. How does that sound?"

"Can't we just go to the inn and tell him to give the money back?" Ozel asked.

"My concern there would be that he'd find a way to slip away at night," Arier said. "I think it's better if you let him think he's safe and happy for the evening, then the Watch will deal with him in the morning. Mr. Barnard will provide us with a note certifying the rightful owner of the fortune, won't you?"

"Indeed," said Barnard.

The doorman reappeared again. "There's someone here to see you."

"You mean, there's someone here to see you, *sir,*" Barnard said testily. "Tell whoever it is that my full attention is on these clients."

"No, sir, someone to see *them.*"

ERGAM WAS WAITING for them in the lobby. He looked tense, but smiled when he saw Ozel and Aysu. They wanted to fill him in on everything that had happened, but everyone realized it would be better to talk elsewhere.

"You will be my guests," Arier said. "Please, I insist." Nobody disagreed. They had no other options. He walked them to his house just a few minutes away. It wasn't enormous, but it had a pleasing walled garden out front. "I'm sorry, I must leave you here. I want to be open for any afternoon shoppers. Relax. Make yourselves at home."

"Thank you, Arier," Ozel said. "For everything you've done today."

"Not a problem. I'm sorry about what happened at the bank. Maybe if we'd gotten there a little earlier we could have avoided this mess."

"That's not your fault."

Arier shook his head in disbelief, then said goodbye and urged them once more to make themselves at home, and was gone.

"Right," Ergam said. "Shall I go first or you?"

Ergam explained his journey and ended by saying, "But when I got back to the fucking gate I was still as transparent as a night-time fart. I had to wait around a few minutes in the forest until I solidified."

"Now there's a problem I've not yet had," Ozel said. Then he and Aysu filled Ergam in on everything they'd been doing.

"It must feel good to be so close to the end of your quest," Ergam said.

"Not really," Aysu said. "We were close, but now it's all messed up."

"Not to worry," Ergam said. "I can find out where Bartu Hamdi is staying."

"You can?" Ozel asked. "Then let's go there and be done with this."

"I think we should leave it until morning. Barnard is a greedy old shit for letting this happen and I don't think he's telling us everything, but he's right—if we tip Hamdi off, he might leave in the night. I would still be able to track him, but it'll be easier if the City Watch make it all legal. Worry not. Even if he were to slip away right now I would still be able to follow him."

"I guess that makes sense," Ozel said. He didn't like it much, but he understood the reasoning. "Ergam, do you think it's possible that Bugra Gurses would kill a man? A merchant?"

"I'm not sure," Ergam said. "He is a wizard, so one would expect him to be dangerous, but he has been in the city of Calan for many years. Before I was alive, even, I think. I've never heard of him killing anyone. When I spoke with my father and Guzul the Fierce, though, they seemed to think he was suspicious ..." Ergam stopped, listening.

"What is it?" Ozel asked.

Ergam put up a finger. A moment later, he said. "There is a town crier in the street. Lord Tebrik will address Calan in one hour. Everyone is to attend. This ... probably isn't good."

"Why not?"

"If they want to make an announcement, it's because shit's on fire. Leaders rarely call everyone together to announce nothing is wrong. Calm speaks for itself."

CHAPTER 32

Bugra Gurses was delighted with the mask of terror he read on the little church primate's face. He must be the highest ranked now that the bishop was no more. The church had sent the primate over to speak for them when they'd heard that Bishop Erkan was no longer an option. The primate was obviously scared that he too would be turned into something small, furry and crushable. He was right to fear as much. But his delicious terror was for the moment, ironically, keeping him alive.

Lord Tebrik wasn't as much fun. He was more or less together. He'd asked Bugra if he could put on his ceremonial sword, the one he always wore when addressing his city. Bugra had allowed it. He could magically replace the sword with a daffodil before Tebrik could do anything serious. Might as well let him have his little sword.

The crowds were filling the palace square. For showmanship purposes it would have been better not to peek out as they turned up, but Bugra was giddy with excitement and couldn't help himself. This was going to be quite a moment.

At last, the time came. Bugra Gurses wasn't fool enough

to think that everyone in the town would attend. The ones who were here would let the rest know what was going on. "Let us begin," he said.

The loudest of the town criers brought the public to order. When they were quiet, Bugra said, "Very well, Tebrik,"

Lord Tebrik stepped toward the stone railing of the balcony and looked down at his city for the last time. "People of Calan, there has been a change in the leadership of the city. I have decided to return to my family's lands, near Dilara. From now on, the city of Calan will be headed by the wizard Bugra Gurses."

A shocked gasp reverberated through the crowd. He waited for it to die down.

"It has been my pleasure to serve you as lord, and as a representative of his Royal Majesty the King in Dilara. I leave you in good hands, and I look forward to visiting Calan again in the coming months." The people were talking amongst themselves excitedly, and they could probably tell that Tebrik's words were bullshit. Tebrik didn't care at the moment. He hoped to get out of Calan with his body in the same shape and not rabbit-like, and his head more round than flat. He turned, nodded to the wizard, and received a nod in return.

Now it was the primate's turn. He was nowhere near as good a speaker as Tebrik. A hush settled over the crowd as they saw him. They all wanted to know what the church intended to do about this.

"I am Primate Sedgewick," he said. "I represent the church in this matter, due to Bishop Erkan's untimely ... because Bishop Erkan is indisposed." He wrung his hands as he looked over his shoulder at Bugra Gurses, who didn't look pleased. "The church wishes it to be known that the wizard Bugra Gurses has its full support of his leadership of the city of Calan."

Again, cries of alarm and surprise rippled through the crowd. They couldn't be blamed. They'd been brainwashed these last few years into thinking that wizards were evil.

Sedgewick stepped back. Bugra Gurses gestured at the musicians, who blew a fanfare. The town crier yelled, "Your new Calan governor, the grand wizard Bugra Gurses!"

Bugra stepped to the railing, thinking he must keep that crier on hand. The man knew how to announce a name and really make it sound good.

Bugra was prepared to be met with collective doubt the first time he addressed the city, and he was correct. The crowd's murmurs sounded apprehensive.

"Good evening, good people of Calan. For any who do not know me, I am Bugra Gurses, your humble wizard. Most of you probably do know me, although lately you have turned your eyes against me in the street. You have drawn your children close, so that they do not get too near. I want you to know that I do not hold these slights against you. They are not the product of the will of Calan, but the manifestations of the church. In their own quest for greater reach, they have maligned me in your hearts. It is only natural that great powers should eventually collide. But I say again, this is not the will of Calan."

This part was important, so Bugra spoke deliberately. "Who better, I ask you, to know the will of Calan, than the man who has been here longer than anyone?" He looked out over the crowd as this point settled in.

"My friends, I owe you an apology. I have sat idly by, working behind the scenes with the merchants, with Lord Tebrik, and even with the church, to set Calan to rights.

That they have tried to turn you against me is a direct attack upon these efforts. I will stand idly by no longer."

He stood up a little straighter. "Calan is not the largest city, but it is a great city. And it can be even greater. The church and I do agree on one important point. The undead citizens of Kanat are an aberration of nature." There were a few supportive cheers. They'd been drilled on this one for a long time by the church.

"But it would be foolish to simply destroy them. Instead, we will harness the undead and use them to power Calan's rise to great wealth!"

In the following silence the people seemed to be considering this. Time to hit them with the part they stood to gain.

"Why should Dilara be the shining city on the hill, when Calan lies at the foot of the mountains? We have the most fertile soil. We have the rich mines. We have the most coveted timber. When we put the undead to work for us, they will harvest day and night. Their picks will ring in the mines at every hour. The axes will never cease to swing. And when the rewards of that *free* labor filter out into the kingdom, my people, three things will come back to us."

Bugra held up three fingers and ticked them off. "Wealth!" he yelled. "Power!" He paused. "And wealth again!" At this there was a proper cheer from the crowd. It hit Bugra like he was gulping powerful spirits. He grinned. He'd done it.

He'd actually done it.

He'd wrested control of Calan from the inferior lord and the sniveling church, and the people loved him for it. He put his arms up. Another smaller, uncertain cheer rose again.

When it finally quieted down, Bugra played his trump card. "In order to celebrate our new future together, I have sent word to the city's taverns. The wine and ale will flow freely tonight, and the church will pay for it!"

The crowd went nuts. He could see workmen hugging one another. Bugra reflected that he should have led with this information as they were eating it up.

"Go forth and celebrate, good people of Calan. Our new future awaits." The cheer at this was earnest and strong. He turned from the rail, an enormous grin on his face, but he was alone on the balcony.

Tebrik and that primate had slunk away. Well. No matter. He could handle things from here.

Below, he could hear a woman calling his name. He turned back. Perhaps one of the whores of Calan wanted to have dinner with him tonight? For free?

It was Guzul the Fierce.

CHAPTER 33

Ergam, Ozel, and Aysu were watching from far enough away that Bugra Gurses wouldn't be able to see them. Ergam was relaying everything that was being said, since he could hear it all.

"I think he's done speaking now," Ergam said. "He's just told everyone there will be free drinking tonight and the church is going to pay for it."

"That explains the cheer," Aysu said.

"Wait," Ergam said. "Something else is happening. Someone's calling for him. Fuck my face. I think it's Guzul the Fierce."

"What?" Aysu asked. "We should go help her."

Ergam shook his head. "No, entirely no. Giant fucking 'no' with teeth and claws. We should get as far away as we can."

"Bugra Gurses!" Guzul called. The crowd hushed as it saw who was calling for him. Some of the older and wiser townspeople made their way hastily out of the square.

Bugra looked down.

"Ah, Guzul the Fierce, what a pleasure. Why don't you join me so we can speak?" He gestured at the palace.

"I can speak to you from here."

"As you like."

"I want you to leave this place and never come back." Her voice, though not loud, was clear.

There were a few shocked gasps. More townspeople realized they were witnessing a disagreement between two powerful wizards. They began to pluck at the shirts of fellow citizens of Calan, urging them to leave.

Bugra laughed. "Come now. That would be silly. I'm about to lead Calan into a new future. Didn't you hear?"

"I heard what you said. I also know what you have done. You are a small, weak man and a murderer, and you will not enslave the people of Kanat."

"Do you hear that, people of Calan?" Bugra called. "She is in league with the undead. It's no wonder she opposes my ideas for your future."

"I challenge you to a duel," Guzul declared. There were a few more gasps, but most of the people were fleeing the square now. They'd all gotten the message. Only the thickest of the thick-headed, or those with a death wish, would hang around for a duel between wizards.

"I'll be right down," Bugra said.

He stalked back into the palace and down the stairs, feeling a bit empty. He'd truly hoped he might someday convince Guzul the Fierce to join him, even romantically. He was not aware of a woman in all the kingdoms who was her equal. But it was time to face the facts. She wasn't to be convinced. Still, there was hope he might talk her out of this duel business.

He walked into the square to find Guzul standing in

exactly the same spot. Her eyes were sharp and, well, it must be said, fierce. He smiled.

"Guzul, my darling. Can we not come to some agreement?"

"No, Bugra. You have stepped over the line. It is up to wizards and witches to police ourselves when we step over the line, for we have no other peers. I have challenged you to a duel. What say you?"

Bugra grimaced. It was time to pull out all the stops. He didn't care what anyone thought of him or his methods anymore. Perhaps there was still time to bring Guzul around to a more amenable position. "Do you not know how I admire you?"

"I know you call your desire to control me 'admiration.' You don't want a partnership, Bugra. You can't abide anyone's will other than your own. That's why I always declined your advances and that's why I must stop you now."

Bugra looked around the square, a sneer on his lips. Only a few citizens were loitering about here and there. "Declined my advances?" he said loudly and laughed. "That's cute. Say what you will, woman. Clearly the undead have touched your memory. But you cannot expect me to duel."

Guzul the Fierce sent a bolt of electricity toward Bugra Gurses which struck the street at his feet, showering him with rock chips and dust. He waved his hands in front of his face to clear the air. He looked angry.

"I don't expect you to do anything besides run your fool mouth," Guzul said.

"Very well, hag," Bugra said. Eyes hard, he rolled his sleeves up.

"Oh, hag, is it? A moment ago you admired me." Then, louder, she called, "Anyone within earshot, clear away."

"Enough talk!" Bugra yelled. He cast a fireball at Guzul that would have torn her limb from limb had it struck her. She was able to bounce the energy up into the sky, where it tore away harmlessly.

"Good," he said. "You still have your speed, I see. Some of it, anyway. Let's see how much." He let rip with a series of fireballs, one after another. He was casting loudly now with short, curt words. "*Augue! Augue! Augue!*" Ball after ball of fire shot into the air after being deflected by Guzul the Fierce.

But near the end of the barrage there was a scream of pain that echoed across the city.

"WHAT WAS THAT?" Aysu asked.

Ergam was hurrying them along the street, trying to get them as far away from the wizard duel as possible. "I don't know, but the best thing we can do is stay away. Otherwise it'll be us screaming into the night. A wizard duel in a forest is bad enough. If this city is much more than a pile of rubble with some reddish stains by tomorrow, I'll be surprised."

"But if someone is hurt, we can help them," Ozel said. "We can drag them to safety. I can give them a healing potion."

A group of City Watchmen nearby were climbing onto horses. Aysu ran over to them. "What are you doing?" she demanded. "You can't leave!"

One of the soldiers grunted. "Didn't you hear the primate, little girl? And the lord? The wizard is in charge now. The best thing anyone can do is leave." The other soldiers nodded in agreement.

"But you're the Watch! The city and the people need you. There will be injuries. Damage to property."

"My wife and son need me as well," the guard replied. "Who will look after them, if I am burned to a crisp between two wizards?"

Aysu didn't have an answer for this. The other soldiers began to ride away.

"Your family needs you too, young miss," the soldier said. He leaned over. "Leave this place to the wizards. Get out while you can."

He rode away.

"I can't," she called after him. "I'm on a quest. And I have some honor." Dismayed, she turned and walked back to Ergam and Ozel.

"You don't have to stay with me," Ozel said.

Aysu balled up her fists and glared. "I am on a *quest.*" Each word came out as hard as the cobblestones.

Ozel nodded. "Ergam, I want you to listen to the duel, help us figure a route around it as best we can. We will do what we can for anyone injured in the fighting, and if we see an opportunity, we will try to help Guzul the Fierce. Agreed?"

Ergam didn't look happy about it. He appeared to be more in the "get out while you can" camp than Ozel and Aysu. But he was nothing if not honorable. "Just so you know, being dead is shit," he said. "Worse than undead."

"We know," Aysu said.

Ergam shrugged. "All right, we will do what we can. I must ask you not to take a pot-shot at Bugra Gurses even if you think you have a perfect chance. An old wizard like that will turn your magic against you before you can blink."

"It's a deal," Ozel said. "Now, is there any way to get back to the square?"

Ergam listened. Ozel could hear barked shouts of magic being cast plus the rumbles, crashes, and the thunder of spells. The battle was well and truly on now. Ergam wiggled his gloved fingers and seemed to make a decision.

"Follow me."

CHAPTER 34

L ieutenant Alper Usta had been dreading giving his after-action report on the conflict with the witch. But then, the witch showed up in town and began fighting with Bugra Gurses, and somehow neither the lord, the bishop, nor even the primate were in charge of the city anymore. He might not ever have to give that after-action report after all. That was good. But overall, things were bad.

He'd been having thoughts about whether he was honor-bound to mention that the witch pinched his bottom. At least his flagpole had subsided.

There were bigger fish to fry at the moment. They had deserters. Not an hour ago there had been a change of leadership of the city and it had caused a mass exodus from his ranks.

Usta had been trained to expect that, in certain situations, there would be deserters in military life. It happened. People signed up for the regular pay and then got cold feet when they were asked to die for a cause they didn't even understand, let alone agree with. However, this was desertion on a completely different level.

"How many?" Usta asked.

"Well, that's just the thing, sir," Alabora said. "It'd be easier to tell you who hasn't deserted."

Usta felt extreme, prickly irritation of the kind that made a grown man want to ball up his fists and bang them on his desk even though he knew the most he could hope for was to dent the surface—and possibly look like an asshole. "Very well, who hasn't deserted?"

"You haven't, sir. And I haven't. And a few more outside."

"You're telling me that my entire command has deserted me?"

Alabora sighed. This was going to be tough on the kid. "They haven't deserted you, sir. They've deserted the idea of being led by a wizard rampaging around the city. It doesn't matter how good an officer is, sir, if the leader to whom that officer reports to is bug-fuck crazy."

"Right," Usta said. "Alabora, you are one hell of a sergeant."

"Thank you, sir."

"In the future, I would rather not be put into the position of imagining how crazy a person would have to be to fuck a bug, please."

"Right you are, sir."

"Let's address the men."

Alabora stood aside and held his hand out. Usta strode out into a twilight sky flashing with loops and sheets of magic. Three men were sharing a cigarette. They snapped to attention.

"Right," Usta said. "Are you men who can be called upon to save a city?"

"Sorry, sir?" one of the soldiers said.

"I said," Usta said, using a loud, clear voice so that there could be no inkling of mistake. "Are you men who can be called upon to save a city? Calan needs men like that. Alabora is a man like that. I pray that I am a man like that. Will you join us or not?"

The men looked at each other.

Usta went on, "There will be townspeople injured. Fires to put out. Elderly, children, and the infirm to evacuate. It will not be proper soldiering, but these people need us tonight. I ask again. Are you men who can be called upon to save a city?"

The three soldiers stood up straight. The one holding the cigarette burned his fingers with it, but stood up straight enough.

"Yes, sir!" they barked as one.

"Good," Usta said. "Judging by the lights in the sky, we need to double-time it to the northeast area of town. We'll do our best to evacuate everyone there. We want to send them west, so that they stay well away from the wizards. Are we clear?"

"Clear," Alabora replied for everyone.

Usta turned and headed out with the sky on fire and thunder in the earth—and his men followed him.

Alabora was impressed.

The man who had burned his fingers on his cigarette wished he hadn't done that.

Usta's route through town where he thought his men could do the most good took them past the church. Usta had it in the back of his mind that trooping past the church would be good for the troops.

After all, the church was an aged, faithful institution. They gave alms to the poor. They even fed the homeless sometimes, didn't they? Surely they'd have set up some kind of response by now. They'd be healing the wounded, or at least caring for them such as they could.

When they rounded the corner in the alleyway that took them to the square in front of the church, it was empty save for someone trying to load a sack into a cart. At first, Usta thought the man had looted the chapel in the chaos of the fighting. Then he recognized Primate Sedgewick.

"Going somewhere, Your Grace?" Usta asked.

"Oh!" Sedgewick said. He grunted as he pushed the sack into the back of the cart. It clanked and pinged as though filled with gold offering plates, candlesticks, and the like. "Well, I have a responsibility to protect these sacred items of the church, you know. Someone could be along any minute to loot the place."

"Indeed," Usta said, icily. "They could."

Sedgewick, his face sweating, squinted. "Are you suggesting anything, Lieutenant?"

"Am I, Primate?"

Sedgewick didn't know how to handle this. He began to climb into the cart, but Usta stopped him.

"What about your responsibility to your parishioners, Primate? Don't you think you or some members of the church might stay back to help with the wounded?"

"Oh no, I shouldn't think so," Sedgewick said. "The church is more concerned with the *spiritual* health of a congregation, you know. And this parish, if I may say so, is fit as a fiddle." He climbed into the driver's seat and took up the reins. "It can certainly find its way through the chaos of life for a few days, I think." Then he added, "By the grace of God." He snapped the reins on an ancient horse's back and it began to pull, clanking and pinging, away. "Bless you all," he said over his shoulder. "And may God have mercy on you."

"And you, Primate Sedgewick," Usta said. His blessing had a rather more meaningful tone than the primate's.

BILAL SAKIR WATCHED the people streaming out of Calan as the sun went down, including most of the members of the military forces which previously would have raided Kanat. Over the city, fire and lightning flashed along with strange lights of all different colors. Occasionally there was a boom that shook the ground even from this distance.

"What do we do?" an aide asked.

Bilal made up his mind. The question of what it would cost him and his people to have made this decision would be answered later. For now, there was only one choice. He turned and faced his small army.

"Men," he said, loudly. "The city of Calan will suffer tonight." He paused to see if a cheer might rise. He hoped his people would be more principled than that. There was silence and the king said a small prayer of thanks. "And though they would have destroyed us all, we must do what we can to help her people." Now there was a grumble. "I ask you to look within your hearts, those of you who still have them." At this there was a murmur of wry mirth. "And ask yourself one question. Though we are proud, though we love our city and we fight as one people, would you wish the death we have all suffered to be inflicted on the innocents of Calan?"

The soldiers of Kanat looked at one another. Bilal knew he'd struck a nerve.

A group of fireballs struck a tall house, knocking flaming debris into the air. It twisted and tumbled on the wind, then eventually landed on the thatched roof of one of the houses outside the city walls. It began instantly to burn.

CHAPTER 35

Sahin and Sansal Hikmet had saved their money working on their parents' farms, dreaming of the day when they could buy their own house. They agreed on many things in life, and one of the biggest was that farming wasn't for them.

So, when they had enough money, they came to Calan to seek work in a town. It wasn't hard to find. They were both strong and well-versed in the broad base of skills any farmer must master to make ends meet. Sahin found work as a stable hand. He didn't love it, but at least he could put bread on the table until he found something that wasn't so farm-ish.

Sansal was without work for longer than her husband, then got some part-time work as a seamstress when she mended one of her new neighbor's dresses as a favor. It was news to Sansal that everyone in the world did not know how to sew.

The house they'd bought was a shambles. Since they'd have been obliged to build a house completely from scratch if they'd started a farm—something they'd helped relatives do a number of times—doing extensive repairs wasn't an issue. Besides, it was all they could afford.

In time, the repairs progressed to the point where it was impossible to tell that their little house had once looked like a pile of garbage with a door on the front. And who knew? With good luck and hard work, perhaps one day they'd be able to live inside the city wall.

All things considered, the big move to Calan was working out nicely. That is, until a couple of wizards decided to get into some kind of a fight, and a collateral piece of burning debris landed on their roof as a result.

Sahin and Sansal began sprinting back and forth with a bucket each. It wasn't enough. The river was close, but not close enough. Sahin and Sansal couldn't get to and from the river with the water fast enough.

Sahin charged through the handful of houses with his bucket yet again, trying not to spill too much, and threw it up at the flames. He was losing the fight.

"Let us help you, my good man," a voice said.

"It's no use," Sahin said. "We only have two buckets. We cannot get back and forth to the river fast enough."

"Not to worry," the voice said. "We can."

Sahin turned to see a group of corpses in various stages of decay, wearing ragged pieces of armor. He fainted onto his wife, who caught him with her arms hooked under his armpits. Her mouth was a round "o" of shock and her eyes were wide in the firelight.

Bilal split his soldiers into two groups: one at the river and one at the house. They took turns sprinting to the river with buckets, then back to the house. It would have gone a lot faster with more buckets, but at least the undead citizens of Kanat were extremely fleet of foot.

Sansal Hikmet watched with wonder, slumped against

the wheel of a cart, fanning absently at her husband. "How are they so fast?"

One of the undead replied, "Truthfully, madam, I don't know. When we lose our lives we gain a good deal of strength. Some of us gain heightened senses as well. Most of us weigh a quarter what we did when we were alive, so we can run very fast. There are few perks to extra-mortality, but that's one of them."

"Oh," Sansal said. What else was there to say?

"I am Bilal Sakir, King of Kanat, madam. We are pleased to be at your service."

Sansal tried to wiggle out from underneath her husband. She couldn't just sit there on her ass. She knew that much about addressing anyone who called themselves a king.

He put out a hand to stay her. "No, no, please. It's quite all right. Let us waive formality for this evening, shall we?"

"As you like, Your Majesty. I'm Sansal Hikmet. This is my husband, Sahin. Thank you for your help."

An aide ran up to Bilal. "Your Majesty. We've contained the fire, sir. Some of the roof is still smoldering, but we believe the house will be saved."

"Very good," Bilal said. "Let's do what we can to contain the smoldering as well."

After a few more rounds of sprinting up from the river, the fire was out. Some steam still rose from the roof, but the home was saved.

"We cannot thank you enough, sir," Sansal said. "We dreamed of this house a long time."

"And you shall live that dream a while yet," the king answered. "Now we must see if we are needed anywhere else."

He gathered his men. They replaced the two buckets by

the front door of the Hikmet home, and were gone into the night. The rumbling and crashing of the magical battle inside the city walls went on. Great sparks flew into the night.

Sansal Hikmet had a very selfish thought, in that moment, about what the price for houses inside the walls of Calan might do over the next twenty-four hours. She chided herself for it immediately.

Her husband stirred. His eyelids fluttered and he moaned.

She leaned over and kissed him on the forehead.

"I dreamed our house was on fire," he said, dreamily.

"Oh, honey," she responded. How to explain it, when she didn't understand it herself?

As soon as the magical lights began shooting into the sky, Bartu Hamdi left his lavishly appointed room and went down to the ground floor of the inn. With a magical fight this fierce going on in the city, and citizens and City Watchmen alike fleeing toward the gate, all bets were off. As a man with several large gold chests with which to concern himself, chaos was his enemy. He'd overseen the innkeeper loading the chests into a strongbox in a back room, so that's where he went.

Lo and behold, the innkeeper was there, trying to drag that very same strongbox across the floor.

Hamdi cleared his throat.

The innkeeper whirled in surprise. "Ah, Mr. Handy." He smiled. "I was just—"

"It's Hamdi. And I saw that you were *just* ..."

"Right you are, sir. Hamdi. Have you seen what's going on outside?"

"I have. That's why I came to check on my investments. Seems I was right to do so."

The innkeeper looked uncomfortable. "I was just about to move only my own small fortune out of the strongbox into my cart." He pointed toward the wall, which Bartu saw had been shifted, designed for when a hasty retreat with a heavy box of coin was warranted. Bartu had to hand it to the man. It was pretty slick.

Beyond the wall was a stable area. The floor of the storage room had been built so that a cart, one of which was already hitched up to a two-horse team, was nearly the same level.

The innkeeper said with a desperate smile, "Why don't we load the box into the cart, and cover it with hay as you see, just there, and then the two of us will be on our way out of town with no one the wiser?"

Bartu had only just been relieved of an unpleasant partnership. He did not want to get into another. But the man had a cart—and a half-decent plan. So, they did as the innkeeper suggested. When the hay was covering the strongbox, there was no way to tell anything out of the ordinary was underneath. They climbed aboard and pulled out into a street thick with people leaving the city.

And blended right in.

CHAPTER 36

Bugra Gurses had fully expected Guzul the Fierce to tire quickly. He thought that he'd be able to pummel her mercilessly with attacks until she showed a weakness of some kind. Then he'd do whatever was needed to exploit that weakness and win the duel.

Not only was she not showing weakness, Bugra had the distinct impression that she was holding back. It had been many years since he'd practiced magic alongside Guzul, or seen her use it, but he knew that she had a peculiar sort of strength. If you needed someone to knock a mountain down, she might not be up to it. If you *counted* on her not being able to do it at all, you might find a mountain landing on your head.

He could feel the same thing in the way she fought. Just when he thought he had found some sort of weakness, and he probed at it—it was only to be slapped away as if there had never been a weakness at all. He'd had to amend his tactics.

If he kept on slamming her with everything he might tire himself to the point where he'd be in danger of revealing a weakness himself. It hurt his pride a little to have to slow down and be a little more careful, but this was not a matter of pride. Only one of them could win this battle.

He hurled a blast at Guzul and she deftly sent it careening into the night. Somehow, over the long years in which she'd lived alone in the swamp, her defense had improved a lot. Not only was she able to block anything he threw at her, she also seemed able somehow to direct the blasts upward into the night sky.

That was it. *That* was her weakness. He couldn't believe it. It had been right there in front of his eyes the whole time and he had missed it. It was so simple it almost made him laugh out loud. He dialed back the severity of his attacks in order to maneuver her into place. She might notice that he had pulled back a little—she was definitely clever. Would it matter? Only time would tell.

ERGAM, Ozel, and Aysu were in a corner of the city where it appeared everyone had found the good sense to evacuate. It was eerily quiet and there was no light. Some of the buildings had loops into which torches could be placed. The few that were in their holders were unlit.

Ozel stopped, squinted at one. Calm. Focus. *Lux.*

The end of the torch shone with a clear white light, illuminating the street.

"Wow, that is a neat trick," Aysu said.

"It's one of the first spells you learn," Ozel said. "Or, one of the first I learned, anyway."

"What are the others?"

"Fireballs, and the healing potion."

Ahead, the street opened into the square. There was trash everywhere. Bits of rock, and hats people had dropped in their haste to get away. Ozel could see the damage to the cobblestones where Guzul the Fierce's magic had torn into it. He was in awe of that level of power. Might he be able to do that someday? Not that he wanted to blast municipal property, but still ...

There was a man on the ground, moaning in pain. It looked like a fire spell had grazed his leg. Lightning spell maybe? A significant chunk of his leg was gone and the wound was weeping blood.

Ozel thought: Calm. Focus. *Potio sanitatum.* He used his speaking voice with a little extra volume to cast the spell. He didn't want to burn himself out of magical energy at the first casualty they encountered. The potion appeared in his hand. It was small, and slightly larger than any he'd made before. He handed it to the man.

"It's a healing potion," Ozel said.

"I don't want no more magic," the man said. He could barely talk, he was gritting his teeth from the pain so tightly. "Get me to the doctor so they can let my bad blood out."

"You've already lost too much blood for that," Aysu said.

"How do you know? Are you a doctor? What do you know about blood?"

"She knows about *your* blood, you pillock. She's standing in it," Ergam said. "Can you even afford a doctor?"

"No," the man said, sucking in air through his teeth. "Maybe if I chopped some wood for him."

"The potion is free of charge," Ergam said.

The man's eyebrows went up and back down. He popped the cork in the bottle and drank it. His body went stiff, and blue-green sparkles appeared in his leg wound. They roved around, turning the blackened skin into pink flesh once more. It wasn't totally healed, but the man wouldn't die, and he might even walk again.

When the man's body went slack, he looked down at his leg. "That does look better," he said. "Is all this blood mine? Disgusting."

"Can you stand?" Ozel asked.

Ergam helped him to his feet. The man tested his weight on the leg. He winced. "Powerful sore," he said. "I think I might be able to walk."

"Head west and wait in the forest," Ergam said. "The west town gate is the farthest from the battle."

The man hobbled away.

"That was amazing," Aysu said. "I'm starting to think I want to be a witch again."

"You'd make a great witch," Ozel said.

"Let's focus on getting through tonight," Ergam said.

"Oi!" the injured man yelled back to them. "There's magic lamps down 'ere. Did you do that too?"

"I did," Ozel said.

"Right nice," the man said.

Ozel turned, smiling, but Ergam's expression was grim. "What's wrong?"

"I hear something," Ergam said.

"What is it?" Aysu asked.

"Coins. Jingling. A lot of them."

"So what?" Ozel asked. "Some rich person is probably just—" He stopped when he realized that Aysu and Ergam were looking significantly at him. "Oh."

It was Bartu Hamdi. He was getting away with the money.

"Perhaps we can catch him," Ergam said. "Before he leaves the city. I could hit him with an arrow from here."

Ozel shook his head. None of this made any sense. The reasons for doing what he was doing seemed to shift every few hours or so, such that he wasn't able to maintain a firm grasp of his next move. What do you do, when you don't know *what* to do?

"No, I don't care about Bartu Hamdi."

"But that's our quest," Aysu said. "We can deal with him, then get back to helping people as we find them. It shouldn't take long, right, Ergam?"

Ozel shook his head again. "No, it's not our quest. My quest is to become a wizard. There is nothing more wizardly in the world than helping people. If we can track Bartu Hamdi down later we will. For now, we help Calan."

Ergam smiled. A half-smile made its way onto Aysu's face too. She hugged Ozel.

"You can track him, right?" Ozel asked. "Later?"

Ergam nodded.

USTA and his men were closer to the fighting than any of them wanted to be. They were having trouble loading an elderly gentleman and his wife into a cart. The wife kept insisting that her husband was afraid of carts. Whenever Usta got near, the woman would scream and cry. He didn't know how to proceed. He didn't want to cause the woman undue stress, as his honor couldn't bear that, and he also didn't want her and her husband to die. His honor could hardly bear that either.

In the end, the old gentleman took a deep breath and whispered, where only Usta could hear, "Sometimes you just have to go forward, son."

Usta put the man in the cart. The old woman screamed and wailed. He picked her up and placed her next to her husband and she quieted down.

There was an ear-splitting boom behind them, and a chunk of boulder nearly the size of a house came rolling down the street. Usta lunged and slapped the mule on its ass, and the animal bucked and heaved forward. The men scattered to get out of the way of the cart and the boulder bearing down on them. In his effort to reach the mule's ass, Usta lost his balance. He tried to hang onto the side of the cart, but couldn't. He fell hard and rolled, ending up in the open doorway of a small house. The boulder was bouncing down the street as though hell itself could never stop it.

Usta crawled into the house, hoping the stone building could protect him. He drastically miscalculated.

When the boulder hit the side of the house, it was like a man kicking in an ant hill. The house collapsed around Usta. He dove under the house's kitchen table, which saved him from being crushed immediately, but a beam pinned his leg cruelly to the floor. Stones struck him all around, and then something hit him hard behind the ear and all was black.

CHAPTER 37

Ergam rounded a corner to find his father supervising a bucket brigade. The soldiers of Kanat were in the streets of Calan, but they hadn't had to fight their way in. They were saving it.

"Father!" Ergam yelled. He ran to meet him. "What are you doing here?"

"The right thing," his father answered. "What are you doing?"

"The same. My young Master Ozel has been healing the wounded where we've found them."

"I'm proud of you, boy," Bilal said. He took his son by his shoulders. "Keep on doing your best, you hear me?"

"I will," Ergam said.

"Carry on then," Bilal said. He turned back to his bucket brigade, urging his men to work faster.

Ergam rejoined Ozel and Aysu, and they kept moving, following in the wake of the battle between the wizards.

"Seems like your father should have said something to you like, 'take care,' or at least 'don't die,'" Aysu said.

"Maybe," Ergam said. "But we've both died once already. Maybe it's not such a big thing anymore."

They found several more people with various types of wounds. Whatever the injury was, it didn't matter with healing potion. Ozel was pleased with the effect of his magic. Only a small amount of healing potion was necessary to make a big difference. He wondered what it would be like to give someone a healing potion of the size Wagast or Guzul the Fierce could make.

He worried about Guzul. Judging by the shaking earth and the flashing magic in the sky, the battle still raged on. Every moment he hoped the fighting would stop and she would emerge victorious, but it just went on and on.

Ahead, men were talking excitedly to one another. It looked like a building had collapsed on itself. Then things became clear, it had been smashed by a boulder rolling down the street. A stout older sergeant was ordering three younger troops to keep working.

"We can't, sir," one of the men was saying. "We've been trying as hard as we can. If we had a couple of dozen more men, perhaps, and we don't even know if he's alive under there."

"What's going on here?" Ozel asked.

"Our lieutenant has been crushed in this house," the sergeant said. "We would break our backs to save him if we could, but we don't know for sure if he's even alive."

The soldier who had been speaking a moment before didn't look entirely ready to break his back to save his lieutenant, but didn't say anything.

Ergam cocked his head and held out a hand for quiet. He listened until there was a momentary lull in the magical onslaught elsewhere in the city. Then he nodded. "Yes, someone is alive under there."

"How can you know that?"

"I have very, very good hearing. I am Ergam." He put his hand out.

"Sergeant Alabora," Alabora said, accepting the handshake.

"Sergeant Alabora, let me ask you a question. What if I could deliver a workforce of very strong, highly trained laborers in the next few minutes who could certainly free your lieutenant, but it would require you to make an allegiance you might never have thought possible?"

"Well, I'd certainly put the life of my officer above any previous misunderstandings—" Alabora stopped talking and his eyes went wide as Ergam removed his mask and pushed his hood back to reveal his head and real face. Alabora gasped. Behind him, one of the soldiers drew a battered sword. Alabora put out a hand to calm his men.

Ergam said, "We are not enemies tonight, Sergeant. We are countrymen facing great evil. You have a man in peril here. My father's men are close, strong, and willing. What say you?"

Alabora stood tall. "I say it takes a strong man to do battle, but a stronger one to be an ally. What say you, men?"

The soldier put his sword away, which was just as well for him, as Ozel's fireball would have hurt quite a lot.

"Right then," Ergam said. "Back in a flash."

USTA HAD the impression that he was weaving in and out of dreams, as if he were sleeping in on a quiet morning, except that in one of his dreams he felt sick and feverish, and in the other there was intense pressure on his leg. When he came into the pressure dream, the pain made him feel ill, which then sent him to the other dream where the bad feeling was different.

He tried to move. Bolts of pain shot up his leg as though it were being impaled on hot pokers. There was a noise around him. Was he dreaming that noise? Something slid and then hit him on the back of the head. There was a tickle near his ear as well.

Some of the noises sounded like shouts. Then the pain in his leg got much worse and he was gone again into the sickness dream. When he came back this time, the air had changed. It was sweet again. Men were shouting. He was being lifted. He was given something to drink. It was like water, ice cold and somehow electric on his tongue. It reminded Usta of a time when he'd once smelled the air after a lightning strike nearby.

Then actual lightning shot through his every fiber. It was like he had sucked in a big breath of cold air, except that every mote of his being had inhaled it all at the same time.

Suddenly, he was standing on the cobblestones, looking at Alabora and surrounded by the undead.

"Well, fuck," he said. "I've died."

A cheer went up, which Usta found to be in poor taste.

Alabora laughed. "You haven't died, sir. You might have, had the undead and the young wizard not saved you."

A skeleton in fine garb stepped forward. "I am Bilal Sakir, King of Kanat."

Usta was at a loss, given that his orders had been to sack this man's—man's?—city and destroy all its inhabitants. On the other hand, given that the man and Alabora had apparently worked together to save him from the crushing ruin of a house ...

Yes, it was coming back to him a bit now. He'd dived into the house to avoid a boulder and had instead jumped right into the blasted thing's path. He looked at the wreckage of the house. He'd certainly have died under there. He shook the king's hand and bowed his head. "Well met, Your Majesty."

"Strange times, eh?" the king asked.

"Quite so," said Usta.

"We've agreed to work together to save as many innocents as we can tonight. Will you join us?"

Usta knew an occasion when he saw one. He put his hand out. "Without question."

As he said this, the boulder jammed into the house disappeared as its magical timer ran out. The house finished collapsing, raining stones down on the space where he'd been lying a moment ago. He realized he'd just lived through the moment when he'd otherwise have died.

CHAPTER 38

Bugra Gurses bided his time like he never had before, conserving his energy. This duel would surely go down as one of the greatest between all wizards. He had little doubt of that much. Unless Guzul was holding something in reserve for him that he hadn't yet detected, they were very nearly perfect matches.

His chance finally came. He drove her back with a barrage of storm winds and a touch of lightning until she was near a three-storey bank building. He let loose with a fierce onslaught of spells he'd been holding in reserve.

Guzul's shielding spell popped into existence, but it wasn't needed. The spells sailed past her into the ground floor of the stone building behind her.

Bugra was using a shield of his own as Guzul counter-attacked. He'd known this was coming and it played perfectly into his hands, because it would take a few seconds for the building to collapse.

Guzul realized the building was going to come down on her in just enough time to save herself with a shield spell directed upward. Timing it perfectly, Bugra let loose with a simple fist of wind spell that sent her tumbling down the street backward like a hat in a windstorm.

When the building was destroyed completely, the rubble blocking the street, all was quiet. The battle was over, surely. His plan had worked. The duel was his.

THE COALITION TEAM OF UNDEAD, Calan soldiers, and apprentices were working their way carefully house to house. Ergam had heard what he thought was a toddler moving.

The battle was uncomfortably close, but they pressed forward.

The baby proved to be only a very squeaky hinge. He went back out and motioned to the team they should retreat again.

Suddenly the wizard battle came roiling into the street behind him.

Everyone dove for cover except Ozel, who was transfixed.

The two wizards were flinging all manner of spells at one another. Guzul the Fierce had a shield technique the like of which Ozel had never even read about. He wished he could interrupt the duel to ask her about it. Guzul moved to the side and some of Bugra's attacks were coming straight down the street. Ozel was yanked off balance when Ergam grabbed his arm and pulled him away.

There was a boom so loud it was a physical blow, not just sound. It pulsed deep inside Ozel's body and made him want to retch.

A white shape bounced down the road and fetched up in a crumpled heap in front of Ozel and Ergam.

"Ergam," Ozel hissed. "Oh, no. No, it can't be!" There was

no way the shape they were looking at could possibly have ever been a human. A white crown rolled away from the heap.

Ergam leaped to his feet, dashed out into the lane and lifted the body of Guzul the Fierce.

"Young master, Aysu, follow me!"

"Go, my son!" the king said. "We'll do what we can to stall."

Ozel was running, doing his best to keep up with Aysu, who in turn was trying to keep up with Ergam. Even carrying the limp body, Ergam could easily have run away from them. They twisted and turned down alleyways until they came to the palace. They ran up the very same stairs where the duel had begun, then through a series of passageways and down deep into the bowels of the building. At every hallway, Ergam would listen intently. Sometimes he made a clicking noise with his teeth, and seemed to listen to that.

At last he came to the end of a corridor. He turned into a darkened room and placed Guzul on a table.

"The door, please, Aysu," he said. She pushed it closed. Ozel cast a light spell onto an empty candle holder on a shelf, then shoved a barrel into the door so it would stay closed.

On the table, the bloody face of Guzul the Fierce was smiling. "Yes," she wheezed. "Yes, this is it. Well done, Ergam."

Ozel cast a healing potion in a loud voice, and placed it in Guzul's limp hand.

She smiled. "Thank you, child. A well-executed spell. Wagast taught you well, I see." She winced. "But I will not heal from this. It is my time to go."

Ozel felt the will to fight draining out of his body as if he were a lake with a broken dam. His quest to tell Bartu Hamdi off at Hamdi's home had failed. His quest to save the world from a wealthy Bartu Hamdi had failed. Now his quest to try to assist Guzul the Fierce had failed too. She was dying. The city would fall. Bugra Gurses had prevailed. And Bartu Hamdi would be rich.

"No!" Aysu said. "You can't, ma'am. We need you!"

Guzul coughed a few times. When she gained her voice again, she said, "It is my time. Now listen to my last words or it'll bloody well be your time too, you ungrateful children."

"Sorry," Aysu said.

"This has always been part of my plan to defeat Bugra Gurses. To complete the plan you must do exactly as I say."

"We'll do it," Ergam said.

Ozel was glad that Ergam still had some will to go on. He felt like lying on the table next to Guzul the Fierce and dying right along with her.

BUGRA GURSES WAS FILTHY, sweaty, tired, and in no mood to be trifled with when he finally climbed over the pile of rubble that lay across the road. He'd had to be careful with his footing. He might be a powerful and victorious wizard, but he was not a young man and he'd twisted his ankle before. Where he expected to see a long bloody smear that terminated in the crumpled body of one Guzul the Formerly Fierce, he saw instead Bilal Sakir and the young lieutenant who had been in charge of Calan's soldiers.

There was a bloody smear as well, but there was nothing at the end of it.

"Where is Guzul?" Bugra asked.

"What Guzul?" King Sakir asked. He turned toward the lieutenant. "Do you know a Guzul?"

"Hmm," the lieutenant said. "Let me see now. There was a Guzul who lived off one of the lanes by the flower market, but I'm sure she's evacuated from the city by now."

There was a distant noise that Bugra had first attributed to something insignificant, but his exhausted brain now recognized it as running feet. These two fools were here to delay him as long as possible while their men scattered in all directions. Well, he had a plan for that too, didn't he? Yes, indeed.

"I will deal with you two later for this insolence," Bugra said. He whirled and stomped off toward his tower. So far, Calan had only experienced an inkling of what being ruled by a powerful wizard might be like.

Bugra Gurses intended to give them full understanding of the matter.

CHAPTER 39

They moved the drums stacked against the far wall of the chamber, then Aysu gave the wall a good strong whack with her hammer. As she hit it, a gout of flame burst forth from the hammer face and the stone shot backwards as if from the barrel of a cannon. From the sound of it, the rock exploded into dust against a far wall somewhere behind.

Aysu slowed her hammer strikes for the next few stones which broke or shot out of place. After a few minutes there was a hole big enough to climb through.

Guzul the Fierce coughed again and they went once more to her side. She smiled through the blood at the corner of her mouth.

"You can do this," she said. "He is strong, but he is also stupid. He will not expect people your age to have the knowledge or the strength to do what I have instructed. Do not lose faith." She withdrew from a fold of her dress a bloodstained piece of parchment. As she unfolded it, they saw that it was one of the drawings Aysu had done for her. Guzul clutched it to her breast.

Ozel felt his eyes sting. A tear rolled down Aysu's face. Ergam's mask looked grim.

"Thank you for these few days," Guzul said. "I bear partial responsibility for this. I thought that Bugra would, in the end, come to some good understanding about himself. I should have fought him years ago, when I was stronger." There was a foreboding rasp to her breathing that hadn't been there a few moments before. Her voice was getting fainter with each word. "Let my mistake be a lesson to you. If ever something needs doing, don't wait. Do it."

"We will, ma'am," Ozel said. He could barely see for the tears.

Guzul the Fierce nodded. She lifted the drawing, looked at it, then clutched it to her breast again and gave a long, deep sigh.

She was gone.

Aysu put her head against the old woman's body and cried. Ozel wiped at his face with the back of his hands.

When Aysu could see again, she looked up into Ozel's face and almost yelped with fear. The wizard apprentice's features were twisted with rage.

"We must mourn Guzul the Fierce later," Ozel growled. "Now we go to war."

BUGRA STOMPED to the top of his tower. He wished he had a few moments to clean himself up, because this moment was one he'd been looking forward to for a long time.

When he'd had this tower designed, the builder had warned him that a completely open top was asking for trouble. A railing was an easy thing to build, and it would pay for itself on innumerable occasions.

"Like what?" Bugra had asked.

"Like, if you have a cocktail party and one of your guests goes up to the top of the tower to have a look around. If they fell and splattered on the street below, it will be a terrible thing," the man had said. He eyed Bugra for signs that the wizard was taking his advice to heart and saw none, so he went on. "What if you have a young family visiting and a wee baby comes up here? You can't watch them at all times, you know. I don't even want to think about what could happen then."

Bugra Gurses continued to fix the man with a cold stare and said nothing.

The man had put his hands in the air. "Have it your way then, good sir. I only wanted to warn you, is all."

Bugra Gurses thought of a few choice warnings for the builder, but kept them to himself. Powerful wizards did not threaten common laborers. It was crass. It showed a lack of control.

In the end, he got the top of his tower built just as he'd requested. As he stepped out onto it now, he surveyed the city. There were a few pillars of smoke here and there. A couple of buildings had been reduced to rubble. That was expected. Now what he needed was some preventative magic.

He stood to his full height and sighed, then calmed himself. He was a bit tired, yes, but he still had the strength to go on. Centuries of practice and refinement had served him well. He began to call to the magic in the loudest voice he could muster. First he reached out to the gates of the city with his mind and bade them crank themselves closed. They obeyed. He heard the wails of people who had nearly escaped. With the gates closed, he began the next phase.

He needed a magical barrier to rise from the walls to protect him from any trickery used to get Guzul out of the city. As long as she lived, he had not technically won the duel. If she had time to rest and recharge, she could come back at him when he least expected it and that would not do at all. This thing needed to end tonight.

So he cast again and again, building and strengthening a magical reinforcement to the city perimeter that would keep everything within the walls until he had searched every possible corner for Guzul the Fierce.

OZEL CAST the light spell on a piece of old burnt-out torch he found on the floor of the tunnel. He led the way around the slight bend ahead with Aysu close behind him. They didn't have far to go before they came to a set of thick iron bars.

Aysu pulled her hammer out again. "You might want to step back a bit. As you saw with the stone, this hammer is unpredictable."

Ozel nodded and backed up a bit while trying to keep some light on the bars. Aysu swung and the bar she struck instantly became red hot. It deformed slightly. She hit it once more and the hot metal blew away in chunks. After a few more strikes she got the hang of using the hammer. Adding that to what she knew of blacksmithing, she was able to work quickly. Soon it only took a few whacks in the right spots to make a hole they could walk through. She warned Ozel not to step on any of the hot metal.

He did his best to keep the light where it was most useful and tried not to hurt himself.

Eventually, they came to a rickety set of stairs that led up to a heavy wooden trapdoor.

Ozel eyed the solid beams. "What if he's put a couch on

the other side? I'm not sure we could lift the trap, even if there's nothing weighing it down from above."

"We don't have to lift it," Aysu said. "These brackets going into the stone here? They're all I need."

Ozel squinted at the trapdoor.

"And the brackets are made of metal," she added.

"Oh!"

She gave one side a small tap with her hammer and the hatch began to sag. When she hit it again, Aysu jumped back under the stone section of the floor to keep from being whacked by falling timber. The trapdoor clattered into the passageway, bringing a small wooden table and a fern in a clay pot with it.

They retreated down the passageway and listened for footsteps. There were none.

After a few moments, Ozel crept forward and peeked into the tower. Bugra Gurses wasn't there. Ozel thought he could hear the distant, barking sounds of the wizard casting some distance away. Good. The plan was working.

He gave Aysu a thumbs-up. She looked worried. He started for the stairway. As he was stepping over the fern, arms encircled him from behind. Aysu was hugging him and he turned around.

"Thank you," he said. "For joining the quest. I couldn't have gotten here without you—"

She kissed him.

ERGAM HEARD the ringing sounds of Aysu's hammer on the metal bars. It couldn't be anyone else. Nobody would be doing blacksmith work in Calan now. It was nighttime, after all. And there was a mad, murderous wizard rampaging about.

At this pace, Aysu and Ozel should be beneath the tower in ten minutes or so. That should be just enough time for him to find a good spot to fire at Bugra Gurses.

Ergam slipped through the door of a house within sight of the top of the tower. He wondered how good the old wizard's eyesight was. Hopefully not that great. And Ergam was fast. Fast enough, though? Well. He'd soon find out.

He waited a few minutes longer until he could just make out the muffled clatter of what sounded like a wooden table falling, along with a potted plant as well. Had he noticed a potted plant in the wizard's home? Yes, he thought he had seen one, positioned incongruously in the middle of the room. He should have seen that as a red flag that something peculiar was going on under the floor, but at the time it had seemed like Bugra Gurses was helping them. Ah, well.

He selected an arrow, spun it in his fingers. It ran true as he twirled it. Of course it did. They all would. He wouldn't have put it in his quiver in the first place, if it had any imperfection. He nocked the arrow in his bow and crouched on the floor. He went through the motions in his mind. Fire, turn, down the stairs, out the back door, left, then doubleback to the next street. Yes. He had it.

Right then. He drew.

CHAPTER 40

The containment magic was proving a little more difficult than Bugra anticipated. That, added to his fatigue after the battle with Guzul the Fierce, meant that Bugra was struggling with some of his spells. His enunciation was suffering a touch, and the magic had a slightly more blunt presentation. Not that anyone would notice the difference. The only person skilled enough in magic to be able to tell that things weren't perfect was precisely the person he intended to kill—if she wasn't already dead.

Something hit his arm. It felt like someone had punched him. He was surprised to see an arrow sticking out of his robe. When he moved his arm to get a better look Bugra cried out in pain. He could hardly believe it.

Someone had shot him with an *arrow*.

He broke the shaft with one hand, then yanked the arrow through the wound and cast a targeted healing spell. His arm instantly felt better.

He scanned the city for the shooter. He wished now he'd taken better care to note which direction it came from, but it had hurt like hell. The street below was deathly still. He stood, watching for a while longer anyway. He needed to finish just a touch more magic to barricade the city in properly, then he could go find whoever had done this. He'd slay anyone in the same vicinity as anything that even looked like a bow, arrow, or a piece of string.

He began to cast again. There was only a little bit left.

Another arrow struck him, this time in the other arm. It went through nearly the same place. Obviously he was dealing with a talented shooter. He searched the street again. This time he saw the next missile coming and was able to block it. More importantly, he'd seen where it came from. He sent a fireball down in the general vicinity. He didn't hear a scream, but that didn't necessarily mean anything. If you killed someone instantly there often wasn't time for screaming. He'd put that theory to the test on the priest by the side of the road.

He yanked the second arrow out, healed the wound, and went hurriedly back to finishing his magic. He needed to do it from this high vantage point so he could see precisely the spot where—

He blocked another arrow. Then there was a flurry of them, but Bugra had been expecting this. The shooter would be able to see that his arrows were hitting their target, but not doing much harm. The obvious answer would be to attempt a volley of them. This would allow Bugra to see exactly where the shooter was positioned. He cast a shield in front of himself, and though the magic distorted the air, he could see a dark blur below. Yes. There it was. He readied his magic.

There was a noise behind him. He whirled, not fast enough to stop a figure from bringing a blade of air down on him like a sword.

Bugra thought for sure this would be the end of his life.

Had he been the one to cast this magic it would have been strong enough to cleave even his tower blocks in two. But no. The spell that bit into his arm had no more force than a wooden practice sword. It broke the skin, then dissipated.

Standing there, looking very afraid, was Wagast's whelp apprentice. He held a toy-like sword and wore a silly helmet.

Bugra began to laugh. A moment ago he had been sure these were the last breaths of his life. How lucky had he been that it wasn't Guzul the Fierce sneaking up on him? He'd have been dead meat then for sure. This lad barely even damaged his robe.

"Is that the best you can do?" the old wizard sneered. "Is this the product of the teaching of the great Wagast? A blade of air that can barely cut a cabbage?" Bugra snorted and laughed again. He'd had about enough of this, whatever *this* was. "Let me show you what a blade of air *should* look like."

He raised his hands over his head and yelled "*Ferrum ex aere!*"

He felt the blade materialize. It was a big one. He brought it down like the judgment of a god on the cowering fool standing before him. It would split the boy in two from his head straight down to his ass, there was no question about that. There would be no more firing arrows from the cover of houses—the ploy to distract him obvious now. There would only be someone who had attempted an attack on Bugra Gurses cut in half.

A fraction of a second before the blade of air struck the boy's helmet, Bugra Gurses saw the sheen on it. He had time for the briefest flash of regret.

THE ENCHANTMENT on Ozel's helmet reflected every ounce of Bugra's magic back into the wizard's hands. The sound was like a bell the size of a city being rung by firing a cannonball into it. At the same time Ozel was driven backward as though he'd been horse-kicked. He lay on his back, barely aware except that his heart was pounding so hard.

When he looked up, the wizard Bugra Gurses was staring at his hands. Except Bugra Gurses didn't *have* any hands. The magic had blown them off his wrists and split his forearms. Bone, flesh and muscle twisted from his elbows. The wizard staggered in a daze. One after another, arrowheads sprouted from his chest, hitting him from behind. One. Two. Three.

Bugra looked down at them and his expression was pitiful. Awareness was leaving the wizard. His eyes glazed as more arrows struck him, and then he fell backward over the edge of his beloved tower—the tower without a railing—and was gone.

CHAPTER 41

Many of the people who had fled the city to escape a wizard battle had nowhere to go. It was many days travel to Dilara and well over a week to Bilgehan, and the trouble had started at night. As a result, there were small camps dotting the surrounding countryside.

As the citizens of Calan awoke, the day was bright, the weather was good. It seemed like the sort of day on which a person was not likely to be murdered, even if the weather, logically, had no direct bearing on their circumstances.

When some intrepid souls crept toward the city gates, they found them wide open and the skies quiet. There were a few pillars of smoke where fires smoldered, but nothing burning in flames. The news on the ground from those who had been trapped inside the walls was that the wizard was dead. The trouble was over. They could return to their homes.

This news spread to the surrounding campsites, and the people began to trickle back into the city.

Some were devastated at the losses their houses and

businesses had suffered. Then in the spirit of a people who have undergone a traumatic night together, neighbors and colleagues pitched in to help one another patch things back up, or at least clear the rubble away from the doors.

As the morning wore on, the townsfolk of Calan recounted their perspective of events. Everyone, it seemed, had a near-miss with disaster. There were smiles. Those who had clean water shared it. Those who had bread shared it. Those who had wine shared the less expensive bottles. All things considered, it was the most companionable day anyone could remember in Calan.

OZEL SAT IN BUGRA GURSES' study. He pulled the wooden cylinder from his pocket and unscrewed the top. He felt a bit like this little device right now, actually. Made of wood. Hollow inside. Maybe some sand in there.

He placed the disc on a work surface, picked up and dropped grains of the sand, and said "*Contactu Wagast.*" He was a little surprised when it worked.

Wagast's face, squinting to see properly, appeared in the flames.

"Ozel? Is that you? How good to see you!" He laughed. He had such a good, hearty laugh.

"Hello, Wagast. Yes, it is me."

"You look years older. Tell me what's been going on. Have you completed your quest? Where did you get a communication portal?"

Ozel told Wagast every part of the quest he could think of. As he did, he felt tears in his eyes. Aysu touched him on the shoulder to let him know she was there, then retreated to give him space. Wagast listened intently, brow furrowed. Ozel spoke of the bear, of Ergam, of Guzul the Fierce. Of

Calan, of Bugra Gurses, and of the battle, and even a little about Bartu Hamdi.

As he was coming to a stop, he realized that Wagast's face was smiling.

Ozel gave him a quizzical look.

"I know," Wagast said. "You are quite right. It is improper of me to smile after a tale like that. You must be feeling a mixture of emotions right now that would be hard for any five grownups to navigate. But, my boy, what a quest."

Ozel thought about that. Wagast had a point. The things he'd seen over the last few days were a far cry from his planned telling-off of Bartu Hamdi. He'd gained two new friends he'd most likely have for the rest of his life.

Wagast smiled again. Even in the tiny, flaming green version of himself, Wagast looked impossibly wise. Ozel hoped to look that wise some day. Wagast said, "There is only one conclusion to be drawn, I think."

"What's that?"

"You are no longer an apprentice wizard. You must come home straight away and begin work on the next phase of your training. We shall have to build a bedroom for you, I think, because Alan isn't likely to relinquish the one here without a fight to the death."

Ozel felt the smile bloom on his face, despite that he'd assumed that the madness of the last few days would qualify as a big enough quest for him to transition to a full wizard. Hearing Wagast say he had a ways to go was still nice. Then his face fell.

"Wagast?"

"Yes?"

"I think there's still one more thing that needs doing before I come home. No, two more things."

THE FUNERAL for Guzul the Fierce was a deeply sorrowful event. Her death seemed so utterly senseless. And yet, her sacrifice was so critical. Without her, Bugra Gurses might have started a reign of terror that would have lasted longer than anyone might survive.

There wasn't a body to bury. When they returned to the room where the tunnel to Bugra Gurses' tower met the palace, there was naught but some light ash inside a white dress. Gone too was the crown she wore, along with the drawing she'd been clutching when she died, which Ozel thought peculiar.

Aysu said a few words over the empty dress, but she had trouble, sobbing the whole time. She held her head high, though.

"We are so terribly sorry, Guzul the Fierce, that we knew you for so short a time. I wish that I had the opportunity to know you better, to learn the art of being a strong woman for a thousand years. But we are also blessed that we knew you at all. As we go forward from this day we will all be, in memory of you and in tribute to your selfless acts, a little more fierce."

Ozel was weeping openly. Ergam looked utterly stricken. The undead prince folded up the dress with care and placed it in a bag. He was taking it back to Kanat, where it would be kept in a place of honor for her service to the undead.

"So passes Guzul the Fierce," Ergam said, placing his hand on the table where she'd died. Ozel and Aysu put their hands on top of his. "Gone, but with us always."

IN THE AFTERNOON, there was a meeting between the merchants of Calan, Lieutenant Usta and Sergeant Alabora, King Sakir of Kanat, Ergam, Aysu, and Ozel. The merchants had held an emergency meeting that morning and voted Arier Enver as their new representative, replacing Odabasi.

Ergam pointed out, "It's no surprise. The old one was murdered by a madman wizard who went on to try to take over the whole town. Arier has a friendly relationship with the three people who took the evil wizard down. Who would *you* choose?"

"He makes a point," Aysu said.

"Right, well," Arier said, speaking loudly so everyone could hear. "Thank you all for coming. This is just a short meeting to determine what to do about Calan for the next few days. I think we can assume that Lord Tebrik will get the message sooner or later that Calan is no longer being oppressed by an evil wizard. When that happens he'll turn around, I have no doubt. Until then, we need to make sure we get people fed, start on rebuilding houses, and try to get life back to normal. Correct?"

There was a general murmur of agreement, but a silence after that went on a bit too long. Arier looked around suspiciously.

Lieutenant Usta stood. "I think that the town of Calan should consider carrying on without a lord. There is a precedent for it. Some of the cities along the southeastern coast do it quite well."

"I think Lord Tebrik might have something to say about that," Arier said.

"He might, sir. But then again, he might not. I don't think he was particularly fond of life here, neither was he particularly fond of governing. We might never see him again."

At this there was a much more confident rumbling of approval.

"There's something else," Usta said. "I doubt we'll have many troublemakers in the city after what we've been through, but if we do, I don't have the manpower to do much about it."

Arier grunted. "Yes, we might have opportunistic looters, or other such lowlifes. Do you have any suggestions, Lieutenant?"

"I do, sir. I suggest we ask our friends from Kanat to help."

There were a few gasps, mostly from the merchants.

"Without their assistance last night, not only would there have been many terrible fires, but I myself would have lost my life. They are men of honor, and Calan is the better for their friendship."

Alabora stood behind his lieutenant and clapped. Then Ozel and Aysu did the same. Finally, Arier and the other merchants nodded their agreement. Bilal Sakir motioned for quiet.

"My friends, Kanat remains your companion. We are pleased to help Calan however possible, but I suggest that we do what we can in a secondary role. We don't want the citizens to feel that they've been attacked by a wizard and are now being occupied by the undead. I suggest that my men and I first put ourselves to the clean-up and rebuilding efforts. When the people of Calan see how quickly and efficiently we can work to put the streets right again, I think it will go a long way to building a bond between our great cities."

"Quite so, Your Majesty," Arier said. "What say we all?"

A chorus of "Aye."

Bilal Sakir nodded and took his seat. Usta sat down as well.

"Well," Arier said. "Sounds good to me, then. Your Majesty, we'll trust you to do as you see fit and work with Lieutenant Usta along the way if needed."

Both men nodded.

"Well, if there's nothing else?"

There was a cough, and Sergeant Alabora got to his feet. "Pardon me, sirs. I'm not an officer or anything as you know, but I figure you asked me to be here so I may as well say what's on my mind."

"Right you are, Sergeant. Carry on," Arier said.

"Speaking as a man of the people, as it were, which is to say of humble means, I think it would be a good idea to have a feast. At the moment out there, people are already sharing what they can with one another anyway. It seems to me that capitalizing on that general spirit of camaraderie with our friends from Kanat in attendance might not be a terrible thing."

Everyone's expressions were variations on the theme of, "that's not a bad idea."

Arier Enver said, "Well, Sergeant, I'd say you'd better nip home around sundown and put your dancing shoes on."

CHAPTER 42

The feast was unlike any Ozel had ever seen. All the inns and public houses gathered their tables and food together in the main square and the people filed past until their bellies were full. A group of musicians set themselves up on a raised platform and as the sun went down they began to play all manner of lively dancing numbers.

Sergeant Alabora had said that he liked to dance and apparently hadn't been kidding. He wasn't a young man, or by any means small or light. Yet he twirled and bobbed on the cobbles like his life depended on it.

"I'll show you," Aysu said, when she saw Ozel watching.

"I couldn't. I don't know a thing about dancing."

"Did you know anything about ridding a city of an evil wizard?"

"Well, no, but ..."

She was giving him that look of hers and grabbed his arm.

When they were in front of the band, she took his hand and began to dance, dragging him along with her. He did his best to keep up. After a few repeated moves he started to get the hang of one or two of the steps. When he got one right, he laughed out loud.

Alabora saw him laughing and called to him. "As long as you're having fun, you are dancing!"

Well. In that case, Ozel was dancing.

THEY WERE all invited back to Arier Enver's house. Bellies full of good food and legs tired from dancing, Ozel thought he was likely to have a very good sleep indeed, especially given that he hadn't had any sleep since the day before. Truth be told, it was a wonder he could stand at all.

"Good night, young master," Ergam said. "I'll leave you here and join my father for a few hours while you rest."

"Thank you, Ergam. For everything you've done for me," Ozel said.

Ergam bowed. "Tomorrow we'll get back on track to finishing our original quest. I quite look forward to it."

"Yes," Aysu said. "That will be fun."

"You know, we could just forget about Bartu Hamdi and go on with our lives," Ozel said. Before he'd finished speaking, Aysu and Ergam both wore expressions of such horror he knew he'd made a grave error. He put his hands in the air. "Okay, all right. Just a thought, that's all."

"See you in the morning," Ergam said, firmly. Then he walked off into the night.

"This has been such a good quest so far," Aysu said. "It feels like I've lived a lifetime each day."

"True enough." He looked at her, intending to say more, but her eyes stopped him. He couldn't quite put his finger on what was different about her in that moment. Perhaps it was the cool, sweet breeze blowing in. Maybe it was his full belly. Perhaps it was the way the moonlight shone in her hair and twinkled in her eyes. She was utterly beautiful.

When their lips brushed one another, Ozel felt a thrill run through him that was unlike any he'd ever experienced before. He'd had a few small bolts of this feeling while he'd been dancing with Aysu. This was like a full-blown lightning storm.

Arier Enver came out of the house. "Ozel? Aysu? If you two don't mind I'm going to say goodnight …" He saw what they were doing and backed into the house. "I say, so sorry."

They laughed.

WHEN OZEL WOKE, he felt like he'd slept a thousand years. The smell of coffee and breakfast were wafting over the pile of blankets Arier Enver had made for him in the front room. He got up, folded the bedding, then went into the kitchen to find Aysu and Arier looking very chipper.

Aysu had an excellent night's rest in Arier's spare bed, which was good news. Ozel felt a bit stiff having slept on the floor after insisting that he should be the one to do so. He couldn't complain too loudly.

Arier was helping them pack a few things to eat on the road when Ergam turned up.

"I think it will be a while before the people of Calan and Kanat are annoyed with one another again," he said. "We've very nearly put the whole city back together."

"Well done," Arier said. "That will help, certainly."

"Thank you for your hospitality, Arier," Aysu said.

"It's my pleasure to provide it. I only ask one thing in return."

"What's that?" Aysu asked.

"Give that Bartu Hamdi a good kicking when you've tracked him down."

ERGAM SPENT MUCH of the first two days worrying about the amount of food Ozel and Aysu had to eat for the journey to Dilara. Ozel went off into the woods by himself for a few minutes and came back with enough herbs and leaves to help out quite a bit. These plus a rabbit here and there made for some agreeable dinners, if not excellent feasts.

"You know," Aysu said, chewing happily beside a camp-fire. "On our next quest, we shouldn't pack food at all, but dried herbs and spices. Just so Ozel has more to work with in terms of ingredients."

"A skillet would be nice," Ozel said. "I could do all manner of casseroles, bread, stews in an iron oven."

"Sounds heavy," Ergam observed.

"Oh, very. And you'll carry it, won't you? I mean, we have to carry these heavy fleshy bodies everywhere. You don't have to carry any food, sleeping gear, anything like that."

"I'm no military mastermind, however something tells me it's not wise to burden a ranger with a giant piece of metal that goes 'clang' every time he moves."

"We'll have to hire a squire then."

"Or an apprentice," Aysu said.

CHAPTER 43

They were a day or two away from Dilara. Ozel was nosing around in the woods for some small fruit to share for breakfast. He could hear a stream somewhere, which might be a good place to try. Something made a snuffling noise nearby. It might be a deer. That would be nice. He'd wanted to see what he could do with deer meat using the local greenery alongside it. He stood stock still and listened.

When the deer nosed its way out of the underbrush near the water—it wasn't a deer at all. It was an enormous bear.

Ozel focused and let a fireball fly. It struck the bear in the chest and the beast roared angrily. Its fur was soaked from the stream. A cloud of steam shot forth, and that was the extent of the fireball's damage.

The bear charged. Ozel yelled.

The bear was apparently so enraged and confused by the fireball that it didn't bite Ozel. It just ran into him, knocking him painfully to the ground. His shoulder slammed against the base of a tree and pain coursed along his bones. He tried to get up. The bear was on him, growling and slashing.

Ozel turned over on his stomach. The bear sank its teeth into his leg. The pain was intense. Ozel screamed, flailing at the bear. He tried beating it with his fists, but couldn't reach behind him.

Ozel twisted around the other way. An arrow shaft appeared in the bear's flank, then another. The bear let his leg go and howled again. Another arrow appeared in the bear's chest. Ergam was on his way, but he might not get there soon enough.

The bear reached a mighty paw out to take a swipe at Ozel. Ozel was filled with the certainty that it was going to knock his head off his shoulders and send it sailing through the air. Ozel fumbled at his belt for his dagger and drew it out of the sheath. He inadvertently dragged the point of the knife across his own stomach. There was a brutal cold sensation, but the fear that he was within seconds of having his head swatted off kept him focused on other things.

He drove the dagger into the bear's neck. A spiderweb of frost grew from the wound into a lopsided shape of cold that enveloped the bear's neck and chest. The animal staggered, fell, and hit the ground. As it did, the block of ice that was now its neck snapped off and blood leaked out. The bear shuddered and bubbles of blood formed at its neck.

Ozel gathered himself. He could hear running feet, but the best help Ozel needed he could provide for himself.

"*Potio Sanitatum!*" he yelled. The biggest healing potion he had created so far appeared in his hand. He popped the cork and drank it, then stiffened with the force of the healing. His body jerked into a plank, causing some of the skin around the frozen part of his guts to rip with searing pain.

He was gasping on the forest floor when Ergam reached him. Ergam saw that Ozel had already given himself a potion, so he scanned the area with an arrow nocked in case there were any more threats. Aysu crashed down beside Ozel and began hugging him and shouting at him, asking if he was okay.

He held his sliced shirt open to look at his belly. It still looked a little blue with cold, but mostly the color was returning to his skin. His breeches were torn where the bear had bitten his leg. Those wounds too seemed to be healing. Blood welled up out of the tooth punctures, but they were closing up.

Aysu was kissing his face and sobbing. He hugged her, saying, "I'm all right," over and over again.

She'd thought he was about to be eaten, which, had he not gotten very lucky, would certainly have been the case.

"I'm all right," he said again. "Look, no wounds anymore. See?"

"That was quite a healing potion, young master," Ergam said. He was impressed.

"Bear bites have a way of focusing one's purpose," Ozel said. He accepted Aysu's help in getting to his feet. His bitten leg was still a little shaky, but it was still attached, which was the important thing.

Ergam nodded, removed his arrow from his bow, and replaced it in his quiver. "True enough, true enough. This evening I think we shall bite the bear instead."

As it turned out, the bear meat wasn't great, but the change from the daily rabbits was nice.

"I've learned a few things today," Ozel declared. "This dagger is an exceptional weapon, but one must take care not to cut one's own belly with it." He patted the sheath on his belt.

Aysu gave him a look that said he shouldn't joke about something that had upset her quite a bit, so he stopped.

"What else?" Ergam asked.

"I dislike bears even more than I thought I did."

CHAPTER 44

Ozel had been amazed when he'd first entered Calan. It seemed nearly impossible that so many people could—or would want to—live so close together.

Where Calan was nestled in a forest, Dilara spread over an entire valley. Next to a great river there was a hill that rose covered by buildings with great spires and domes. There was a wall around the hill as well. Around the foot of the hill and shouldering up next to the river there were still more dwellings, again separated by another wall. Outside of this the houses diminished in size and proximity until patches of farmland took over.

"Why do they have so many walls?" Ozel asked.

Ergam tilted his head side to side. "I can only guess, but I suspect it's because a city spreads faster than stout walls can be built."

The traffic on the road grew as they walked down into the valley. Soon they were standing in a long line. Ergam was nervous.

"Are you all right?" Ozel asked.

Ergam had been listening intently. "I think we should back up a touch."

They crossed the road and headed back the way they'd came, which put them into the path of a cart. The driver had to pull his horses up slightly and he made an irritated noise.

"Ugh," he scoffed. "Mountain people."

"Mountain people?" Aysu asked aloud, offended.

Ergam motioned at them to move on. They hurried back up the road a bit until they came to a crossroads that was a little quieter. There was a stone nearby big enough to sit on.

"What's wrong, Ergam?" Ozel asked again.

"I am fine," Ergam said. "But I cannot accompany you inside Dilara. It would be unwise."

"Why not?"

"We might not have gotten quite close enough for you to see it. There is a man at the gate with a magical artifact which, I believe, enables him to detect undead fuckers like myself. Detection would be a problem. As in possibly fatal."

Ozel looked toward the city gate, even though it was the best part of a mile away now. "That is a problem."

"Why would they do that?" Aysu asked.

Ergam grimaced. "My people are slaves in Dilara. There have been attempts to free them from time to time. Some might call those attempts 'violent uprisings.'" Ergam smiled sheepishly. "Anyway, the Dilara guard is careful about letting undead inside, and they never allow someone to bring an undead slave inside the city without paying the proper tax."

"Proper tax?" Aysu said.

Ergam shrugged. "I know. It doesn't make much sense on the face of it. If you delve a little deeper and come to understand Dilaran politics, it doesn't get any better." He sighed deeply. "However, we're not going to sort the problem out today. What we can do is find out where Bartu Hamdi might be."

"How do we do that?" Ozel asked.

"First, go to the city guards, show them your document so they'll keep an eye out for Hamdi. Next, try the palace records. They might tell you if anyone has arrived and started sniffing around about land or titles for sale."

"You can just buy nobility?" Aysu asked.

"Not really. It's complicated. You can unquestionably buy land and a manor. Those things often come with a lesser title. If there are any such things for sale, or have been sold recently, palace records will know about them."

"What are you going to do?"

"I'm going to find another way into Dilara."

"How?"

"I'm going to listen for moving bones. If I find a way in and I think it's safe, I'll find you. Otherwise, I suggest we all meet back here this evening, at sundown."

Ozel and Aysu nodded.

"It feels terrible to leave you behind," Aysu said. "Like we're participating in this Dilara ugliness."

"Ah, but if we don't participate, Bartu Hamdi will keep the fortune. The ugliness will spread."

ERGAM HAD BEEN RIGHT about the man at the gate with a magical artifact. It was only a carved piece of wood, but to Ozel's eye there was certainly a sheen to it that only a magical item could have. He needed to spend some more time reading Wagast's books dedicated to enchantment. He'd ignored them until now because he thought enchantment boring when compared with combat or healing spells.

Now that he knew how powerful passive magical items could be, Ozel was much more interested.

The man holding the device didn't look like a guard, more like a monk. Why did they need him as well as the guard for this job? It wasn't even a one-man job. Half a man could have managed it.

They asked the gate guard where to find his guard house and he gave directions in the least interested voice Ozel or Aysu had ever heard. It was as if the man was asleep inside his armor, but his mouth was still making sounds of its own accord. Testament to the boredom of two men doing one-half-a-man's job.

They were waved on through the gate.

Ozel was amazed at the Dilaran's choices of clothes. Almost all of them wore some kind of colorful garment as if every one of them was a merchant. That simply couldn't be true. He looked at his own clothes and Aysu's. They were muted colors, made of materials that could keep a person warm and would last a long time. That must be why the man on the road had called them mountain people. They weren't wearing enough colors.

"It's so loud here," Aysu said over the din of people. "I hear a hammer, though. Do we have time to follow it? I'd like to see what a blacksmith shop in the big city looks like."

They followed the sound. When they rounded the corner, they both gasped. The blacksmith's shop was nearly as big as the entire town of Bilgehan. There were anvils of every size arranged around a multi-sided forge in the center and a small army of apprentices and journeymen running to and fro.

Aysu's eyes were wide, but she also looked concerned. "I never thought a blacksmith shop could be this big, or that I could miss my shop so much."

Ozel put an arm around her shoulders. "Let's get this business finished. I'd like to be home as well." He also thought that hopefully Alan was doing most of the gardening these days so he could spend his time learning advanced wizarding.

They tore themselves away and headed toward the city's guard house. It turned out to be a small castle in the town, very nearly as big as the palace in Calan. They were directed to a man behind a high table.

The man listened to their tale and had a look at the document Barnard provided. Then he took the parchment to his superior, who returned with it to the table. The superior guardsman said they'd certainly be willing to have a word with Bartu Hamdi as soon as they ran across him. However, they were preoccupied with pressing issues of policing already.

"So if we find him, we can tell you where he is and you'll help us sort it out?" Ozel asked.

"That's correct," the supervisor said.

"But you're too busy to look yourselves?" Aysu asked.

"That's correct," the supervisor said again, unfazed. Then he added, "Stolen currency is certainly a problem. It's just that people are killing one another in certain parts of the outer Dilara area and we have to focus on that. We may be able to make some queries later in the day, as long as no one kills anyone too important before then."

"I see," Ozel said. "We'll do our best."

"I advise that you don't," the supervisor said. "It could be dangerous."

"That's okay, we're used to danger," Aysu said.

The supervisor apparently didn't really listen to this. "Right you are. Now, if you'll excuse me ..." he handed the bank document back to Ozel, who rolled it up and stowed it away.

Outside, Ozel and Aysu conferred.

Aysu looked annoyed. "Well, that was a waste of time."

"I'm not so sure. At least now if we get into some kind of scuffle we'll be able to say we tried to do things the legal way. Besides, we do have another possibility."

"I guess you're right. Let's go see those records."

THE RECORDS WERE KEPT in what looked like a library except that the library part was sectioned off. If they'd found the motivation of the city guard lacking, the records department's level of interest was nearly nonexistent.

On the far side of a bench counter, men in light-colored robes shuffled to and from tables, reading scrolls, running their fingers down the pages of books. Occasionally one would dip a quill in an ink pot and make a note on a scrap of paper. The overall mood of the room was like the elderly men who worked there: quiet, dry, slow.

At the rear of the room a man in white robes was turning a crank which operated a system of wheels and leather belts. These worked to turn some air-moving devices mounted to the ceiling. Ozel was wondering how long the man could turn the crank before he had to take a rest, then he noticed how thin the man appeared to be.

The realization that this was an undead slave landed on Ozel like a great weight.

Aysu looked horrified.

They stood at the bench for a few minutes and waited for someone to come speak to them. They tried not to stare at the robed slave in the corner. No one came to ask what they wanted. Ozel cleared his throat. Still nothing.

"You just have to wait," a voice behind them said. There was a man sitting on a seat and wearing a typical farmer's clothes. "If you don't go away, sooner or later one of them will come over and ask what you want."

"How long have you been waiting?" Aysu asked.

"A while. They know what I want. Come, sit." He scooted over so there was plenty of room. Ozel and Aysu sat.

"I'm Ozkan Aytac," the man said. He had a friendly smile. In fact, he looked and sounded like the sort of people Ozel and Aysu had grown up around. He also wore muted colors and functional clothes.

"What do you do, Mr. Aytac?" Ozel asked.

"Oh, nothing too special. I'm just a farmer. My family has owned and operated one of the biggest farms in the region for generations. At least, it used to be one of the biggest."

"What happened?"

Aytac gave a sort of laughing sigh. "It's a long story. Probably not the sort of thing I'd bore a couple of nice young people with. Lots of politics and budgets, and so forth. Speaking of boring, what brings you two to the records room?"

"That's a pretty peculiar story," Aysu said.

CHAPTER 45

Aysu gave the highlights of their quest to find Bartu Hamdi. "It looks like he might get away with it after all," she finished.

Aytac looked wistful. He was staring through the high arched windows in the far wall. "Yes, things can be that way sometimes. You try your best to do the right thing, but sometimes you end up on your backside in the mud anyway, eh?"

"Do you think these men will be able to tell us if anyone has tried to buy a title?" Ozel asked.

"Oh, I expect so. They do know almost every little bit of business that takes place around here. They might walk over to one of those tables, look it up, and get back to you in no time at all. Or they might take six months to research the matter. More likely the former than the latter in your case, though."

A young woman in a blue dress stuck her head in the doorway and saw Aytac. "Papa, you're still here."

Aytac nodded. "Aye. Might be for a while yet, I expect. I'll find you girls when I'm done." When the young woman was gone, he said, "My daughters. Best thing ever happened to me, those three. If it weren't for them I'd have packed it all in and left Dilara for good years ago, and that's a fact."

"Why's that?"

Aytac frowned. His eyes went left, right. There was no one too near, but he lowered his voice anyway. "There are just a few things going on I don't care for. Used to be a farmer could make an honest living, working the land, employing good people. New there are these farms with their *extra-mortal* workers." He plainly didn't care for them. "Well, it's so you can't make a living any more. I've sold off parcel after parcel till there's hardly any land left, all in the name of maintaining a nice dowry for my daughters. It looks like even that's not too likely with these tariffs and fines. That's what I'm here to ask about. Tax rates."

"Extra-mortal workers?" Ozel said. "We heard about that."

"Nasty business. I don't care if a man is dead or alive. If he can plant a seed in the ground, he deserves a fair wage and time off just like everyone else. I honestly thought the people of Dilara would prefer food from a proper farm where the workers are treated fairly, but people buy on price alone. The farms with round-the-clock free labor are running us out of business. They say they take the proper precautions to make sure food isn't handled directly by their undead workers, but there's no way to know if that's true and the market doesn't seem to care in any case."

"What happens if your daughters don't have dowries?" Aysu asked.

"Well, they won't be able to marry into society. Far as their old dad is concerned they can live with me forever, mind you, but their mother would have wanted them to have a fine husband. I don't like to think about what could happen, if they end up on their own."

"What *could* happen?" Aysu asked.

Aytac scratched the back of his neck, uncomfortable with the question.

Aytac was saved when an ancient man in rough robes the color of eggshells approached the bench and cleared his throat.

As Ozel stood up he heard Aytac let out a sigh of relief.

"Hello, sir," Ozel said, with Aysu next to him. "My name is Ozel. A man has stolen a fortune from me and we believe he may seek to purchase land and titles. Can you tell us if anyone has tried such a thing in the last few days?" He unrolled the document from the bank. The old man didn't seem interested in it.

"How many days?"

"Just recently. Within the last few."

"Exactly how many days?"

"Four," Aysu said.

"Yes." The old man folded his hands as though he expected the matter to be concluded.

"Yes what, sir?" Ozel asked.

"Yes, I can tell you."

Ozel and Aysu were puzzled.

"They despise ambiguity here," Aytac explained from behind them. "Actually, that's not true. They enjoy it quite a lot. It affords them opportunities to be pedantic, which is rather like a sport for these men of the records department."

"Thank you very *much*, Ozkan Aytac, sir," the old man said, loudly.

"Not at all," Aytac said.

Ozel tried again. "Sir, we would like to know, please, if

anyone has asked in the last four days whether there is land and titles for sale."

"One person has."

"What was that person's name?"

The old man turned, walked to a table, flipped a page, stooped so that his face was nearly touching the paper, then stood and shuffled back to the bench. "Burak Hanem."

Ozel's face fell. He pounded the bench in front of him. The old man looked appalled at this display.

"We're sorry," Aysu said. "We're just at the end of a long quest."

The old man's face was so utterly bereft of interest he could have been a statue. "Mr. Aytac, perhaps I can help you?" he said at last.

Aytac stood. "Bad luck, friends. Why don't you wait a moment? I won't be long here, and then I'm due to have lunch with my daughters. You could join us."

"That's very kind of you, sir, but we should keep looking."

"No, please. I won't take no for an answer. Just wait by the door for a moment or two and I'll be right with you." He widened his eyes significantly.

Ozel got the message, nodded.

Aytac was right, it didn't take him any longer than a moment to speak to the old man, then he stepped outside and spread his arms to shepherd Ozel and Aysu down the street.

"I didn't want to talk about this in there. I wanted to tell you that I've lived here all my life and I don't know any Burak Hanem."

"But surely Dilara is a big city?" Aysu said.

"It is, it is. But I am old and I've been a landowner all my life. If anyone is in a position to buy something like what you're looking for, I would know it. I'm in the records office more than anyone else in Dilara who doesn't work there."

"So who could that person be?"

"Well, I couldn't help but notice that Bartu Hamdi and Burak Hanem start with the same letters."

"We would never have thought of that," Aysu said and laughed.

Aytac shrugged. "Sorry to say it, but I have dealt with some shifty people in my life. Now, listen. If you really do want lunch, please join us."

Ozel said, "Thank you, but I think we should get this information back to the city guard and see what they have to say about it."

"I think so too. If you need a place to stay tonight, ask around for the Aytac house, all right? It's not far."

"We'll do that, sir. Thank you."

Aytac nodded. "Good luck."

CHAPTER 46

I t took Ergam longer than he'd expected to find what he was looking for. It had, at least, been on the side of the city he'd guessed it would.

He was looking for the way into the city used by enslaved undead. It had to exist, because he knew something about the living, having been one once: they are lazy.

Somewhere in Dilara, he reasoned, there was a wealthy person who had themselves an undead slave to do menial tasks around the house. Some of the tasks that slave was required to do would take them outside the walls of the city and into the outlying streets. And since the law of the city was that an undead slave required a massive amount of tiresome and expensive paperwork to do this, it stood to reason that someone, somewhere, had come up with a loophole to allow their undead slave to get unmolested in and out of town.

All Ergam had to do was skulk about and hope to hear something that sounded like a desiccated, undead body moving around where it shouldn't be.

He caught the first whisper of the sound when he was

wending his way through the houses on the northeast side of the city. The sound wasn't enough, of course. He also needed to see something.

Ah, there. A very thin man moving carefully so as not to accidentally bump into anyone. Ergam followed the figure as he entered what looked like a tavern. Picking up the previous day's earnings, perhaps? Likely.

It wasn't easy hiding in broad daylight, but Ergam managed. It helped that, unlike the living, he could be completely motionless for long periods of time. He could also assume a squatting posture and fold himself up almost as small as a barrel. Not having much flesh really paid off sometimes.

The figure emerged from the tavern. Ergam had positioned himself well. He waited a moment before rising to follow. He had time. He could hear the motion perfectly well. Had his target doubled back or anything like that, he'd have known. He followed at a careful distance.

When they neared the city walls again, Ergam hurried to close the gap. He wanted to be close enough to catch his target just before he disappeared into whatever mechanism allowed for getting through the wall. The opening would surely be hidden from prying eyes.

He was hurrying and catching up. The way the man was angling his body it looked like he was about to duck into a doorway just up the street. At that moment, a cat darted out in front of Ergam and tripped him. The cat yowled noisily as Ergam stumbled to catch his feet, blocking the finer details of his hearing momentarily. When he'd regained his balance, the man was gone.

Ergam's hood had come away. He had his mask on, but the back of his head was still a charred mess. He fumbled with the hood to get it back up—and heard a man's voice.

"Hey! Why aren't you with your master? Excuse me!"

Ergam felt sure his target had ducked into the doorway. Right now the citizen challenging him was deciding how civic-minded he really wanted to be. Did he want to chase an apparently unattached undead slave up the street, or had he already done enough by shouting and so on?

The undead man couldn't have gone up the street any farther or he'd still be in sight. Ergam went to the nearest alleyway anyway, but judged it to be too far away. He doubled back to the doorway and tried the knob. It opened. This riled the citizen.

"Hey!" he yelled again, hurrying after Ergam. Now it sounded like he meant to come sort this out after all. Ergam had only seconds to figure out what to do.

This was made somewhat easier by the fact that there was nothing in the room other than a barrel. But when Ergam tried to shift the barrel to expose what he assumed was a trap door underneath, it didn't budge. There must be some release. He tapped on the wood around the perimeter of the barrel listening for—there!

He tapped a few more times, then pressed on one of the staves on the side. It swung out. He pulled on it, and the barrel swung away to reveal a ladder down into a narrow passageway.

Ergam pulled the barrel shut over top of the tunnel just as he heard the door open.

"Now see here ..." a voice said. There was a surprised noise and shuffling sounds as the man looked around for a minute. Then apparently satisfied he'd made an effort, he left.

Ergam listened to his footsteps retreating, then he opened the barrel again, climbed out and went outside. The man was walking down the street again, shaking his head.

Ergam let him get just far enough away and called, "Did you need something, sir?"

The man turned, peered, looked surprised.

"Oi!" He began hurrying back.

Ergam dashed into the alleyway, then making several right turns quickly navigated his way back to the same street.

He returned to the barrel room and let himself down into the passage. He hung around for a few moments to see if the man came back, but he didn't. With luck, he never would.

Ergam headed down the tunnel which was, by his reckoning, easily long enough to get him under the wall. He hoped there wouldn't be a group of guardsmen at the other end, but he doubted it. Whoever made this thing had kept it secret, surely. If they were smart, the tunnel could be easily flooded or caved in, so that the owner wouldn't be left answering some very uncomfortable questions if an invading army used it to gain access to the city.

At the other end was another fake barrel. Ergam listened a moment. There was the usual bustle of a city, but it didn't sound like anyone was lurking near the barrel waiting to hit him on the head with something heavy. At least, if they were, they were doing a good job of being quiet. Which, considering he was pursuing an undead man, he'd be able to do.

Oh well, he thought. Might as well get it over with.

He tripped the catch on the barrel, pushed it aside, climbed out of the hole—and wasn't hit on the head with anything. He replaced the barrel and took stock of his surroundings.

He was in a tiny alleyway between two buildings. It looked perfectly nondescript except, if you thought about it, why was there an alleyway here at all? Surely the owners of the buildings on either side would have liked the extra room. Strange.

He walked to the mouth of the alleyway and listened for his friends.

CHAPTER 47

I t was lucky that the same guard was on duty when Ozel and Aysu returned to relay the info about the possible name change, but now the guard still didn't seem terribly interested.

"Burak Hanem," he said, absentmindedly, as he made a note on a scrap of paper. "We will do what we can."

"It doesn't seem like you are doing very much," Aysu said.

"It might not seem that way, but you haven't been killed, have you?"

"You can see that I haven't."

"Right, well, that's one of the things we endeavor to prevent. In your case, we've been successful so far."

The wooden door of the guardhouse banged open. A woman in a very revealing dress stormed in. Judging by her expression, she intended to kick the shit out of everyone in the building twice. The black eye forming on her face suggested she'd already been fighting.

"There you are, Guardsman Duman, I'm glad it's you on duty," the woman declared. She marched right up to the high table. "You're always saying how proud we should be because we're not murdered. Well, what do you say about a man who beats a lawful lady in the face?" She pointed at the bruise on the side of her face as evidence.

Duman put his quill down and straightened up. "I say we'll have a word with the gentleman right away, if you can show us to him."

"Oh, I can. Don't you worry about that. He's reclining on his fat ass at the Spotted Duck, probably thinking of the women he'd like to smack around tomorrow, if the guard lets him get away with it."

"Not likely," Duman said. "Does this person have a name?"

"Oh, yes. Burak Hanem."

OZEL AND AYSU weren't allowed to go up to the room, but Duman did let them tag along to the Spotted Duck. They waited outside. By the sounds of the shouting, Burak Hanem, whoever he was, was fairly sure that he was above any sort of recrimination for smacking a lady around. Duman, however, was sure that he wasn't.

"It's him," Ozel said. "I'd know that voice anywhere. It's Bartu Hamdi for sure."

The woman with the black eye came back down the stairs with a satisfied look on her face and walked away down the street.

A few moments later, Duman appeared with one very irritated-looking Bartu Hamdi, wrestling him out the front door. When Bartu Hamdi saw Ozel, his eyes went wide.

"You!" he said.

"Me," Ozel said.

"What's this whelp doing here?" Bartu asked the guard.

"He's been making up lies about me, has he? You can't believe a word he says."

"Even if I didn't believe a word of it, you still can't go getting rough with a lady in Dilara and expect to get away with it. Just so happens, this young man's got a writ from the bank that says you're an imposter and a thief."

"Writ from the bank?" Bartu shrieked. "What could that be worth?"

"It'll be worth a year or two in the king's finest, deep dark hole, I'd imagine."

"You can't do that!" Bartu screeched. His voice was so high now and his face so red that Ozel thought it might actually pop. "That is my gold. Mine! You can't just hand it to any piece of trash that blows up the street."

"Mr. Hamdi, I assure you—" the guard began.

"What could you possibly assure me? *What?*" Bartu snapped at him.

"Well," Duman said quietly. "I can assure you that admitting to using a false name in Dilara is another serious offence."

Bartu's face in the next moment, for Ozel and Aysu, was a treasure beyond any fortune. Duman enjoyed it quite a lot as well.

When Bartu started screaming again, he changed tactic. "There is four thousand in gold at the Spotted Duck!" he yelled. He waited a moment, then shouted it again as Duman hustled him to a cart and shackled him to an iron bar. He kept yelling it repeatedly and a sardonic grin formed on his face.

"Why is he doing that?" Ozel asked Duman, as the guard climbed into the driver's seat.

"Perhaps he hopes to incite thieves to take the money from you?"

"Will they try?"

"Probably," the guard said.

"Can't you stay to help us?"

"I have to get him sorted out, but I'll be back. Just stay in the inn. You should be safe there."

"Should be?" Aysu asked, but Duman was pulling away.

There was a clinking sound behind them. A man, presumably the innkeeper, was stacking wooden chests on the porch outside the front door. He said, "Excuse me, are these yours?"

"Yes," Ozel said. "They certainly are."

"Ah. Very good. I'll thank you for removing them as soon as possible." He smiled thinly and turned to go back in.

"But, sir, couldn't we wait inside? We'll pay for a room."

"I'm very sorry, but the Spotted Duck is a fine establishment. We cannot associate ourselves with these ..." he paused. "These matters. Good day to you." He shut the door.

Ozel banged on the door. "What if we get robbed and murdered out here in the street?"

A muffled voice said, "Would you mind moving down a few doors, please? Thank you."

"Might I be of some assistance?" someone asked conversationally.

Aysu was lifting her hammer out of her belt as Ozel turned around.

"Now, now, young miss," the man said, one hand out, "There's no need for that with Big John."

Big John, as he'd sort-of introduced himself, was indeed big. He was wearing a lot of leather, the effect more fashionable than functional. He wore a cape and boots with folded-over tops just below his knees. "I couldn't help but overhear your little predicament. I can offer my protection services for a mere, say, one hundred gold."

"No, thank you," Aysu said. "We can protect ourselves."

"Perhaps so," Big John nodded. "By the look of that hammer you might have a few tricks up your sleeves. You might be able to protect your property ... for now. But night will fall. You'll have to sleep at some point. Besides, you'll need a cart to get that much heavy old gold anywhere. I can help with transportation as well." He smiled, showing a gold tooth, and spread his hands.

"No, thank you," Ozel said. "Please move along."

"I would love to, but I feel this has become something of a matter of civic duty for me. You see, I'm the best man in the city when it comes to protecting life and limb. My team and I are peerless in that regard. Regrettably, though, my price has gone up to three hundred gold."

"We already said no, thank you," Ozel said. "Why would we pay even more?"

"Because now you'll need to pay Quetzal and Bones as well." He raised his hand to someone behind Ozel and Aysu.

Ozel glanced with the corner of his eye, trying not to take his eyes off Big John. There were indeed two figures behind them, silently coming from nowhere.

"Now you see?" Big John said. He took a few steps closer. "Doesn't it seem like we can come to an arrangement? I think we're going to be great friends. In fact, I think perhaps young miss and I are going to find a way to be very, very good friends. There might even be a discount in it for you."

There was a loud "chock!" sound as an arrow struck a wooden beam close to Big John.

Aysu let out a pleased gasp.

Ozel said, "I recommend that you and your friends melt back into the shadows. That was a warning arrow."

"Hah," Big John said, looking over his shoulder. "That was just a fluke. I don't see anyone close enough to—"

"Warn them again," Ozel said loudly.

Chock-chock! Two arrows struck the wall of the Spotted Duck.

Ozel turned to see Bones glaring up at an arrow pinning his hat to the boards. Quetzal's shirt was similarly caught.

"Uh, Big John, I think we need to regroup," Quetzal said.

"Yes, I think you need to regroup, Big John," Aysu said.

Big John started to say something. Two more arrows appeared in the beam in front of him. Chock-chock!

He frowned at them, took a step back, nodded. "Very well, my young friends. Just remember that you had the chance to do this the easy way with Big John."

Ozel looked over his shoulder again. Bones and Quetzal had crept quietly away. All that remained of their presence were two arrows embedded in the woodwork. One of them had a scrap of a dirty blue shirt still attached.

Ergam ran up with a small cart, stopped in front of Ozel and Aysu, and grabbed the coin chests. He had them all loaded in seconds. Ozel wasn't sure the old cart could hold up under the weight, the way it was creaking and groaning.

"Now what?" Ozel asked.

"Take the cart to the gate, this way," Ergam said, showing Ozel how to lift the handles. "I will cover you from a distance, then meet you outside the gate. Hurry now, please."

Ergam hauled on the handles and the cart threatened to run Ozel over. When Ozel and Aysu worked together, it became manageable. They hauled on the thing. Ergam cocked his head, then fired an arrow into the air. There was a distant scream.

"Hurry now, young master."

Ozel and Aysu hauled for all they were worth on the cart. Luckily, the Spotted Duck was near one of the city gates. It wasn't the one they had entered, but any gate leading out of Dilara at that moment was a good one. Since it was the end of the day, the line to get in was almost nonexistent. There were a few other carts headed out, but the guards didn't seem as concerned with what was leaving Dilara. There was another man in a monk robe waving his device around, though.

Ergam melted into an alleyway and was out of sight by the time they reached the gate. The guard didn't even look at them. The monk waved his device, and that was it. In the distance, there was another scream. Ozel and Aysu kept pulling the cart for all they were worth.

"They're coming," Aysu said, grunting with the effort of trying to speed up.

Ozel looked over his shoulder. A small wedge of rough-looking men was walking toward the gate with Big John at the front of them. As Ozel watched, there was a loud noise and the gate guard's helmet fell off. The guard turned to see Big John and his men advancing toward him.

"What's this?" the guard yelled. "You'd attack a city guard in broad daylight, Big John?"

Big John's smile disappeared. He shook his head, protesting. Ozel and Aysu didn't wait around to see how the rest of the exchange worked itself out. They kept tugging and pulling on the cart, urging it up the road with every ounce of strength. There was a slight rise in the road here, making things even harder.

A familiar figure was sprinting down the road toward them. Ergam grabbed the cart handles and began single-handedly pulling it up the road as though it were empty. Ozel and Aysu shared a look of amazement, then jogged to catch up.

CHAPTER 48

They took a circuitous route getting back to the road to Calan. The sun had gone down, but the moon was bright. They'd all agreed that they wanted to be clear of Dilara and headed back up onto the high ground before they camped for the night, but Aysu stopped short when she saw the sign at the entrance to a farm.

"Hey," she said. "This is the Aytac place."

"Aytac place?" Ergam asked.

"He was at the records room in the palace when we went to ask about Bartu Hamdi. He's the one who gave us the idea that Hamdi might have been using a false name," Ozel said.

Ergam said, "People can be tricky."

Ozel was looking at the farmhouse. The glow of firelight came from within, and the sound of laughter floated over the fields.

"They are eating supper together," Ergam said. "Sounds like rice."

"You can't hear rice, you liar," Aysu said.

"I have an idea," Ozel said. "Ergam, I'll need your help, if you're amenable."

"What's that? I couldn't hear you over the rice."

OZKAN'S DAUGHTERS WERE ARGUING, but in a companionable way. He'd learned years ago not to listen too closely to his children, but rather to pay attention to the general tone. This way he could appear in a doorway before anyone got too angry. The content might have been mildly offensive tonight, but the tone was generally agreeable.

These were the nights he lived for. The evening was nice enough to let the air blow into the house from across the fields. The girls could prepare supper for all four of them. He could sit down at the table and relax.

How many more of these nights would there be? He had promised his wife he would do everything in his power to get the girls married into society so they wouldn't have to live the life their mother had in her early days. "Digging and scratching at the ground," is what she'd called it. Ozkan thought of farming rather more fondly than that, but he also thought of his wife quite fondly, so he respected her point of view.

Even if he didn't manage to get his daughters married off into society, they'd surely match up with a laborer sooner or later. Then they'd be off to start their lives without their old man. He was sure he'd be allowed to come visit them, of course, but it wouldn't be like tonight. He smiled, and a tear rolled down his cheek. He wiped it away.

He was being foolish, getting wistful about his evening instead of enjoying it.

Something made a bizarre chonk-tinkle sound. A pouch of coins had appeared on the table. He stared at it. As he did, two more pouches plopped down next to it. They'd been thrown through the window, of all things.

He leaped up from the table, or as close to leaping as a man his age could manage, and tore open the door. There was a distant flicker of what looked like a dark man-shaped figure sprinting away. Whoever or whatever that was couldn't possibly have been responsible for the pouches. The shape was much too far away. No one could run that fast.

He walked around the perimeter of the house. There was nothing to be seen. The ground was too dry and hard to hold much in the way of footprints.

When he returned to the door, he went inside to find his daughters had pulled the strings on one of the pouches.

"It's gold," his eldest said. "Oh, Papa. You found some way to come up with dowries for us!" She ran to him, hugged him around the middle, jumping up and down and crying. The other two girls hugged him too. Everyone was crying and laughing.

Ozkan wondered what the hell was going on. He thought back to earlier in the day when he'd met those two kids looking for someone who was trying to buy a manor house and title. Someone with that kind of money could throw a purse or two around, couldn't they?

But no. There had to be some other explanation. That couldn't be it.

Could it?

CHAPTER 49

They had a good journey without mishap returning to Calan. Lord Tebrik hadn't yet returned, so the coalition between Usta and Arier Enver was doing its best to get on with running the town. King Sakir had returned to Kanat.

Where it had once been like a vast city to Ozel, now, having been to Dilara, Calan seemed more like a town. It was a much cleaner and more orderly town than the one he'd left. The streets were positively sparkling.

They deposited the remaining gold with Barnard, who promised to make up the difference between what Bartu had spent and the remaining total. They told him about the gold they'd given to Ozkan Aytac and his family, at which Barnard's eyes glazed over. He apparently couldn't fathom such a thing.

That done, the group traveled to Kanat. Ozel had assumed that they would leave Ergam there, but Ergam insisted on carrying on to just outside of Bilgehan, lest some denizen of the swamp set upon them.

When they drew close to Bilgehan, Aysu stopped everyone.

"I think you should let me go on my own from here," she said. "And if you're intending to visit, Ozel, which you'd better be if you value your life, I would advise you to wait a week or two."

"Why's that?" Ozel asked.

"Because my dad, being my dad, probably thinks we've eloped, which probably means he'd like to tear your arms off and use them to bludgeon your legs off."

"Oh, I see."

"Very descriptive," Ergam said.

"Would you excuse us a moment, Ergam?" Aysu asked.

Ergam bowed and removed himself a few paces.

Aysu kissed Ozel. He hugged her.

She said, "If you start on another quest and go without me, it'll be your last mistake."

"This goodbye is rather more filled with threats than I'd like," he said.

She kissed him again. Ozel decided she was the best friend and most attractive person who had ever lived.

"Goodbye for now, Ergam," she called.

Ergam rejoined them, took Aysu's hand. "I hope to see you again soon."

She kissed him on his masked cheek. He put the tips of his fingers there and looked shocked.

"I suppose I shall leave you here too, Ergam," Ozel said. "It's only a little more than an hour to Wagast's house."

"I'll be by in a few days," Ergam said.

IT FELT weird to be walking alone. Ozel gave Bilgehan a wide berth, lest Aysu's father come out swinging something sharp, or heavy, or both. Soon enough, he was back on the road. It looked a lot narrower than he'd remembered it.

A little over an hour later, the stonework of the house appeared between the trees. Ozel could hear the sounds of dirt being worried at with a gardening implement. As he wound up the path he found Alan was doing the worrying.

"Ho there," he said. "Is this where the wizards live?"

Wagast came out of the house. His smile was a mile wide. "Look at this, Alan. A journeyman wizard. We've got a full complement around here now, I dare say. One apprentice, one journeyman." He laughed and clapped Ozel on the back. "Come on and tell us all about it, won't you? We've been expecting you. We'll have such a feast tonight, won't we, Alan?"

Alan beamed.

"Oh, has Alan learned to cook too?" Ozel asked.

"Not one bit," said Alan, happily.

Wagast said, "We were hoping we could convince you to cook, Ozel. We've nearly starved to death on our cooking."

"He tried to make me eat a raw potato when it was his night to cook," Alan said.

"There are people who say that you should only eat raw food," Wagast said, indignantly.

"I bet they're skinny," Alan said.

OZEL DIDN'T MIND COOKING. In fact, it was nice to be able to ply his culinary hobby in a proper kitchen, with a proper work surface for preparations. Of course, in order to do it properly he'd had to begin with a thorough cleaning of everything. Alan and Wagast were apparently content to get everything that looked kitchen-ish into a pile and call it good.

They had roast vegetables with pork and baked potatoes. Wagast found a bottle of wine. He offered a sip to Alan and a glass to Ozel, but neither had a taste for it. Alan said he thought it smelled like paint.

When the food was served, Ozel told them everything that had happened. They oohed and aahed appropriately, but not convincingly since he'd obviously survived every bit of danger relatively unscathed.

Wagast was delighted that Ozel had a newfound interest in enchantment.

"You know," Wagast said. "By ancient wizard law, you are now the wizard of Calan."

"I'm what?"

"No, it's true. You defeated Bugra Gurses, so his tower and his library, the lot of it, all becomes yours."

Ozel felt his mouth hanging open. "That seems terribly barbaric."

"Perhaps. If you look at it another way, it discourages needless dueling. If you duel with someone and lose, not only are you likely to die, but they get all your things."

Alan also looked horrified. "What if someone dueled with you and *you* lost, Wagast? What would happen to your apprentice?"

"Mmh, apprentices come and go. The law isn't concerned with them. And given that we are very far away up in the hills, it probably doesn't matter too awfully much."

Ozel said, "I would think the more cruel elements of Calan will have looted Gurses' tower by now."

"I doubt it. He probably had some enchantments to keep prying eyes out anyway. Some of it might still exist. Actually, now that I think of it, Guzul the Fierce's place might be yours as well, since Gurses defeated *her*."

"I'd rather have Guzul the Fierce back than any old house."

Wagast nodded somberly. "Indeed. But there may come a time when her library offers knowledge that mine or Gurses does not." He patted Ozel on the back. There was a silence.

Ozel remembered something. "Oh! There is something she wanted me to show you." He got up from the table and dug around in his pack a bit until he came out with the wooden disc and his dagger. He took it to the table and set it in front of Wagast, who unscrewed the top and looked at it, his face bright with wonder.

"This is positively magnificent," he said. "Puts that giant old thing I have to shame. Guzul made this?"

"She did. She wanted you to know that. And this." He set the dagger down on the table. Wagast studied it.

At this he was positively dumbfounded. "An unparalleled masterwork of enchantment," he declared. "You keep that close to hand. It's worth more than this house, I should think. I had no idea she'd been studying enchantment so assiduously. What a woman she was."

Ozel nodded, looking sadly down at the table.

"Well, at any rate, this has been a truly magnificent dinner. Thank you, Ozel. We are glad you're back safe. After a quest like that I think you're going to make one hell of a journeyman wizard."

"Thank you, Wagast. It's nice to be back."

"Now, Alan, what say you handle these dishes?"

"Right you are, sir," Alan said.

Ozel didn't trust him to do them properly, so they did them together.

CHAPTER 50

Deep in his private chambers in the massive Cathedral Yetisk, at the center—spiritually, politically, and geographically—of Dilara, Cardinal Vural Uysal steepled his fingers. He listened to a primate from some mountain shithole blabbering on about some sort of wizard nonsense. The man was obviously lacking in the spine it took to manage a city properly.

"Remind me again, please, Primate," Uysal said. "How did you come to be in charge of ... what was it?"

"Calan, Your Eminence."

"Calan. Yes."

"I wasn't in charge, sir. Bishop Erkan was."

Erkan, Uysal thought. That name did ring a bit of a bell. He seemed to recall that he liked Erkan for some reason. He couldn't remember the man's face. He looked to Hablok, his secretary.

Hablok whispered in his ear. "Erkan was converting the town of Calan to be under church control with an eye to conquering the neighboring undead stronghold of Kanat for workers to use in the mines."

Uysal nodded, waved Hablok away. "And what has become of Bishop Erkan, Primate?"

"The wizard Bugra Gurses turned him into a rodent and crushed his head."

"Oh, really?"

"Indeed so, yes, sir."

"And this wizard is running Calan now?"

Uysal thought that would be annoying. Wizards were always annoying, because they couldn't be taken by brute force. They couldn't be bribed, or swayed by devotion to any religion other than themselves. Also, they tended to live a lot longer than Cardinals. They could simply hole up in a tower and wait you out.

All this would mean the loss of the revenue they'd forecast from the Calan area mines, which would be an inconvenience. More than that, it could become a festering sore in the kingdom.

"No, Your Eminence. Word from our friends in Calan is that the wizard has been defeated."

"What, already?"

"Quite so, sir."

"How did that happen?" Uysal asked.

"I'm told a boy did it. An apprentice wizard."

"A boy? A boy killed a full wizard called Bugra Gurses?"

"I'm told that Gurses was rather softened up by Guzul the Fierce, but the boy did the actual final killing, yes."

"So Guzul the Fierce is dead as well?"

"Indeed, sir."

"Well," Uysal asked. "That is a lot of news." He fixed the primate with an expressionless stare as he considered everything.

The primate shifted uneasily. Uysal figured his knees were probably hurting. Good.

"You will go back to Calan. You will keep a close eye on developments. And you will report anything immediately to me."

"But it is a wild place now, Your Eminence. The undead walk the streets. I could be killed."

"You shall have to weigh the possibility of being harmed in Calan against the certainty of repercussions if you don't go."

The primate's face drained of color. Uysal savored the sight.

"Yes, Your Eminence."

"Go then. And the next time there is trouble in Calan, do not run from it. The church does not run when a storm comes. We *are* the storm."

The primate bowed and nodded as he backed out of the room.

What an ass, Uysal thought. But ultimately, he was pleased.

A storm was coming. "We are the storm." He quite liked coming up with that.

It would be good fun.

AFTERWORD

Hi! Thanks for reading. I hope you liked Apprentice Quest. If so, you can continue the journey in book 2 of the Ozel the Wizard series, "Journeyman's Trial."

Reviews are critical. If you have a moment, do leave an honest review on Amazon.

I have lots of other work to read as well, which you can find at http://readmyfuckingbooks.com. It's really jimhodgson.com but the other one is easier to remember I think you'll agree.

Jump on the mailing list to be notified of new work plus all manner of other shenanigans I get up to. http://eepurl.com/cSEhNL

Writing work like this is a dream for me. It can only ever be reality because of the support of people like you. Many thanks!

94572423R00165

Made in the USA
Middletown, DE
20 October 2018